One Special Christmas

A Sweetwater Crossing Novel

Amanda Cabot

ByDand Publishing

Chapter One

Saturday, November 1, 1884

Mama used to say that Christmas was the season of miracles, but Christmas was almost two months away. Greta Engel tried not to wince when she heard her brother coughing. For the three days that Otto had breathed normally she had let herself believe that Dr. Fletcher had been wrong and that Otto would live to be an adult. But now ... She shuddered as the coughing intensified. This was different from the horrible wheezing he'd had in Houston, but it was no less frightening.

There was no question about it: the cough was worse, much worse, and the way Otto gasped for breath worried Greta more than Nigel's threats had. Otto's face, which Mama said resembled the porcelain their grandfather used, was now flushed; his fair hair was darkened with sweat; and his eyes—the same light blue as Greta's—were dulled by pain. This was the sickest her brother had been since they left Houston.

Greta tried to calm her nerves. She and Otto might not need a miracle, but if he was going to have his dream of the perfect Christmas come true they needed to find a town with a doctor who could stop the coughing. And to reach that town, the wagon that had started making ominous creaks earlier today had to hold together long enough for Blackie to pull them there. And then, once they found the town, the doctor needed to be in his office and willing to help them, even though Greta had only a few coins to pay him.

Maybe they did need a miracle.

"Where are we?" Otto asked between coughs. "I don't see any mountains."

That was because they hadn't reached Colorado. Yesterday when they'd entered the Hill Country, Otto had smiled at the sight of gently rolling hills, limestone outcroppings, and the live oak canopy they'd discovered on one stretch of the road. Today he seemed to have forgotten that they were still in Texas, hundreds of miles from Colorado Springs.

The road they'd been traveling reached a T intersection, forcing Greta to choose a direction. The route to the left appeared smoother and better traveled, probably leading to a larger town. She tightened the reins, preparing to turn Blackie that way, then stopped. *Turn right.* No one had spoken, and yet she heard the words as clearly as if someone had been seated next to her.

As the wagon lurched toward the right, Greta spotted a small wooden sign almost obscured by a prickly pear cactus. The letters were faded, but she could still make out the arrow and the words, "Sweetwater Crossing 3 Miles." Surely the wagon could hold together for another three miles until they reached the town whose name made her smile for the first time since Otto had begun coughing. There was something almost fanciful about the name, and today more than ever Greta needed a reason to smile.

She turned to look at her brother. "We're going to Sweetwater Crossing," she told him.

Though Otto's only response was renewed coughing, Greta's spirits rose at the prospect of reaching the town in a few minutes. It might not be their final destination, but her instincts told her it was where they needed to be today, and she trusted her instincts.

"C'mon, Blackie." Greta wouldn't force the animal to trot, but she hoped he could pick up his pace a bit. Otto needed a doctor, and he needed that doctor soon. Greta had done all she could.

The sun went behind a cloud, the sudden darkening of the sky causing her doubts to resurface. What if she was wrong? Greta took a deep breath, telling herself that leaving Houston had been the right thing to do—the only way to protect Otto and give him a chance to see Pikes Peak before he died. Greta knew that, but no matter how often she told herself that, she hadn't been able to dismiss the fear that Nigel would be angry enough to search for them and that he'd do what he'd threatened.

She couldn't let that happen. That was why whenever she ventured into a town to buy the supplies they so desperately needed, she'd kept Otto hidden under a blanket in the back of the wagon, why on rainy nights they hadn't dared stay in a hotel, even if they could have afforded a room. But now there was no choice. They had to find a doctor and pray that if Nigel was having them followed, his tracker wouldn't discover them.

It wasn't yet Christmas and what Mama called the season of miracles, but there was no longer any question about it: Greta and Otto needed a miracle.

⋅≫⋅⋅◆⋅⋅≪⋅

"Sweetwater Crossing's residents deserve a choice," Matt Nelson told his brother as they exited the livery.

Earl Dodd, who served as the town's blacksmith as well as the owner of the livery, had assured them that Neptune would be reshod by the time they'd picked up their mail. "You know Jake Winslow likes to talk," he'd said, "especially now that his brother is running for sheriff. He wants to ensure that everyone in town votes for Byron." Earl clicked his tongue in apparent disapproval. "It's an awful shame that Sheriff Granger had that fit of apoplexy."

Matt couldn't argue with that—it was indeed unfortunate that the man who'd been Sweetwater Crossing's lawman for over a decade was now bedridden, unable to move anything on the left side of his body—but Matt could argue with the fact that ever since the War Between the States, when their term of office expired, neither the mayor nor the sheriff had an opponent. When Matt had asked longtime residents why, they'd simply said, "That's the way it's always been." But not the way it should be.

"Uncontested elections don't seem American to me," Matt said. "Folks deserve more."

As his brother nodded, his lips curved upward in what Matt had heard described as a fatuous smile, revealing the direction of Toby's thoughts. "And I deserve a bride." It didn't matter that they were discussing the town's need for a lawman. These days Toby had only one thing on his mind: courting Rose Hannon.

It was far from the first time Toby had been infatuated with a young woman. When they'd lived in Galveston, the object of his fancy had changed as often as the moon had hidden its face, but this was the first time Toby had fixed his attention on a girl since they'd arrived in Sweetwater Crossing earlier this year. And while he'd spouted the same sentiments Matt had heard a dozen times before, Toby seemed different this time. More earnest, almost desperate.

"Rose is the one for me," Toby continued. "I'm as sure of that as I am that you'd be a good sheriff." He gestured toward the next building on Main Street, the one that housed the sheriff's office, held the town's one jail cell, and served as the sheriff's home. "I can picture you living there."

So could Matt. From what he'd heard, the apartment on the second floor would be more than adequate for his needs. "You don't have to convince me. Pa's the one who doesn't approve of what either of us wants."

He crossed the street, preferring to walk through the park rather than next to the building that might never become his home, wishing there were an easy way to convince the man he and Toby owed so much that they were old enough to know their own minds. Because, despite the Bible's admonition to honor thy father and thy mother, the decision of how to spend the rest of their lives—in Toby's case, married to the woman who'd caught his eye the day she'd come to Sweetwater Crossing, in Matt's, serving as their adopted hometown's sheriff—should be theirs and only theirs.

Clearly oblivious to the beauty of the deep blue sky and the puffy cumulus clouds that drifted across it, Toby clenched his fists, then slowly relaxed them in what Matt knew was an attempt to control his anger. "Pa's being unreasonable. I know it's in the Bible, but just because Laban tricked Jacob into marrying Leah rather than Rachel because the eldest had to marry first doesn't mean I should have to wait for you to marry. Those were Laban's daughters. Nowhere in the Bible does it say that the oldest son has to marry first."

"True." Matt wished Pa hadn't been so adamant, announcing that he would not give Toby his blessing to marry unless Matt was married or at least engaged.

His brother shook his head in apparent disgust. "You're so stubborn you'll never fall in love."

"That's not true." At this time of the morning, the park was empty. It would be an ideal place to stroll, to clear his mind, but Matt's mind continued to whirl, trying to find a way to help his brother. "I'm not stubborn. I simply haven't met the right woman."

Though there were a number of single women in Sweetwater Crossing and several matchmaking mothers had done their best to encourage his interest in their daughters, none had stirred Matt's fancy. He might be twenty-six years old, old enough to be wed according to his mother, but he had no intention of marrying unless he found someone who made him as happy as Ma made Pa. Theirs was the kind of love Matt wanted ... eventually.

"I don't have time to think about courting a lady," he told Toby as they strolled through the park, neither in a hurry to reach the post office. Even if Matt had the time, he wouldn't consider courtship until he had a secure future to offer a wife. A man owed that to the woman he wooed. The problem was, despite what Pa thought, Matt's future was not living and working on the family's ranch. "What I want is to leave the ranch in your and Pa's hands and run for sheriff."

Owning a ranch had been their father's dream. That was why when Matt had learned about one for sale near the town where his friend had become the schoolmaster, he had come to Sweetwater Crossing, assured himself that the ranch was a good one, then helped his family sell their haberdashery in Galveston and move here.

Pa was happier than Matt had ever seen him, which meant that Ma was also happy. So was Toby. His brother had taken to ranching as if he'd been born to it. But Matt missed living in a city and having daily interactions with people outside his family. Ranching was not for him, no matter what his father believed.

"I know what I want, and you know what I want. I want you to help me win Rose. I want to become engaged on Christmas Eve like Ma and Pa."

Matt shouldn't have been surprised by the timing, because each year their mother told them that Christmas Eve was extra special for her because it was the day Pa had asked her to marry him and placed a ring on her finger.

"I suppose you want to give Rose the family ring."

His brother shook his head. "I don't care about that. All I care about is making Rose my wife. That's why I need you." When Matt did not respond, Toby grabbed his arm and pulled him to a stop, demanding his full attention. "You don't have to actually marry. I think Pa would be happy if you simply took an interest in someone. If you did, he might agree to let me marry Rose."

Matt stared at his brother, wondering if the morning sun had somehow addled his brain. He and Toby were the same six feet tall and had the same dark brown hair and eyes, but it appeared that they did not share the same sense of honor. "Are you suggesting a false courtship? By now you ought to know me well enough to know I wouldn't do that. It wouldn't be fair to anyone."

"But it would help Rose and me. Look, Matt, I'm not asking you to compromise your principles. Just promise me that you'll consider it. If you show interest in a lady, I'll try to convince Pa that we don't need you on the ranch, and I'll do everything I can to help you become Sweetwater Crossing's next sheriff."

The way Toby phrased it, it sounded almost reasonable. From the number of times that they reminded him that he was more than a quarter century old, Matt knew his parents were concerned that he was still single. They wanted him, whom Pa called the steady one, to settle down and give them grandchildren. He understood that, and he wanted to honor their wishes, but he wanted to do it on his own schedule, not theirs. Today was one of the times when he wished he didn't owe them so much, but the truth was, he and Toby could never repay them for what they'd done.

"All right," he said, his attention snagged by the sight of a wagon hurtling down Main Street. One of the wheels wobbled as if it were ready to fall off, and the horse pulling it was so scrawny Matt was surprised it could move that quickly. "If I can find a woman who appeals to me, I'll court her."

"And I'll help you win the election." Toby extended his hand. "Do we have a bargain?"

"We do." As they sealed their agreement with a handshake, Matt heard a loud gasp. He turned and saw Beulah Douglas, the girl many in town called simple, running back toward her parents. Had something disturbed her? He'd speak to the Douglases later, but right now there was someone who needed him: the woman who was driving the decrepit wagon.

⇉ ·•· ⇇

"You'll be fine, Otto." Greta infused her voice with as much confidence as she could muster, even though her heart feared that her brave words would be proven false. "I like the looks of this town."

They'd entered on what appeared to be the main road, a street lined with businesses and offices. The buildings were well maintained, the boardwalks swept clean. Greta slowed Blackie, searching both sides of the street. Surely Sweetwater Crossing had a doctor. There it was!

"Whoa, Blackie." She reined in the horse, turned to look at her brother, then pointed to the building on the street corner across from the church. "There's the doctor's office." It was what she'd sought. Moreover, the front window bore a sign announcing that the doctor was in. "He'll make you well again."

When Otto's only response was another painful-sounding cough, Greta offered a silent prayer that whatever was causing her brother's cough would be easily cured. The truth was, she was even more frightened than she'd been in Houston when Dr. Fletcher had delivered his ominous prognosis. Otto was coughing almost constantly, the force wracking his small body and filling her with dread. She couldn't lose him. Surely God wouldn't take her only remaining family member so soon. Surely he'd let him live long enough to spend Christmas near the snow-capped mountain that had filled him with hope. Surely this doctor would know what to do and wouldn't demand a large fee.

"Can you walk?"

When Otto struggled to pull himself upright, Greta knew that his legs would not support him even for the short distance from the wagon to the doctor's office.

"It's okay," she assured her brother as she climbed out of the wagon and reached for him. "Wrap your arms around my neck. I'll carry you inside."

Otto was thinner than he'd been when they'd left Houston, because try though she might, Greta hadn't been able to convince him to eat more than a little each day. She doubted that Otto's appetite had decreased and suspected he knew how little money they had and was doing his best to help her conserve it. Mama's death and all that had occurred afterward had forced Otto to grow up too quickly, making him wiser than most ten-year-olds. He might be wise, but though he'd lost a few pounds, he was still too heavy for her to lift.

"Let me help you, ma'am."

Greta turned, startled by the deep voice. She hadn't heard anyone approaching, but there he was. He didn't look like Nigel. This man was taller than Nigel, with dark brown hair and eyes rather than blond hair and gray eyes. He wasn't as handsome as Nigel, his features strong rather than classically sculpted. He wasn't Nigel, and yet the way the stranger looked at Otto, as if assessing everything about the child, reminded her of the reason they'd left the Channing residence.

She started to shake her head, to insist she could carry Otto, but before she could speak, the man lifted her brother into his arms and turned toward the doctor's office. He'd no sooner cradled Otto in his arms than the boy who was so dear to her began to cough, his cough ending with a spray of sputum that wet the man's shirt.

Cringing at the thought of what retribution the man might invoke, Greta said, "I'm so sorry, sir. Please don't blame him."

The man shook his head, and to her relief his expression was concerned rather than angry. "There's nothing to worry about. My shirt can be washed. All that's important is getting this young man inside." He took a step toward the door. "You're in the right place, ma'am. Sweetwater Crossing has the best medical care in the state."

If only that were true. As she remembered the urging she'd received to turn right at the intersection, Greta wondered if this was the reason. She had thought the doctors in a city like Houston would be more skilled than the one in a small town, but for Otto's sake, she hoped the man wasn't exaggerating when he touted this physician's expertise.

When the man she'd begun to think of as the Good Samaritan reached the door, he nodded toward it.

Recognizing his unspoken request, Greta opened the door and heard the tinkle of a bell as the door swung inward. She followed him inside, blinking to help her eyes adjust to the comparative darkness. As a woman who was greatly with child emerged from the door on the left, Greta said, "I'm looking for the doctor."

The woman nodded as if she'd expected that. "I'm Louisa Porter and I'm a doctor."

Greta tried not to stare. Though she'd heard that there were a few women doctors, she hadn't expected to find one in the Hill Country, and she certainly hadn't expected one to be so young. How was it possible that this woman who appeared to be no older than her own twenty-three years had gained enough experience to be an expert in anything?

"I need this young man"—the lady doctor tipped her head toward Otto—"your brother?" When Greta nodded and murmured, "Otto," the brown-haired woman whose eyes were a deeper blue than either Greta's or Otto's continued. "In order to see what's wrong, I need to examine Otto." She led the way into the room she'd just exited.

It looked like the doctors' offices Greta had seen in Houston, with a desk, bookcases, cabinets filled with bottles, and a table. It was toward that table that the doctor gestured. "Please lay him there, Matt."

So the stranger who'd proven to be a Good Samaritan was Matt. The name fit him. It was as firm as he appeared to be, a man who was confident in his abilities.

"Otto's been coughing for a couple days," Greta told the doctor. "I hoped it would stop on its own, but he's much worse today." She wouldn't admit that she'd hesitated to consult a doctor lest he take the little money they had left and be as unable to help Otto as Dr. Fletcher had been. But when the coughing intensified, she'd worried that she'd made the wrong decision and they might not reach a town in time.

Greta closed her eyes and sent a prayer that this doctor would be able to help Otto and that Greta would be able to pay her fees winging toward Heaven. As she did, the sound of piano music began to fill the room. *Music in a doctor's office?* That was something Greta had never experienced. She couldn't identify the song. All she knew was that the notes wrapped around her, comforting her like a warm shawl, and she started to relax. So did Otto. Though his coughing continued, he no longer appeared to be struggling for each breath as he had before.

The doctor fitted a stethoscope into her ears, then listened to Otto's chest. "Your brother has an inflammation of the lungs," she told Greta, "but you're fortunate you stopped here. My partner has a special interest in lung diseases. I'm not boasting when I say he probably knows more about them than any other doctor in Texas."

So that was why Matt had said Sweetwater Crossing had such good medical care. There were two doctors, one with the specialized knowledge Otto needed. For the first time since her brother had begun to cough, hope blossomed in Greta's heart. It appeared her prayers were being answered.

Matt, who'd been standing quietly at her side, spoke. "When I told you you were in the right place, I wasn't exaggerating."

"Burke will know what to do." The doctor turned from Greta to hand Matt a towel and a small pitcher of water. "For your shirt," she said. When he'd cleaned it, she continued. "I don't want to keep you from whatever brought you into town today. Miss ..." She let her voice trail off, waiting for Greta to reveal her name.

"Engel. I'm Greta Engel."

"Miss Engel"—the doctor returned her attention to Matt—"and I will be fine on our own. Thank you for your help."

It was a clear dismissal of the man who'd carried Otto into the office. As if he'd expected it, he gave the doctor a quick nod, then favored Greta with a reassuring smile before striding toward the front door.

"All right, young man, let's see what we can do to make you feel better."

Greta took the seat the doctor had indicated and watched as she measured the contents of one of the colored jars from the largest cabinet into a glass of water, then raised Otto to a sitting position so he could sip it. "This will ease his pain," she told Greta. "When Burke—he's my partner—returns, we'll move your brother to the infirmary and probably put him in a steam tent. That will help him breathe more easily."

She laid her finger on Otto's wrist to check his pulse. "It's possible Burke may believe something else is required, but based on what I've seen so far, I think you got your brother here before there was any permanent damage. While we wait for Burke, the medicine I've given Otto will make him sleep."

"Then you don't think he'll die." Greta voiced her greatest fear.

"Not from this."

Relief flowed through Greta. "Thank you, Dr. Porter."

As the music continued and Otto's breathing became more regular, the peace that had settled over Greta increased. Perhaps Matt was correct. Perhaps she was in the right place.

⟫ ·•· ⟪

"Well done, brother." Toby was laughing when Matt rejoined him in front of the schoolhouse. "Helping a damsel in distress is a great first step. If you had a suit of armor, you could have been a knight from one of those stories Ma used to read us."

Matt tried not to let his annoyance show. What had happened to Miss Engel and her brother was no laughing matter. Though Louisa had kept her expression calm, Matt sensed that she was concerned by the boy's condition, as was Matt. He'd never heard such painful coughing. "You could have helped, you know."

Toby shook his head. "It was obvious you didn't need any help. What could I have done?"

"Open the door."

Once again Toby shook his head. "Your lovely damsel in distress did that. You didn't need me." His expression turned sober. "What's wrong with the boy? Is he her son?"

"Her brother." Matt wasn't certain why the fact that she was single had made his pulse race a bit, but it had. It wasn't simply that she was, as Toby had said, lovely. With her blonde braids wrapped around her head like a crown, highlighting those clear blue eyes and flawless features, she was more than lovely. She was beautiful. That shouldn't have mattered, but somehow it did.

"Louisa says the boy has some kind of lung ailment." Perhaps if he focused on Otto Engel's illness Matt would be able to forget the way his first sight of Miss Engel had made his heart skip a beat.

"Then they'll be here for a while."

Toby's assessment was probably correct. The little Matt knew about lung diseases was that they were often slow to heal. He wished the boy weren't ill, but he couldn't deny that something about Greta—Miss Engel, that is—had touched him. It was more than her appearance. Perhaps it was the fear she'd tried to hide, a fear that he wanted to erase. Perhaps it was her obvious devotion to her brother, a devotion he understood, for he felt the same way about Toby. Perhaps it was simply the fact that it had felt good to be able to help her.

Matt couldn't explain it. All he knew was that Greta Engel was the most intriguing woman he'd ever met. He almost laughed at the irony that he would feel this way about someone who was passing through town. The joke was definitely on him. But even though Miss Engel wasn't the woman for him, perhaps Pa and Toby were right. Perhaps it was time for him to consider courting a lady.

Hadn't Ma said that everything required practice? When it came to wooing a lady, Matt had little practice. Talking to customers' wives wasn't the same as flirting with young ladies the way Toby did, but he could learn. While he waited to find the right woman, there was no reason Matt couldn't spend a little time with Miss Engel. Not courting her, of course. Simply getting to know her. And if by some chance she and her brother decided to remain in Sweetwater Crossing and if his feelings for her continued to grow, well ... He'd cross that bridge if he came to it.

As the thought lodged in his brain, another one assailed him. Was the interest he felt for Miss Engel the way Toby had felt all those times when he'd declared that he'd found the woman he would marry only to change his mind a few weeks later?

Matt refused to follow in his brother's footsteps. Toby's infatuation had caused the ladies distress when he'd stopped wooing them, and that was something Matt would not to do anyone, especially someone who appeared as vulnerable as Miss Engel. He would take a different approach, a prudent one. He would ensure that she understood that all he sought was friendship.

It was a good plan. Matt would go so far as to say that it was an infallible plan. As long as he followed it, nothing could go wrong.

Chapter Two

"He's here."

Although Dr. Porter had said she was confident in her diagnosis, Greta could see she was reassured when a tall man with auburn hair strode into the office, his confident demeanor leaving no doubt that this was Sweetwater Crossing's other doctor, the expert in diseases of the lungs.

"I'm so glad you're here, Burke. Miss Engel's brother needs you." Dr. Porter gestured toward Otto, who was still coughing, although the intensity had diminished once the medicine had taken effect. "Oh, excuse me. I've forgotten my manners." She gave Greta an apologetic smile. "You've probably already guessed that this is Dr. Burke Finley, the man I told you about. He knew what to do to heal my sister's lungs, and I'm sure he'll be able to help Otto too."

Though Nigel would have preened at the praise, Dr. Finley, whose green eyes reminded Greta of spring foliage, said only, "I'll do my best," and turned back to his partner. "What's your diagnosis, Louisa?"

For the first time, the lady doctor revealed her lack of confidence. "I'm not certain, but I suspect capillary bronchitis."

The way his expression grew solemn told Greta this was a serious condition, but Dr. Finley remained silent until he'd listened to

Otto's heart and lungs. Then he nodded. "Your diagnosis was correct, Louisa. It is capillary bronchitis. A steam tent will help."

"That's what I thought." Dr. Porter's relief that her opinion had been confirmed was evidenced by the slight smile that curved the corners of her lips. "I would have moved Otto to the infirmary, but ..." She laid her hand on her swollen abdomen.

"You were right not to. There's no reason to take unnecessary risks." Dr. Finley gave Greta an assessing look. "Can you help me?"

"Of course." She would do anything she could for her brother, anything except agree to Nigel's demands. "What should I do?"

Together she and Dr. Finley carried Otto across the hall to the room the doctors called the infirmary. Smaller than the office where they'd examined Otto, it held two beds, a small table with two chairs, and an even smaller stove. Dr. Porter began heating water on the stove while Greta and Dr. Finley settled Otto on one of the beds.

Within minutes, the doctors had constructed the steam tent, and all the time, the beautiful piano music that invigorated Greta at the same time that it filled her with peace continued. As she sat next to the table watching the doctors care for Otto, she marveled at the way they worked together, their movements as carefully choreographed as she'd heard ballets were. Perhaps the music was the reason they moved so smoothly.

Greta tipped her head to one side, wondering where the piano was hiding and who was playing it so masterfully.

"That's my wife," Dr. Finley said when he saw Greta searching for the source of the music. "The piano shares space with our supplies." He gestured toward the rear of the building. "The last doctor's wife insisted that her daughter learn to play, but they couldn't get the piano upstairs, so it's been in the storage room ever since. I know it's unusual, but Louisa and I have discovered that music helps our patients—and us—relax." He stuck his head into the steam tent to check on Otto, then said, "Joanna must have seen your wagon and known you'd need her."

Dr. Porter shook her head. "She was here before Miss Engel and her brother arrived. We were talking about Curtis's sniffles and whether he might give them to Prudence." Another sheepish grin crossed the lady doctor's face. "I owe you another explanation. Joanna isn't only Burke's wife. She's also my sister. Curtis is Burke and Joanna's son, and Prudence is my other sister's daughter. If you can keep all those straight, you're doing better than most folks."

Though Greta managed a weak smile, Dr. Finley did not. "What did you tell Joanna about Curtis?" he asked his partner.

"Probably the same thing you did, that young children recover quickly from minor ailments and often seem stronger afterward, so she needn't worry that Curtis might be contagious."

Greta stared as the other doctor nodded his agreement. This was far different from anything Dr. Fletcher had said. He was convinced that all illnesses needed to be quarantined. Greta's spirits rose at the thought that if he was wrong about that, it was possible that he'd been wrong about Otto's condition.

Dr. Finley gave his partner a rueful smile as he headed toward the door. "Now that we have young Otto settled, I need to leave. I promised Herb Oberle I'd check on him today, and you know that he doesn't like waiting." He turned to Greta, his expression reassuring. "You're in good hands here, Miss Engel. My partner knows what to do for your brother."

When the other doctor left, Greta turned toward Dr. Porter. "Can you tell me more about what's wrong with Otto?"

Dr. Porter took a seat on the second chair. "As Burke and I said before, it's called capillary bronchitis. That means there's inflammation of the smallest air tubes in the lungs. We typically see it in children younger than your brother or in the elderly, but whenever it occurs, it's important to treat it quickly."

The doctor rose and lifted the edge of the canvas tent to listen to Otto's breathing. "If his disease follows the normal progression, we'll keep him here for two or three days, but I need to caution you that it'll take several weeks for a complete recovery."

Weeks. Greta tried not to let her dismay show. They didn't have weeks to spare if they were going to reach Colorado by Christmas.

"How many weeks?" As much as she wanted to make Otto's dream come true, his health was more important than seeing a mountain. What had happened today had shown her how fragile it was.

"For a complete recovery, I'd say six weeks." Dr. Porter's voice resonated with sympathy. "I know you were on your way somewhere, but your brother shouldn't travel again until he's fully healed."

"We were going to Colorado. Otto wanted to spend Christmas near Pikes Peak."

The doctor frowned. "You could try leaving sooner than six weeks, but I'm not sure that's wise. Colorado Springs is at a much higher altitude than Texas. That could be harmful for Otto's lungs."

Greta was confused. "I read that people went there to heal their lungs."

Dr. Porter nodded. "The climate in Colorado Springs is beneficial for those with tuberculosis, but your brother isn't tubercular."

"Are you sure? Greta hated to question the woman who'd been so kind to Otto, but she couldn't forget what had happened in Houston. "Dr. Fletcher said he had galloping consumption. Isn't that the same as tuberculosis?"

"It is," Dr. Porter confirmed, "but your brother shows no sign of it. What were his symptoms when that doctor diagnosed consumption?"

Greta shuddered, remembering the horror of the day Dr. Fletcher had been summoned. "Otto could barely breathe. He wasn't coughing like he was today. Instead, he was wheezing. It was like he couldn't get the air out of his body."

"I see. Did he have chills or fever?"

"No."

"Was his face very pale with red spots over his cheekbones?" The doctor pointed to her own cheekbones.

"No."

"Had he lost a lot of weight?"

For the first time, Greta could not give a definitive answer. "Some, but I thought that was because he was working so hard and couldn't always come in for meals."

"What about weakness?"

"If anything, he was stronger after he started working in the stable. He had to lift a lot of heavy things."

Dr. Porter's expression softened. "I don't know what caused your brother's breathing problem, but I can tell you that he did not have tuberculosis."

Greta blinked to keep the tears from falling. Happy tears. Relieved tears. "Then he won't die?"

"We all die eventually," the doctor reminded her, "but I don't believe your brother is in any immediate danger." She paused, her expression solemn. "I won't speculate about what happened to Otto in Houston and why the doctor believed he was on the verge of dying. All I can say is that it doesn't sound like tuberculosis. There's always a chance that whatever it was may recur and that it could threaten his life, but unless it does, I recommend that we consider whatever it was a one-time event and not worry about it. If you stay here long enough for Otto to make a full recovery from his bronchitis, you should be able to take him to Colorado."

As the tears leaked from her eyes, Greta brushed them aside. "I don't know how to thank you, Dr. Porter."

"I didn't do anything other than tell you that based on your answers, it appears that you were given an erroneous diagnosis."

Greta reached out to touch the doctor's hand. "You did much more than that. You gave me hope."

"I'm glad I could do that." She rose to check Otto's breathing again, then walked to the window and looked out. "Is that your wagon?"

"Yes. Why?" The doctor's serious tone raised Greta's concern.

"I'm not an expert, but from what I can see of it, I doubt that wagon will make it all the way to Colorado."

The hope that had risen like a balloon on the breeze faded, punctured by Dr. Porter's assessment. Not even the beautiful music that was still coming from the room next door soothed her.

"The news about Otto's health is wonderful, but I didn't expect this." That wasn't completely true. Greta had known that most wagons did not creak the way theirs had, but she hadn't realized that those creaks were the sign of irreparable damage.

"I don't know what we'll do. Otto has his heart set on seeing Pikes Peak, but without a reliable wagon ..." Greta bit her lip, not wanting to admit how precarious their situation was but knowing she owed Dr. Porter honesty. "We have very little money."

Buying the wagon and horse had cost more than she had expected, leaving little for food and nothing for lodging, which was why she and Otto had slept in or under the wagon each night of their journey. Now it seemed they would need a new wagon.

"It's not only the wagon. I don't know how I'll pay your fees or how I can afford to rent a room for us while Otto recovers."

The doctor seemed unconcerned by Greta's confession. "I'd offer you the other bed, but Burke will need it tonight. When we have a patient as ill as your brother, he spends the night here to check on them."

Greta must have looked discouraged, because she continued. "I know you'll want to be close to Otto, and you can. There's an apartment upstairs that was the former doctor's residence. You can stay there while Otto's in the infirmary. Don't worry. There'll be no extra charge."

Accepting charity when she was an able-bodied woman went against everything Greta had been taught. "It's not right not to pay you."

The doctor was silent for a moment. "I'm not sure what condition the rooms are in." She gestured toward her midsection. "The stairs are steep, so I haven't climbed them recently."

Greta understood her need for caution. "When is your baby due?"

"Early December, and that can't come soon enough." Dr. Porter let out a laugh. "I'm the town's midwife as well as a doctor, so you'd think I'd be well-versed in the stages of pregnancy. I can't count the number of times I've advised my patients to be patient, and now I'm the impatient one."

"I imagine that's normal." Greta remembered Mama complaining about swollen ankles and difficulty sleeping during the last few weeks before Otto was born.

"It is. Still, I find it humorous that I can't take my own advice. If you don't mind some dust, you're welcome to use the apartment."

It was a generous offer and one Greta had no intention of refusing. Even though the canvas covering of the steam tent muffled sound, she could tell that Otto's breathing was easier and that the coughs that had frightened her had lessened in severity. Still, she wanted to remain as close to him as she could.

"I'd be happy to give the apartment a thorough cleaning, but I need to find a way to earn enough money to pay your fees and buy a new wagon. Is there a restaurant in town where I might work?"

When the doctor raised an eyebrow, Greta explained. "My parents used to own a restaurant, and I helped them. I can do everything from cooking to serving to washing dishes."

"We have one restaurant here, but I don't believe Mrs. Tabor needs any help."

The music stopped abruptly, and seconds later a tall woman with dark brown hair and eyes entered the infirmary. The doctor smiled. "Greta, this is my sister, Joanna. She's Burke's wife and, as you've heard, an accomplished pianist."

Searching for but finding little resemblance between her and the doctor, Greta smiled at the woman who'd made the time pass so quickly. "Your music is wonderful. At times it soothed me; other times it encouraged me; still other times, it made me want to dance with joy. I've never experienced anything like that." She extended her hand in greeting. "I'm pleased to meet you."

"Not as pleased as I am to meet you." Joanna returned Greta's smile as she clasped her hand. "You're the answer to prayer."

"You've caught it bad." Toby gave Matt's arm a playful punch as they left the post office.

"What are you talking about?" As he'd expected, it had taken far more time than it should have to get their mail because there had been a line of people ahead of him and Toby, and each one had had to listen to Jake Winslow's stories of how qualified his brother was to become sheriff.

Though he'd tapped his foot in impatience, Matt hadn't contradicted the postmaster or suggested that Byron might not be running unopposed. It was too soon to do either. Before he announced his plans, he needed to tell his parents what he'd decided. As annoying as the delay at the post office was, the truth was Matt hadn't paid too much attention to Jake's ramblings. His thoughts had been focused on what might be happening next door in the doctor's office.

Toby's chuckle turned into a laugh. "I wish I had a mirror so you could see yourself. You're obviously thinking about that girl, your damsel in distress."

Unwilling to let his brother know how accurate his assessment was, Matt said, "You'd be concerned about her too if you'd seen how sick her brother was." That had concerned him almost as much as the worry and the momentary fear he'd seen in Greta's lovely blue eyes. Otto's illness was taking a toll on her, and though he wanted to help, Matt knew there was nothing he could do. Or was there?

"Look at that." He gestured toward the wagon parked in front of the doctor's office. The rim of one wheel was so badly bent that he wondered how long it would be before it fell off. Even if it didn't, the misshapen wheel had to have made the ride uncomfortable. And, as if that weren't enough, the wooden sides were splintered, seeming on the verge of disintegrating. A piece of canvas covered what appeared to be a few possessions, while the pile of blankets suggested that Greta and her brother had spent their nights sleeping in the wagon's bed.

"I'm surprised this hasn't fallen apart. Do you suppose Earl can fix it?" Matt asked when he'd rejoined Toby on the board-walk after studying the wagon from all sides. "And what do you think about the horse?"

When they'd first arrived in Sweetwater Crossing, folks had told Matt's family that the livery's owner could fix just about anything that moved—wagons, carriages, even babies' peram-bulators—and that he took excellent care of the horses that were stabled with him. While Matt would trust Earl's opinion of the wagon, he wanted his brother's assessment of the animal that had pulled it. Toby's affinity for animals was one of the reasons he was finding ranching so rewarding.

Toby's frown confirmed Matt's assessment. "I don't think there's much hope for the wagon." He gave the gelding an appraising look. "The horse will probably be all right with more food and a couple weeks' rest, but the wagon? I doubt it's salvageable. My guess is Earl would say it would be cheaper to buy a new one than try to fix this one."

"That's what I thought." Were the horse and wagon part of the reason for the fear he'd seen in Miss Engel's eyes? If the state of their wagon was any indication, the Engel siblings were on the verge of poverty, and that made Matt's heart clench. There had to be something he could do to help them.

When Matt saw Burke Finley emerge from his office, he approached the doctor who'd become a friend. "I won't ask you to divulge anything about your patient, but it looks like the boy isn't the only one in need of help." He pointed toward the horse that stood patiently in its harness, even though it was obvious that he needed water, food, and rest. "The Engels' horse should be in the livery. They'll probably want their belongings out of the back of the wagon, but if you'll take care of that and getting the horse to him, I'll tell Earl to put his board on my bill."

"Are you sure?" Burke appeared surprised by the offer. "They could be here for a while."

Which was exactly what Matt was hoping for. He wouldn't make the mistake Toby had so many times and declare that he'd found the woman he wanted to share the rest of his life with only to change his mind a few weeks later. Toby was impetuous. Matt was not. A week or two, maybe longer, would give him a chance to get to know the pretty blonde better.

Casual conversations would be the first step in discovering whether his unexpected feelings for her were more than infatuation. And if they were and if she was still here after the election was over, he would take the second step.

There was no reason for Burke to know that this was part of Matt's plan. Instead, he said only, "It's the neighborly thing to do."

His expression seeming to see more than Matt had said, Burke nodded. "All right. On behalf of the Engels, thank you."

When the doctor was out of earshot, Toby clapped his brother on the shoulder. "I knew it. You're smitten, Matt. Smitten."

Chapter Three

"Breakfast is ready. I hope you are too."

The tantalizing aromas of bacon and coffee followed Louisa's voice up the stairs. Though Greta's mother would have disapproved of her addressing the doctor by her first name, Dr. Porter had insisted that they dispense with formalities. "My friends call me Louisa," she'd said yesterday afternoon when they'd left Otto sleeping in the infirmary, "and since I hope you and I will become friends, you should too."

Dr. Finley had said something similar upon his return to check on Otto, urging her to address him as Burke. Greta had been surprised by the informality Sweetwater Crossing's residents seemed to have adopted, but her surprise turned to astonishment when Burke told her that Matt Nelson, the Good Samaritan, had arranged for Blackie and the wagon to be taken to the livery and had offered to pay for Blackie's board.

"I can't let him do that," Greta had told the doctor. Strangers—especially strange men—did not make generous gifts unless they expected something in return. That was one of the reasons etiquette prohibited men from giving a lady anything other than flowers, books, and candy until they were affianced.

"I'll find a way to repay him." Greta frowned, once again wondering how she would earn enough money to cover all the expenses she was incurring.

"Don't worry about that," Burke urged her. "Matt and his family moved here from Galveston earlier this year, and in the months they've lived here, they've proven to be caring and generous people. Matt personally paid for new primers for the schoolchildren when he saw how shabby the others were."

A wave of relief flowed through Greta at the realization that Matt Nelson did not appear to be like Nigel. His kindness, it seemed, came without expectation of repayment. Despite that, she would repay him ... eventually.

"Let's concentrate on getting your brother well again," Burke continued, oblivious to the detour Greta's thoughts had taken. "My advice to you is to sleep as much as you can tonight. You need to be rested and strong for Otto."

Greta had tried to take his advice. Once she'd cleaned the apartment, a task that took far less time than Louisa had feared, she'd eaten a light supper, then after she was assured that Otto was sleeping, had climbed into bed. Now, more than twelve hours later, she descended the stairs, more anxious to see Otto than she was to sample the delicious smelling food.

Though Burke had assured her that he would waken her if Otto's condition worsened, Greta had slept fitfully, memories of her brother's wracking cough echoing through her brain along with worries about how he would react when she told him they would not reach Pikes Peak by Christmas.

"Otto is still sleeping," Louisa told Greta when she reached the foot of the stairs, "but I've set the table in the infirmary, because I knew you'd want to be close to him."

As they entered the room where Otto had spent the night, Louisa lifted the edge of the steam tent so that Greta could hear her brother's steady breathing. Though he coughed occasionally, there was none of the rasping sound that had so alarmed her.

"He seems better."

"He is. Burke confirmed that Otto slept fairly well." Louisa gestured toward a covered plate that she'd placed on the small table. "I hope you like pancakes and bacon. My sister didn't want you to worry about cooking today, so she sent breakfast for you."

With her worries about Otto relieved, Greta found that she was hungrier than she'd realized. After giving thanks for the food and for the care Otto was receiving, she uncovered the plate and took a bite, savoring the delicately browned pancakes and the crispy bacon. "Your sister cooks as well as she plays the piano."

To her surprise, Louisa chuckled. "It's a different sister. Joanna isn't much of a cook, but no one can match Emily." As if she sensed Greta's questions, Louisa explained, "Emily's the oldest of us; I'm the youngest."

"And Joanna is in between." Greta cut another piece of pancake. "I hope you don't mind my saying so, but if you hadn't told me Joanna was your sister, I wouldn't have realized you were related. There's not much resemblance between you. Her hair's much darker than yours, and her eyes are brown."

Once again, Louisa chuckled. "Wait until you meet Emily. She's a petite blonde with blue eyes like mine."

It appeared the three sisters were very different in both appearance and talents. "I'm surprised. I thought most siblings shared similar coloring and features the way Otto and I do." Not only did they have the same blond hair and blue eyes, but Greta and her brother's noses were the same shape, and they both had heart-shaped faces.

"You're right. Most siblings do resemble each other. We're an unusual family." Louisa sipped the coffee she'd poured for herself. "My parents were widowed before they married each other. Emily was Mama's daughter from her first marriage, and Joanna was born to Father's first wife. I'm the only one of the three of us who was raised by both of her parents."

With the War Between the States leaving so many widows, few women had had the opportunity to marry a second time the way

Louisa's mother had. And some women, including Greta's mother, did not even consider marrying again.

Greta had often wondered what her life would have been like if Mama had sought a husband rather than a position with the Channings. Since the only thing Greta knew for certain was that her life would have been different, she told herself there was nothing to be gained by speculation.

"No wonder you don't look alike."

"The three of us were fortunate for so many reasons." A smile accompanied Louisa's words. "First of all, Father and Mama treated us all the same—there was no favoritism. Just as importantly, we were able to grow up with two parents. The war left so many children fatherless."

Greta nodded, remembering the women who brought their children to the restaurant for a rare treat. They'd often struggled to put food on the table and had confided to Mama that money wasn't their only worry. It was equally difficult to raise children without a father.

Only a week after Papa's death, one of their regular customers had asked Mama to marry him, saying Otto needed a father, but Mama had refused. "All he wants is the restaurant," she had told Greta. "I know I have to sell it, because I can't bear the thought of living here without your father, but I won't sell it to that man. This is a family restaurant. It should be run by a man and his wife."

Within a month, Mama had found a couple who'd worked in another restaurant but wanted to own one. She'd sold the restaurant for far less than Greta thought she should have and had announced that the three of them would be working for Mrs. Channing.

Oblivious to the direction Greta's thoughts had taken, Louisa continued. "Are your parents still alive? Since you and Otto were traveling alone, I'm assuming they aren't."

She was correct. Greta laid down her fork, grateful for the delicious breakfast that had assuaged her hunger. "Papa died five years ago. That's when my mother sold the restaurant and took a position as a cook in one of the city's largest homes." Greta tried to keep her voice even, not wanting to burden Louisa with what she considered her mother's biggest mistake. "I helped her in the kitchen." Though the days had been long, the work wasn't difficult. "Six months ago Mama died, and things began to change. Eventually it got to the point where Otto and I couldn't stay there any longer."

Louisa's expression radiated sympathy. "I won't pry into your past. What's important is that you're here now." She rose and pulled back the steam tent to examine Otto. "Your brother will sleep for another hour or two if you'd like to go to church with my family."

"I would." When she'd seen the church from her bedroom window, Greta had wondered if it would be possible for her to worship there today. She had so many reasons to give thanks: finding doctors as competent and compassionate as Louisa and Burke, seeing Otto's improving health, and receiving Matt Nelson's kindness. Greta hadn't had time to thank Matt properly, but surely he'd attend services this morning.

Heavy footsteps announced the arrival of a man. Louisa smiled at the tall blond whose eyes were a darker shade of blue than Greta's. "Greta, I'd like you to meet my husband. Josh has already heard about you and your brother."

Greta returned the man's friendly smile. "And I've heard about you. I know your name is Porter, so when Louisa mentioned that you own the mercantile as well as a teashop and tearoom, I wondered if you were connected to Porter & Sons in New York." Even though New York was thousands of miles from Houston, Greta had heard of the establishment that called itself the New World's answer to Fortnum & Mason.

Josh nodded. "That's my family's business. I used to work there, but my cousin is in charge now."

"You're quite a ways from New York."

"You're not the first to say that." Josh's chuckle made Greta suspect it had been a frequent topic of conversation when he'd first arrived in Sweetwater Crossing. "It's a long story and one best saved for another day. Let's just say that breaking my leg was the best thing that ever happened to me, because it led me to Louisa."

The smile he gave his wife reminded Greta of the looks her parents had exchanged, looks that left no doubt of their love. Would she ever find a love like that? She certainly hadn't with Nigel.

"Ready for church?" Josh asked.

"Almost." Louisa hoisted herself to her feet, muttering something that sounded like, "I feel like a whale."

When both women had donned their hats and gloves, Josh offered each an arm to escort them across the street toward a trio of adults and a young boy. Greta recognized Burke and, based on the description Louisa had given, suspected the other adults were Louisa's older sister and her husband.

"You've already met Burke, and if you're wondering where Joanna is, she's our pianist, so she's already inside." Louisa's mouth turned upward into a wry smile as she gestured toward the couple whose watchful gaze left no doubt that the boy was their son. "You've probably guessed that this is my sister Emily and her husband. Craig's our schoolmaster, and this is their son Noah."

Emily was every bit the petite blonde that Louisa had described, the only resemblance between her and Louisa being the same vivid blue eyes. Craig stood almost a foot taller than his wife, his dark brown hair and eyes echoed in his son's. By any standard, they were an attractive family.

"I'm so glad to meet you." Emily extended her hand toward Greta. "Joanna told me about you when she came to pick up Curtis yesterday. You'll get to meet him and my Prudence some other time. They're both a bit cranky today, so Mrs. Carmichael is keeping them at home."

"Emily's not only the best cook in the family," Louisa continued her explanation. "She also runs a boardinghouse and cares for my sister's son as well as her own daughter." She cupped her midsection and smiled. "In another month, Josh and I'll be adding another to Emily's nursery."

Greta felt a twinge of envy at the sisters' obviously close relationship. As a child, she'd wished she had a sister or even a brother, someone to be her playmate, but that hadn't happened. Her mother had lost several babies before Otto was born, and by then Greta had been old enough that he was more like her child than a sibling.

Emily's smile was self-deprecating. "I don't do it singlehandedly. We have Mrs. Carmichael living with us. She started by serving as Noah's nanny and has expanded her responsibilities."

"You're fortunate to have her," Greta told Emily. "My mother admitted that it was a challenge working in the restaurant and trying to take care of me when I was little." When Otto arrived, Greta was old enough to help in the restaurant and in caring for her brother, something Mama had said made her life easier.

"We're a very fortunate family," Louisa said with a fond glance at her sister and the three men in her life. "I won't claim there have been no hard times—there certainly have—but we survived and are stronger as a result."

Greta could only hope that would prove true for her too. When she'd left Houston, she had had only one thought: reaching Colorado before Christmas. Now that that seemed impossible or at least unlikely, she needed wisdom to find a new path and strength to follow it. Her brother was depending on her.

When the church bell rang, Josh laid his hand on Louisa's back. "We'd best go inside now."

As he and Louisa led the way to the second pew from the front, Greta spotted Matt with an older couple and a man about his age. Though the older couple bore no resemblance to Matt, the woman boasting auburn hair almost the same shade as Burke's and the man with blond hair as light as hers and Otto's, the young man looked so much like Matt that he must be his brother. Still, Greta guessed that this was his family. There was no time to speak to Matt now, but she hoped he wouldn't leave before she could thank him.

The church was smaller than the one she had attended in Houston, but between Joanna's playing, which made ordinary hymns

31

seem sublime, and the minister's sermon, Greta found even more comfort than she usually did in worshiping her Lord.

Pastor Lindstrom chose the third verse of Psalm 23 as the foundation for his sermon. Although Greta had recited the words, "He restoreth my soul," more times than she could count, she had never pondered them the way the minister urged the congregation to do. Was the feeling of peace that had surrounded her while Louisa treated Otto and that had only increased as she worshiped today a restoration of her soul? Perhaps it was.

* * *

Matt said a silent prayer of thanksgiving when he saw the pretty blonde who'd occupied his thoughts since yesterday follow Louisa and Josh Porter into the pew reserved for the three sisters and their families. He'd thought about and, yes, worried about her, for it was obvious that Greta was at a difficult time in her life. Her presence here with Louisa told him Otto was well enough to be left alone for an hour or so, and that was an answer to prayer.

Now if only his other prayer would be answered. He was still trying to decide how to tell Pa of his decision to run for office. As much as he hated to disappoint him—and Pa would be deeply disappointed that Matt didn't share his dream—the sense of rightness that had filled him when Craig told him there would be a special election to replace Sheriff Granger could not be denied.

Being a lawman was different from working in a haberdashery, but both involved serving other people and that, Matt had discovered during the months he'd spent working on the ranch, was important to him. While both Pa and Toby found satisfaction in raising cattle and exploring every acre of the ranch, Matt did not. He missed being with people outside his family. More than that, he missed helping others.

Perhaps the fact that he'd been able to help her was the reason his thoughts turned to Greta so often. He hadn't been a knight in shining armor, simply a man who found satisfaction in lending a helping hand. That's what he had to make Pa understand.

Pastor Lindstrom's sermon resonated within him, reminding Matt that as much as the Bible admonished the faithful to honor their parents, doing God's will was of even greater importance. He would speak to Pa and Ma today, then do whatever was necessary to make his candidacy official tomorrow. Maybe then he would feel that his soul had been restored.

As Matt emerged from the church, he looked around, telling himself he wasn't looking for anyone in particular, though the way his pulse raced when he saw Greta told him he'd been deluding himself. There she was, with Louisa and Josh Porter. He hoped he wasn't deluding himself into believing she'd been looking for him, but when she spotted him, Greta said something to the Porters, then walked toward him, determination in her pace as well as etched on her face. The distraught and fearful woman he'd seen the day before had been replaced by one who exuded strength, and that transformation only increased his desire to learn more about her.

"Good morning, Mr. Nelson. I hope you can excuse my poor manners yesterday," she said when she reached him. "I'm very thankful for the help you gave my brother and me and should have told you so before you left."

Though a smile accompanied her thanks, the slight tremor he heard in Greta's voice told Matt that, while her worries may have lessened, she was still concerned about Otto's condition. That was understandable, given how ill the boy had been when Matt had carried him into Burke and Louisa's office.

Wanting to see that smile again, he shrugged, then smiled at her. "No apologies are needed. I was simply being neighborly."

Toby's laughter caused Matt to swivel and glare at his brother. Leave it to Toby to arrive at the wrong time. Matt hadn't heard him approaching, but there he was with Ma and Pa next to him, and while Matt saw nothing amusing about the conversation he and Greta had been having, apparently Toby did.

Mindful of the etiquette lessons Ma had given him and Toby, Matt turned back to Greta. "I'd like to introduce you to my family," he began. "These are my parents, Daniel and Mary Nelson, and my brother Toby." As she gave them a small smile, he continued. "This is Miss Greta Engel. When she and her brother arrived here yesterday I helped take him into the doctor's office."

"And he arranged for our horse to be boarded at the livery." Greta looked at Matt, those pretty blue eyes shining with so much gratitude that he felt humbled. "I assure you that I'll pay you back, but in the meantime, saying 'thank you' seems inadequate."

When Matt shook his head, indicating that he did not expect to be reimbursed, Greta turned her gaze toward Pa. "Your son was a Good Samaritan."

"I see." Matt could not decipher the look Pa exchanged with Ma, but their silent communication made his mother raise her eyebrows.

Seemingly oblivious to their parents' reaction, Toby grinned. "That's our Matt, a Good Samaritan, always ready to serve others. If all goes the way I predict it will, in another month he'll be serving Sweetwater Crossing as its new sheriff."

No, Toby. No. This wasn't the way Matt wanted their father to learn that he planned to run for sheriff.

This time there was no question about Pa's reaction. The way the blood drained from his face, then rushed back in told Matt he was both shocked and displeased by the news and the way it had been delivered. It was probably only Pa's refusal to involve others in their family's affairs that kept him silent.

Toby clapped Matt on the back, then took a step away, seemingly unfazed by their father's obvious anger. While the public announcement wasn't the way Matt would have told his parents, he had to admit that there was some merit to Toby's approach. Pa would have a chance to cool down a bit before he was alone with Matt. His anger flared quickly but rarely lasted long.

Deliberately not addressing his candidacy, Matt turned back to Greta. "How is your brother, Miss Engel?"

"Better this morning. Louisa—that is, Dr. Porter—said he's recovering faster than she thought possible, but she warned me that he shouldn't travel for at least six weeks."

"If you're staying that long, you should plan to be here for Christmas." Though Matt had thought Toby was leaving, he'd simply moved a few feet away. "It'll be my family's first Christmas in Sweetwater Crossing, and it would be nice to not be the only newcomers."

The way Greta's smile faltered told Matt that while Toby might be looking forward to Christmas here and possibly continuing the family tradition of becoming engaged on Christmas Eve, she must have had other plans.

As if sensing Greta's unease, Ma addressed her for the first time. "Your name sounds German."

Her smile once more in place, Greta nodded. "It is. My parents and grandparents were among the first emigrants from the old country. They were drawn by the promise of a better life, but they stayed in Houston rather than coming to the Hill Country with many of the others."

But now she was in the Hill Country, at least temporarily. Rather than ask where she'd been headed, since that might distress her again, Matt said simply, "We were almost neighbors. My family lived in Galveston until earlier this year."

Before Greta could respond, Pa spoke. "I doubt this young lady is interested in our family's story. She's probably anxious to see how her brother is faring." It was as close to a dismissal as Matt had ever heard from his father.

He tried not to let his surprise show. It wasn't like Pa to be so rude, but then again this was the first time he'd learned that his older son was hoping to leave the ranch.

Deciding it was best to get Greta away from what might become an unpleasant situation, Matt crooked his arm for her. "May I escort you across the street?"

"Thank you." She bade his family farewell, then turned toward the doctor's office.

When they were out of earshot, Matt said, "I want to apologize for my father. He's not usually so curt."

Greta gave him a reassuring smile. "I know it wasn't directed at me. He's obviously concerned about your running for sheriff."

"You're right, but how did you know that?"

"My mother taught me to read people's expressions. We owned a restaurant in Houston, and she said it was important to watch people's faces, because sometimes their expressions contradicted their words."

It was an interesting observation. As he thought about some of the customers they'd had at the haberdashery, Matt remembered several occasions when customer had said they were pleased with the service they'd received but had never returned. Had their expressions revealed something their words had not? Perhaps.

"That's good advice. I'll have to remember it when I'm campaigning. And now that I know you're so observant, I'll have to be careful around you."

Greta raised an eyebrow, then gave him the warmest smile he'd seen. "So far you've passed the sincerity test. Your words and your expressions said the same thing. You're not trying to mislead anyone."

The flash of pain that deepened her eyes made Matt suspect someone had misled her and filled him with the determination that he would never cause her that kind of distress. For however long she was in Sweetwater Crossing, Matt would do his best to ensure that Greta's face was wreathed in a smile, not a frown.

Chapter Four

Louisa joined Greta and Matt as they reached the front door of her office. When she'd unlocked it, rather than enter, Matt said, "My family's waiting for me."

The slight frown that accompanied his words told Greta he wasn't looking forward to being with his father but that he knew it was time.

Nodding as if she understood although she had not been privy to Mr. Nelson's reaction to his son's candidacy, Louisa led the way into the infirmary. "Let's see how our patient is doing."

Though Otto was coughing, even to Greta's untrained ear, it seemed like a less painful cough than a few hours ago. "That sounds different."

"It is." Louisa confirmed Greta's observation. "And that's good. The medicine and the steam are softening the phlegm that was blocking his capillaries. That's making it easier for him to breathe." Louisa walked toward the bed. "He's responding more quickly than most patients. I think it's safe to say that your brother is a very determined young man."

"That's Otto, all right." And that made Greta dread telling him that he wouldn't be spending Christmas near Pikes Peak.

"Let's see how he does without steam." The doctor removed the canvas and withdrew the pots of hot water that had filled the makeshift enclosure with moisture, and as she did, Otto stirred. "Good morning, young man. How do you feel?"

Thrilled that he was awake, Greta moved to Louisa's side, but her brother had fixed his gaze on the doctor, confusion written on his face. "Who are you?" His voice was hoarse, perhaps because of all the coughing he'd done.

"This is Dr. Porter." Greta tried to reassure him. "She's been helping you get better. You were very sick when we arrived here." When Otto looked around, as if trying to understand where he was, Greta said, "This is the doctor's office. You spent the night here."

His gaze returned to Louisa. "A lady doctor?" Otto punctuated his question with another burst of coughing.

"Yes, indeed, and she's a very good one. She and her partner knew exactly what to do to help you."

While Louisa pressed her finger to Otto's wrist to check his pulse, Greta studied her brother's face, noting that the pallor that had contributed to her worries yesterday had been replaced by a healthy pink. Though she knew that could be due to the warmth inside the steam tent, she chose to believe that it was a sign that Otto was improving.

Otto continued to stare at Louisa. "Did you play the music?" Apparently he recalled that much.

"No. That was my sister. Now I'm going to listen to your heart and lungs." Louisa pulled out her stethoscope and continued her examination. When she finished, she said, "You're doing better, but it's time for a bit more medicine." She rose and poured a dark-colored liquid into a cup, then helped Otto sip it.

Though he grimaced at the taste, when he'd drunk it all, he fixed his gaze on Greta. "I want to play the piano like the lady."

Of all the things Greta might have expected him to say, that was not one. Music had not been part of their life at the restaurant, and Otto had never paid any attention to the Channings' grand piano. Perhaps that was because no one there had played with Joanna's skill. She was more than talented; she was truly gifted, able to turn even a simple hymn into glorious, soul-touching music. Though Greta wished she could promise her brother that he would have the opportunity to play a piano, that was one of many promises she could not make. "We'll see, Otto. Right now, you need to get well."

As his eyelids began to close, he nodded, then coughed again.

"He'll sleep for a while. Even though he's doing better than I expected, there's still a long road ahead before he'll be fully recovered." Louisa made her way to her office.

Greta followed, thinking about the changes she'd seen and heard in her brother. "That's more than he's talked in several days."

Louisa laid a protective hand on her abdomen as she lowered herself into one of the chairs in front of her desk, then indicated that Greta should take the other. "Otto can talk more because his throat doesn't hurt as much now that he's coughing less often. It's all part of the healing process."

A process that might not have happened without Louisa. Greta didn't want to consider what might have happened if there had been no doctor in Sweetwater Crossing or if the doctor had been like the one in Houston. "I don't know what I would have done if I hadn't found you."

"But you did."

And it wasn't happenchance. A shiver made its way down Greta's spine as she thought about yesterday. "When we reached the last crossroads, I almost turned left, but something told me to turn right. It's hard to explain, but I felt as if I was being led here."

Louisa smiled. "You were."

⋙━━◆━━⋘

"Is this some kind of ploy to make me more agreeable to Toby courting the Hannon girl?" Though Ma usually sat next to him on the front bench of the wagon, today Pa had insisted that Matt share it with him, relegating Ma and Toby to the seat behind them. While his anger appeared to have faded, his voice was still harsher than normal, making it clear that he was not happy over the prospect of Matt's candidacy.

Matt shook his head. "It's true that I think Miss Hannon might be the right woman for my brother. Toby's been happier than I've ever seen him since she came to town, but ..."

"So you admit it," Pa said before Matt could finish his sentence. "Either you're trying to distract me or you're trying to convince me that Toby's the right one to carry on the family name and that he should marry and start producing grandchildren."

If it turned out that Toby's feelings for Rose Hannon were more than infatuation, Matt saw no reason why he shouldn't be the first to marry, but that wasn't the issue today.

"No, sir. Neither of those is the reason I want to become Sweetwater Crossing's next sheriff." Matt kept his voice low and even, not wanting to reignite Pa's anger, though he knew his father would not be pleased by what he had to say. "Having a ranch is your dream and Toby's, but it's not mine. I want to keep the town safe. I want to ensure that justice is done."

When Pa started to scoff, Matt continued. "Toby was right when he said that I want to serve. I do. Ever since we moved here, I've been searching for a way to make a difference in people's lives. When Craig told me about Sheriff Granger's resignation, I knew that running for sheriff was what I was meant to do."

Matt studied his father's expression, searching for the slightest softening but not finding it. "There's no guarantee that the townspeople will elect me, but I want to try. No, that's not correct. I *have to* try."

A long silence followed Matt's declaration. Finally Pa spoke. "That's all the more reason why you should think about marriage. The right wife would make your job and your life a lot easier."

He paused for a second, then turned toward the back of the wagon and looked at Ma and Toby, neither of whom made any pretense of not listening. "Once you're settled, it'll be Toby's turn."

Chapter Five

Greta blinked in surprise at the sun streaming through the window. Even though Burke and Louisa had said it wasn't necessary, she'd wakened several times during the night and had gone downstairs to check on Otto. Both doctors had told her that her brother was progressing well but that another night under the steam tent was needed to continue the healing. She trusted them, but worries about how she was going to pay both them and Matt Nelson and how Otto would react when he learned that their trip to Colorado was being delayed had kept her awake.

Finally Burke had insisted she go back to bed, assuring her that her brother was doing better and that the best thing she could do for him was to get some rest. After that, Greta had slept longer than she'd expected, and now not only had the sun risen, but she heard two women's voices coming from the first floor.

Five minutes later, she descended the stairs to find both Louisa and Joanna apparently waiting for her in the hallway between the infirmary and the office. Once again, Greta was struck by the differences in the sisters' appearance, although today she noticed that their noses were the same shape, something they must have inherited from their father.

"Your brother is still asleep," Louisa told her as she started to move toward the infirmary, "so I thought you could eat breakfast in my office." When the three of them were inside the office, Louisa pointed to a covered bowl on the desk. "I'm afraid it's only oatmeal this morning. Burke said you were up too late and might sleep in, so Emily made something I could reheat easily. Coffee's ready."

Louisa gestured toward one of the chairs in front of the desk and waited until Greta had taken the seat she offered. "While you eat, Joanna and I want to discuss something with you. You could say we have a bargain to propose."

Joanna took the remaining visitor's chair, while Louisa settled into her chair on the opposite side of the desk.

"It feels good to be off my feet," she said with a long sigh. "The baby has been unusually active this morning, but that's not what we wanted to talk about."

Greta raised an eyebrow as she savored her breakfast. The coffee was as good as it had been the day before, and the addition of raisins and a bit of molasses made the oatmeal anything but ordinary. The food was delicious, but what intrigued her was the sisters' mysterious bargain. She took another swallow of coffee before she spoke. "A bargain? What kind of bargain?"

"One that will benefit both you and me." Though Louisa had initiated the conversation, Joanna replied. "When I said you were the answer to prayer, I wasn't exaggerating."

Dimly Greta recalled Joanna having said that the day she'd arrived, but she'd been so worried about Otto that she hadn't asked what Joanna meant.

Louisa nodded, as if she agreed with her sister's assessment. "You know that my husband Josh owns a tearoom. One of my friends has been managing it, but Caroline's baby is due any day now. She jokes that she's winning the baby race with me, but that's not important. What is important is that Caroline won't be able to work for at least two months. She told Josh she wants to make this Christmas a special one for her baby."

Though Greta was tempted to point out that a child less than two months old would not remember Christmas, she understood the desire to create a special Christmas for a loved one and remained silent as the sisters continued their story.

"Caroline admitted that the girls who help her cook and serve are good at what they do, but they're not ready to handle everything." Joanna wrinkled her nose and twisted her lips into a wry smile. "That's where my problem started. I never thought I'd run a tearoom, but someone has to, so I volunteered."

As Greta took another spoonful of oatmeal, Louisa reached across the desk to touch her sister's hand. "Joanna's a good sister, but I know she wouldn't be happy there even though it's only for a limited time. We didn't know what else to do, so Josh and I discussed closing the tearoom temporarily."

The solution surprised Greta. If the tearoom was like her parents' restaurant, the upcoming Christmas season would bring more customers than usual. Though she wanted to say so, she didn't want to interrupt the story the sisters were telling, and so she continued savoring the oatmeal, interspersing bites with sips of coffee.

"I knew that closing wasn't a good idea for them or for the ladies in Sweetwater Crossing who enjoy their teas at Porter's." This time Joanna smiled, and as she did, she became not simply pretty but beautiful. What a difference a smile could make. "That's why, even though I volunteered to help, I've been asking God for another way to keep it open."

"And then you arrived." This time it was Louisa who spoke. "You said you'd done many things in your parents' restaurant, so it seems you know how a restaurant is run."

"It's true. I do. I helped my mother cook and serve and"—Greta wrinkled her nose—"clean up. My father taught me how to order everything we needed." If there were aspects of running a restaurant she hadn't learned, Greta could not imagine what they were.

Louisa nodded. "That's what we thought. You have the skills and the time, since Burke and I believe you shouldn't leave Sweetwater Crossing for at least a month. Ideally you'll stay for six weeks or more. All three of us—that's Josh, Joanna, and I—are hoping you would consider extending your time here a bit longer."

"Exactly." Joanna's smile encompassed both her sister and Greta.

Greta marveled at the way the sisters were taking turns telling the story. Either they'd rehearsed it or a lifetime together had resulted in their knowing what the other was thinking.

"What we're proposing," Joanna said, "is that you take over the tearoom until the first of the year. To be perfectly honest, Louisa doubts Caroline will ever return to the tearoom, so if it turns out that you like Sweetwater Crossing as much as we do, we could make this a permanent arrangement, but if you decide that isn't what you want, staying until January will give Josh time to find someone else."

Although what she had seen of the town pleased Greta, remaining in Sweetwater Crossing permanently wouldn't give Otto the opportunity to see Pikes Peak. She had already resigned herself to the fact that their trip would be delayed, but she couldn't abandon it, not when it was so important to her brother. Still ...

Her brain had been whirling the whole time the sisters were speaking. They were right. Managing a tearoom was something she could do. Moreover, it was something she would relish doing. Even before Nigel had returned and made life at the Channings' intolerable, Greta hadn't felt completely comfortable living and working there. Being part of her family's restaurant had been wonderful. Oh, it had been a lot of work, but it had been satisfying to watch their customers savoring their meals and saying how welcome they felt whenever they came to the restaurant.

She had loved almost every aspect of running a restaurant. That was why she had tried so hard to convince Mama not to sell, but she'd failed. And so for five years, Greta had missed the joys and even the minor crises that had been part of a restaurant's life. A tearoom could provide the same satisfaction.

"It's an intriguing idea," she admitted. "I can't agree to stay past the first of the year, because I still want to take Otto to Colorado, but since we can't get there by Christmas without risking his health, we might as well stay here."

Greta frowned. "That sounds ungrateful, which is not how I feel. I appreciate your faith in me." A faith Nigel had never shown. "And I appreciate the opportunity. Whatever I earn will go toward paying my bill here and reimbursing Matt Nelson for Blackie's care, but there's still one problem: Otto and I need a place to live once he's well enough to leave the infirmary."

The smile Louisa exchanged with Joanna told Greta they'd anticipated this. "That's not a problem," Louisa said. "I think I mentioned that Emily turned our family home into a boarding-house. Even before Joanna and I moved out, she had more than enough room for you and Otto, and now she has a practically empty house. When we asked her, Emily said she'd love to have you stay there."

"What do you think?" It was Joanna's turn to speak. "Is it a good idea?"

Greta felt as if an enormous weight had been lifted from her shoulders. "It's more than a good idea. It's an answer to my prayers." It wouldn't be the Christmas she and Otto had envisioned, but somehow, someway she would make it a Christmas filled with happy memories for her brother.

"Then we have a bargain." Joanna made it a statement rather than a question.

Greta nodded. "We do."

Now came the hard part: breaking the news to Otto.

⇥ ⋯ ✦ ⋯ ⇤

"It's official," Matt told Toby as he exited the mayor's office. "I thought there might be papers to fill out, but all I had to do was tell Mayor Alcott that I wanted to run for sheriff. He seemed surprised."

Toby shrugged, as if the reason should be obvious. "Probably because there hasn't been a real election in years."

45

"Probably. He warned me that as a newcomer I didn't have much of a chance, but he took me through the sheriff's office and apartment. I'll probably whitewash the office—the walls are dingy from all the cigar smoke—but the living quarters are fine." More than fine. Matt had no trouble imagining himself living there, and the presence of a second bedroom meant that if he married and started a family, there would be room for them.

Marriage! He was beginning to sound like Toby, and that was more than a little alarming. To distract himself from the unexpected thoughts, Matt continued. "The mayor told me frankly that I had about a one percent chance of being elected."

The lack of enthusiasm might have bothered Matt, but knowing how close Mayor Alcott and Jake Winslow were had prepared him for it. It was only natural that the mayor would want his friend's brother to win.

As they started walking west on Main Street, Toby shook his head. "We're going to prove him wrong, starting with this." He paused long enough to pull a sheet of paper from his pocket and hand it to Matt.

Matt opened it and read, "'Make the right choice. Choose Matt Nelson for sheriff.' I like the sentiment, but what do you propose we do with this?"

"*We* aren't going to do anything," his brother said. "This is the first step in my part of our bargain. Today I'll make a dozen copies. Tomorrow I'll go to each of the businesses here"—he gestured both directions on Main—"and ask them to put one in their windows. It'll be harder for them to refuse me than you. I can tell them what a good sheriff you'd be, but if you said the same thing, it would sound like bragging."

"What exactly are you planning to tell them?" Toby had a habit of exaggerating.

"I'm going to start with the time Pa made a mistake and overcharged a customer. You noticed it and rode five miles to return the extra nickel."

While that had happened the way Toby said, it wasn't a story Matt would have considered telling anyone. "You make that sound heroic. It was simply the right thing to do."

His brother nodded. "That's my point. You do the right thing. And right now the right thing is to start courting Greta Engel. She'd make you a fine wife."

"She and her brother are just passing through town." That was one of the reasons Matt had tried to squelch his thoughts of Greta.

"They're going to be here while her brother recuperates," Toby countered. "You could make it your mission to convince them that Sweetwater Crossing should be their home."

"Toby, you're jumping ahead far too fast. Greta and I've exchanged only a few words." Admittedly, thoughts of her had occupied far too much of Matt's waking hours, and he'd even dreamt about her last night, a dream that had had him waking with a smile on his face. But there was no need to tell his brother that. Matt's thoughts and the dream resembled the stories Toby had told about the women he'd fancied in Galveston, and look how those had ended. Matt had no intention of making the same mistake.

Toby's expression became more earnest. "It's true that you haven't had much time with her, but you can change that. She's probably still at the doctor's office."

Matt glanced across the street, nodding when he saw the "Doctor Is In" sign displayed in the front window. He suspected it was too soon for Otto to be released, which meant that Greta was probably with him. She might have left her brother alone so she could attend church yesterday, but Matt couldn't imagine her going anywhere else without him.

"Even if she's there, that's not an ideal spot for a pleasant conversation." When Matt spoke to Greta, he didn't want her to be distracted by her brother's illness, nor did he want them to be surrounded by the accoutrements of a doctor's office.

Ignoring the way Toby nudged him to cross the street, Matt looked in the other direction. When he saw that school was in recess, he knew he'd found his reprieve. "I need to see Craig. He stopped me as we were leaving church yesterday and said he wanted to talk." When Toby raised an eyebrow, Matt shrugged. "I don't know what he has in mind, but I'll meet you back at the livery."

He climbed the schoolhouse steps and entered the building where his friend taught Sweetwater Crossing's children the three R's and so much more.

Craig, who'd been sitting with his feet propped on his desk, lowered them and rose to greet Matt. "I didn't expect to see you so soon, but I'm glad you came."

Though their features differed, the fact that Craig's hair and eyes were the same shade as Matt's and Toby's and that they were all the same height had made more than one person in Galveston believe they were three brothers.

"I was in town this morning to talk to Mayor Alcott about running for sheriff," Matt explained.

His friend nodded, then resumed his seat behind the desk when Matt perched on the corner.

"I hope you win. Byron Winslow is a good man, but the town needs someone with new ideas."

Matt couldn't help but chuckle at Craig's statement. "I thought you told me some of the residents didn't appreciate your new ideas. As I recall, you said you were ambushed."

"That's true." A shrug accompanied the admission. "Some of the adults didn't like my approach to teaching and discipline, but their children did. Holding an occasional class outside and removing the dunce stool may have seemed like revolutionary concepts to a few of the parents, but it didn't take me too long to win them over. I predict you'll have the same success."

"If I win."

"There's no guarantee, but I think you have a chance. Maybe even more than a 50-50 chance."

"That's a substantially higher probability than the mayor gave me. He said I had a one percent chance."

"I'm more optimistic. I won't say it'll be easy, but even though I'm a relative newcomer, I believe you'll be able to convince many of our men to vote for you."

"Is that what you wanted to talk about?" Matt wanted to get back to the ranch. With both him and Toby gone for the morning, Pa would have more work than he could handle. "I'm sorry that you had to learn that I was thinking about running for sheriff the way you did, but I didn't realize Toby was going to make an announcement." Matt wrinkled his nose as he remembered what his brother had done. "He certainly wasn't quiet about it. I don't think he'd have been any louder if he'd had a megaphone."

Craig chuckled. "You're right about that. I suspect he didn't want you to change your mind, but—no—that's not the reason I was hoping to see you privately."

"Then what was?"

Though Craig was clearly attempting to keep his expression neutral, his eyes sparkled with mirth. "I saw the way you looked at Miss Engel. I've known you for more than fifteen years, and that's the first time I've seen you look like that."

As Matt recalled how Greta had said she'd learned to read expressions, he could only hope that his feelings hadn't been as obvious as Craig claimed. "Like what?"

"Like she was the most wonderful woman in the world and you were trying to figure out how to convince her that you were worthy of her."

Matt blinked and tried to corral his emotions. That was how he'd felt, but he wasn't ready to admit it to anyone, not even Craig. The feelings were new, overwhelming, and quite possibly fleeting.

"I just met her," he said, hoping his friend would accept the excuse. "It's too soon to form any opinions about her when we're practically strangers."

Craig shook his head, dismissing Matt's explanation. "Sometimes it only takes a minute or two to know you've met the right one. You looked the way I did when I first met Emily. I didn't believe I was ready to love again, but I was."

No one seeing Craig and Emily together would doubt the strength of their love for each other. "How did you know she was the one for you?"

That was something Toby had never been able to explain. "I simply knew," Toby had said. "Just as I knew when she was no longer the right woman for me." Matt hoped Craig would be more helpful.

The smile that crossed his friend's face told Matt he was remembering his first days with Emily. "I couldn't stop thinking about her. It didn't matter what I was doing. Emily was always on my mind. I won't ask if that's how you feel about Miss Engel, because your face tells me it is."

Craig leaned forward, resting his forearms on his desk. "You need to spend more time with her to learn whether your feelings are true or as transitory as Toby's used to be. That's why I'm inviting you to have supper at Finley House tomorrow. Emily tells me her sisters are planning to convince Miss Engel to stay in Sweetwater Crossing until the new year and to live at Finley House."

Craig gave Matt a second to absorb the news that made his pulse race before he asked, "So, will you come?"

"With pleasure."

Chapter Six

"Well, young man," Louisa said as she removed the stethoscope from her ears, "you've done even better than Dr. Burke and I expected. You won't need the steam tent again, so we're releasing you from the infirmary."

As Otto's eyes brightened, he grinned at Greta. "Can we leave for Pikes Peak today?"

Greta exchanged a look with Louisa. This was the question she'd been dreading. As much as she would have liked to postpone the conversation, she could not.

"I'll be back in a few minutes," Louisa said as she exited the infirmary and closed the door behind her.

Otto swung his legs off the bed, then stopped when he realized they were bare. "Where are my clothes?"

"Right here." Greta picked up the garments Louisa had placed on the other bed. "You were so sick that the doctors wanted you to wear things that were easier to wash." In his case, it had been one of Burke's old shirts that covered Otto from his neck to his knees.

It seemed that even though Otto had spoken to her yesterday and had appeared coherent and cognizant of his surroundings, he had not noticed that he'd been undressed. More than anything else, that convinced Greta that Burke and Louisa were correct in saying that Otto would need time to fully recover from his bronchitis.

When Otto was once more clad in his own clothes, Greta sat on the bed next to him. "I know you want to see Pikes Peak," she told him, "but you've been very ill." After what happened in Houston, she hated reminding him that his health was fragile, but it couldn't be helped. Otto needed to understand the severity of the situation.

"You're healing," Greta said, trying to encourage him, "but the doctors don't want you to travel for at least six weeks. That means we won't reach Colorado by Christmas."

Furrows formed between Otto's eyes, and his expression became mulish. "You promised."

"I said I would do my best to get you there," she corrected him, "and I did, but I can't risk you falling ill again. We were fortunate to find doctors as skilled as Dr. Burke and Dr. Louisa, but that might not happen again. Not all doctors are as good as they are." If what Louisa said was true—and Greta had no reason to doubt her—Dr. Fletcher had been wrong in his diagnosis of Otto's breathing problems.

"But we'll go when I'm better. Right?"

"It'll be a while. We need to stay here long enough for me to earn the money for a new wagon."

His eyes widening in surprise, Otto began to cough. When he stopped, he looked at Greta. "What happened to our wagon?"

"It fell apart." That was what Burke had told her.

"What about Blackie?"

"He needs time to recover from bringing us here. We all need time."

Otto was silent for a moment before he nodded. "All right. I can wait."

That was easier than Greta had expected.

⋅⋅⋅ ⋅✦⋅ ⋅⋅⋅

"This is where you live?"

After a short detour to show Greta the tearoom where she would be working, Louisa had turned the buggy around and headed east on Creek Road, pointing out the house she and Josh had built, then stopping in front of a drive flanked by two large pillars. Greta stared in astonishment at the magnificent home at the end of the drive. Three stories tall in addition to the raised cellar, it boasted verandahs on the first and second floors as well as twin curved staircases leading to the front door. Though she hadn't traveled every street in Sweetwater Crossing, Greta guessed that Finley House was the largest home in the town. It was even larger than the Channings' house, and that was considered a mansion.

"It's where the three of us grew up. You've seen Josh and my home." Louisa tipped her head in the direction of the modest house on the corner. "Joanna inherited a small house from her former teacher, so Emily's the only one of the three of us still living here."

"It's magnificent."

"Some people call it ostentatious," Louisa admitted with a wry smile, "but we like it." She guided the buggy past the stone pillars and along the curving drive that led to the house. "As you can see, there's plenty of room for you and Otto."

Otto, who'd been uncharacteristically silent as he sat between them, spoke for the first time since they'd left the doctor's office. "Is there a piano?" Apparently he had not forgotten Joanna's music or that he'd developed a desire to learn to play the piano.

"Yes, there is." This time Louisa's smile was genuine.

"Then I like the house." Otto nodded solemnly, protesting only feebly when Greta helped him out of the buggy.

After Louisa hitched the horse to a post, the three of them approached the house. Even before they reached the front door, Emily opened it, her lovely face wreathed in a smile.

"Welcome to Finley House. I'm so glad my sisters convinced you to stay here," she said as she ushered Greta and Otto into her home.

"It's big." Otto stared at the entry hall with its twin curving staircases.

It was indeed large. The wide hallway extended the full length of the house, ending with a door that Greta assumed opened onto grounds leading to the creek that gave the street its name.

Otto tugged on Greta's hand. "Where's the piano?"

"I'm sorry, Emily." Though he'd managed to climb the front steps, he was breathing heavily, and Greta feared he'd begin another coughing bout. "My brother's been obsessed with music ever since Joanna played while Louisa was treating him."

"Both of my sisters are talented." Emily turned her attention to Otto and gestured toward the room on their right. "The piano is in the parlor, but your doctors said you have to rest unless you want to go back to the infirmary, so there'll be no playing today. Burke will be here shortly to check on you." She chuckled when the front door opened and the doctor entered. "Even more shortly than I'd expected."

"Ready for me?" Burke asked Otto.

Though he nodded, Otto protested when Burke started to carry him up the stairs. "I can walk."

Greta gave her brother a reproving look. "Not if you want to touch the piano."

Admitting defeat, Otto nodded again and was silent while they all climbed to the second floor, then followed Emily to the left.

She stopped at the entrance to the second room from the end on the rear of the house and directed Burke to lay Otto on the bed.

"I've given you separate rooms," Emily told Greta. "They both open onto the back verandah, but yours is larger."

"We can share," Greta said. Though there were clearly several empty rooms at Finley House, she did not want to create additional work for Emily and extra expense for herself.

Louisa, who'd been silent, joined the conversation. "You'll sleep better if you have your own rooms, and that'll help Otto's healing."

Greta wouldn't argue with that.

After Burke left, declaring that his partner knew what to do next, Louisa opened her medical bag and started preparing

Otto's medicine. When Greta raised a questioning eyebrow, she mouthed, 'to sleep.'

"You need to drink this," Louisa said, holding the glass to Otto's mouth. "I know you want to get up, but it's important to rest."

When Otto started to protest, Louisa held up a cautioning hand. "I'll check on you this afternoon. If you're doing well, Mr. Craig will carry you downstairs to the dining room."

"I can walk. I'm not a baby."

"No, but you're still weak. You have a choice. You can nap for a while and be carried or you can eat up here in bed."

"I'll sleep." Even as he spoke, Otto's eyes began to close.

Louisa ushered Greta and Emily out of the room, explaining, "The medicine I gave him will make him sleep for a couple hours. Greta, you might want to take a nap too. I know you didn't get much rest last night."

When Louisa left, Emily led Greta to the room next to Otto's. Simply furnished with a bed, bureau, nightside table, and a rocking chair, it was a comfortable room, one made special by its windows on two sides.

"This was mine when we were growing up," Emily explained. "Joanna stayed here when she returned from Europe, but since she and Burke married, it's been empty ... waiting for you."

"It's lovely." And far nicer than either the room Greta had had above her parents' restaurant or the one Mrs. Channing had assigned her. "I can't recall the last time I took a nap, but that bed looks inviting."

Emily nodded. "Take advantage of the time to rest. You'll need a lot of energy tomorrow."

For tomorrow would be Greta's first day at the tearoom, a building that was almost as distinctive as Finley House. When Louisa had driven past it, she'd explained that Josh had converted two small houses, turning one into the tearoom, the other into a shop that sold tea and other specialty goods. The individual houses were charming, but the addition of the covered porch that connected them turned them into a building that could have been part of a fairy tale.

The nap proved to be a good idea. Greta slept longer than she'd expected and woke feeling refreshed and ready for what Emily had warned might be a raucous supper. As she'd expected from the elegant entry hall, the dining room was beautiful, with wainscoting and crown molding. Tonight the table that could have seated a dozen had seven place settings plus a highchair where Emily and Craig's daughter Prudence was sitting, banging her fists on the tray to announce that she was ready to eat. So was Otto, who'd been pleased when Louisa had declared him well enough to go downstairs on his own, though she'd warned him that Craig would carry him back to his room once the meal was complete.

"You've already met Craig and our son Noah," Emily said as Greta and Otto entered the dining room. "I'd like to introduce you to Mrs. Carmichael," she said, gesturing toward the gray-haired widow who cared for Noah during the day, "and this is Beulah Douglas." Though the older woman responded to Greta's greeting, the young girl with the almond-shaped eyes and a single blonde braid simply studied her before nodding.

Noah was less reticent. He tugged on Otto's hand and said, "My baby sister is asleep. She's too little to play. Will you play with me?"

Before Otto could reply, Beulah frowned. "I play with you." She paused, then looked toward the parlor. "I play the piano."

"You do?"

Otto's question turned Beulah's frown into a smile. "Mrs. Joanna is teaching me."

Before Greta could caution him, her brother turned to Emily, his eyes bright with excitement. "Will she teach me too?"

"Otto." Greta used her 'you know better than that' tone.

"It's all right, Greta," Emily reassured her. "Joanna can teach two almost as easily as one." She turned back to Otto. "Once you're well enough, I'm sure she will give you a lesson."

He grinned. "I'm gonna get well fast."

Chapter Seven

"Someone likes blue," Greta said as Caroline showed her around the tearoom the next morning. Not only was the exterior sign blue, but so were the tablecloths and the rims on the china.

"All that blue wasn't my idea." Though no one would call Caroline Knapp beautiful, she bore the same glow that Greta had seen on other women who were with child. And Caroline was most definitely with child. Even her skillfully tailored dress could not hide the fact that her midsection was larger than Louisa's. It was no wonder she no longer wanted to work at Porter's. Being on her feet all day would be difficult for a woman so close to giving birth.

When she'd arrived at Finley House to escort Greta to the tearoom, Caroline had declared that walking even the block and a half had become a challenge. "I feel like a whale," she told Greta, repeating the same complaint Greta had heard Louisa voice. But whales didn't have glossy dark brown hair and green eyes, nor were their faces wreathed in an anticipatory smile.

"Louisa's the one who chose the blue," Caroline continued, "but I have to admit that I like the way it turned out, and so do the ladies who come here." She gave Greta a conspiratorial smile. "Working at Porter's has been the most fun I've had since I was a little girl playing with baby dolls." Her smile broadened as she cupped her midsection. "Soon I'll have a real-life baby."

"Very soon, if what Louisa said is true." She'd confided that she expected Caroline to give birth within the next week, which was the reason she and Josh were grateful Greta had assumed responsibility for the tearoom.

Caroline led Greta to the rear of the building. "As you can see, this is our kitchen." The room was equipped with everything Greta would have expected other than a place to store supplies. Caroline must have read her mind, because she said, "These Sunday Houses were designed for farmers to have a place for their families to sleep on Saturday nights when they came into town for Sunday services, so no one worried about storing much. We keep extra china, linens, and foodstuffs upstairs." She pointed toward the ceiling. "The only problem is that the staircase is outdoors, so when it's raining, it's a bit of a challenge to climb down with our arms full. That's why Josh comes by each afternoon to help us."

That was something Papa would have done for Mama. Everything Greta heard told her this was an exceptionally well-run restaurant, one where she'd enjoy working. Half an hour later, Caroline had finished her explanation of the menus, given Greta hints on how to best bake scones, and had her sample each of the teas that Porter's offered. By the time the two girls who served as waitresses arrived, Greta knew that working here would be even better than helping in her family's restaurant. Not only would she be doing something that gave her satisfaction, but she'd be in charge, not simply a helper.

What a wonderful opportunity she'd been offered! Even though it was only for a few months, Greta knew it would be an unforgettable experience and one that would help her find employment in Colorado Springs if she and Otto decided to remain there.

"So, what do you think?" Caroline asked as Greta pulled the last pan of scones from the oven.

"I don't just think, I *know* that I'm going to have as much fun as you did." The classic English high tea menu was different from the food her parents had served and the surroundings were more elegant, but the fundamentals of preparing and serving food were universal. So too was the satisfaction of watching customers savor their meals.

"I'm glad my responsibilities include serving as hostess," Greta told Caroline. "Greeting customers was always my favorite part of working in a restaurant."

"For me it's hearing someone say they've never eaten such good food." As the front door opened, Caroline gestured toward it. "Here's your chance to be a hostess. That's our first party."

The three women who entered Porter's could have been three generations of the same family, although—thanks to Caroline's explanation—Greta knew the woman whose hair was fully gray was not related to the other two, who were indeed mother and daughter.

"Welcome to Porter's, Mrs. Albright." Greta addressed the oldest woman. "We're honored that you brought your guests here. I'm Greta Engel."

Caroline had explained that the Albrights lived diagonally across the street from Finley House and were hosting friends from San Antonio, Mr. and Mrs. Hannon and their daughter Rose.

Mrs. Albright inclined her head in a gracious gesture. "I've heard about you. You're the gal who moved into Finley House."

While she led the trio to their table, Greta said, "My brother and I are fortunate to be living there. We count ourselves fortunate to be living anywhere in Sweetwater Crossing. It's such a welcoming town."

As she pulled out chairs for each of the women, Greta wondered whether Colorado Springs would be as welcoming. It was considerably larger than Sweetwater Crossing. While that could give her more opportunities for employment, would its greater size mean that she and Otto were simply two among many newcomers and that they'd feel like strangers rather than being accepted as readily as they were here? Only time would tell.

Rose Hannon, who appeared to be about Greta's age, spoke. "I agree that this is a special town. I like it better than San Antonio. Much better. That's why I don't want to leave."

"Now, Rose, you know we can't impose on the Albrights forever, even though you fancy yourself in love with that rancher." Mrs. Hannon chided her daughter.

"You know you're not imposing, Harriet. Having you visit has helped Wilbur and me more than I can express." As if suddenly aware that Greta was still standing next to her, Mrs. Albright shook her head. "Miss Engel doesn't need to hear our stories. She wants us to decide which tea we'd like." She turned toward Greta. "What would you recommend?"

"I'm fond of Earl Grey, but some people don't care for the bergamot. If you want a lightly flavored beverage, you might try our green—I describe it as delicate—and for a traditional tea, you can't beat our China black." When the women remained undecided, Greta added, "You could each order a different one. That's why we have individual pots."

Rose nodded as solemnly as if Greta had negotiated the end to a war. "Let's do that. That way we can taste them all."

When Greta returned to the kitchen to place the order, Caroline was beaming. "You're a natural at this. Now I won't feel guilty if I don't come back to work." She took a bite of one of the small tea sandwiches that Greta had rejected, saying it wasn't cut properly. "I'm glad you came to Sweetwater Crossing."

"So am I."

⇒ ·•· ·•· ⇐

"How was your first day at the tearoom?" Emily asked when Greta entered the kitchen after assuring herself that Otto was resting in his room. As she'd expected, he claimed to be bored, but as a result of the additional sleep and the medicine Louisa gave him each evening he was coughing far less frequently than he had only a few days ago.

Greta was tempted to clap her hands in response to Emily's question but was afraid that that might disturb the children. Joanna's son Curtis was sleeping in a basket, while Prudence was playing quietly with a rag doll, and so Greta contented herself with saying, "It was wonderful! I'm impressed with what Louisa and Josh have done there. I can't imagine a tearoom in a large city being any better than Porter's."

Emily shrugged as she finished peeling the carrots that would accompany tonight's chicken and dumplings. "From what Louisa said, Josh took the concept from the one in his family's store in New York but made it more inviting."

"Inviting. That's an excellent way to describe it." Greta shook her head when Emily offered her a cup of tea or coffee and a slice of pumpkin bread. After all she'd sampled at Porter's, she wasn't hungry, but she took the seat Emily indicated at the table, grateful for the chance to rest her legs.

"I enjoyed meeting more of the town's residents," she said when Emily had settled into one of the other chairs, a cup of coffee in front of her. "Mrs. Albright was there with her guests."

"The Hannons are a lovely family." Emily's expression turned somber. "Having them visit has helped the Albrights recover from their daughter and son-in-law's deaths. That was such a tragedy, but let's talk about something happier. I know we still have seven weeks, but I'm starting to think about Christmas. I want this one to be extra special, because it'll be the first for Prudence and Curtis as well as Louisa's baby."

Greta gazed at the babies, who looked more like siblings than cousins. Emily's daughter Prudence had her father's brown hair but her mother's blue eyes, while Curtis had dark hair and blue eyes and bore no resemblance to Burke with his auburn hair and green eyes. Would Louisa's child resemble Prudence and Curtis? Since both Louisa and Josh had blue eyes, it was likely their baby would be blue-eyed, but he or she might inherit Josh's blond hair rather than Louisa's brown.

Even though they would be too young to remember this Christmas, Greta understood Emily's desire to make this a memorable holiday. The babies might not recall their excitement over brightly decorated gifts and holiday foods, but the adults would.

"I agree," Greta told Emily. "I'm hoping this will be a special time for Otto too. He was looking forward to seeing snow in Colorado."

Emily wrinkled her nose. "I can practically guarantee that you won't see snow here, but there have to be ways to make the day special. Do you have any suggestions? Even though Louisa and Joanna have their own homes, they've agreed to spend Christmas Day here, so we'll have a full house."

"What do you usually do?"

"We have a tree, of course, and I make dozens of cookies, including Pfeffernusse."

Greta's mouth watered at the memory of the small cookies that contained a bit of pepper, giving them the name pepper nuts. "Those were one of my mother's favorites. Is your family German?"

"My mother was. We girls weren't especially fond of Pfeffernusse, but I bake them in her honor."

"An excellent tradition. What about the tree? Do you have any special decorations?"

Emily shook her head. "We use the same ornaments we've had since I was a child. They're pretty, but I wouldn't call them special. We were going to have some of the glass ornaments that Josh brought into the mercantile last year, but he sold them all before I could get one."

Greta was silent for a moment, considering. "Instead of buying a lot of new things, you might want to start the tradition of adding one ornament each year." Her family had done that. Many years Mama made the ornament, but one year Papa had purchased one of the glass balls from Germany that had become so popular.

Emily sipped her coffee, then said, "I like that idea. Maybe I should replace the star. One of its points was broken when Noah dropped it last year."

"That's a problem my family never had. We had an angel on top of our tree." And even though Papa had lifted Otto so he could place it on the top branch, he'd ensured there was no danger of it being dropped or broken.

"An angel." Emily refilled her cup. "How very appropriate, since unless I'm mistaken Engel is the German word for angel."

"You're not mistaken. That's how it started. My grandfather was an artist who made porcelain figurines back in Germany. His most popular creations were angels designed for the top of Christmas trees." Somehow, Greta kept her voice even, although inside she was aching as she tried to repress the pangs that always came when she thought about the angel that had graced her family's tree. She'd done the right thing, she told herself, the only thing she could under the circumstances.

Unaware of Greta's inner turmoil, Emily nodded. "It must have been beautiful. This may sound strange, and now that I think about it, it *is* strange, but there are no angels in my family's collection of ornaments."

There would be this year, Greta resolved. She couldn't make porcelain ones like Grandfather had, but Mama had taught her to crochet, and one of the things Greta had learned to make were angels. She would create an angel for each of the sisters and Mrs. Carmichael, plus smaller ones for Beulah and Noah, and tiny ones for the three infants. And since Otto had told her it wouldn't be Christmas without an angel, the one she crocheted for him would be the size of the one that had been the focal point of their tree. It wouldn't be the same—nothing could take the place of Grandfather's masterpiece—but Otto would have an angel, and there would be angels on the Finley House tree this year.

Chapter Eight

Matt knew he was gawking, but he couldn't help it. "I feel like I ought to be in formal clothes," he told Craig as he set foot in Finley's House's entry hall. Even though the house his parents had bought from the Albrights was large, it could not compare to this. The high ceiling and dual staircases that mirrored those on the exterior were impressive, telling him no expense had been spared in creating this home. "This is a mansion."

Craig wrinkled his nose. "It can be a bit overwhelming when you first see it, but now we accept that even though it's large and a bit elaborate, it's our home." He turned to the left and ushered Matt into the dining room where the other Finley House residents had gathered. "I think you've met everyone."

Matt looked around, and for the second time in less than a minute, he gawked. Greta was standing next to Prudence's highchair, listening intently as the baby babbled something that sounded like total gibberish to him. Even though he knew she couldn't understand it any better than he could, Greta smiled, nodded, and said, "Yes. Of course. You're right." And as she did, Craig and Emily's daughter grinned, then chortled with pleasure.

Matt had little experience with babies—few customers brought them to the haberdashery—but his instincts told him that Greta had played a large role in raising Otto and that that was part of the reason was she was so protective of him now.

"Our guest has arrived."

Craig's words reminded Matt that there were others in the room. In addition to Craig's immediate family—Emily, Noah and the baby—he recognized Mrs. Carmichael and Beulah. And of course he knew Greta and Otto.

Greta straightened up and walked to Otto's side, putting her hand on his shoulder, drawing him away from Beulah.

"Thank you for inviting me to join you." Matt flashed a smile at the group before he approached Otto. After scrutinizing the boy for a second, he said, "You're looking much better than the last time I saw you." He was still pale and too thin, but he no longer appeared seriously ill.

"I'm feeling better." A short cough punctuated Otto's words. "Thank you for helping me the other day. Greta said she couldn't have gotten me into Dr. Louisa's office without you."

"I'm glad I was there and could help."

Emily smiled. "I'm glad you could come tonight." As the others moved to what were obviously their usual spots around the table, she pointed to a chair across from Greta. "I put you here."

Matt felt a momentary disappointment that he and Greta weren't seated side-by-side but realized this might be better. This way he had an unobstructed view of her and would be able to observe her reaction to everything that happened. That was an important part of learning about a person, wasn't it?

"I hope you like chicken and dumplings," Emily said when Craig had offered a blessing for the food.

"I do."

"Me too." Beulah chimed in from her seat next to Matt.

It was one of the most enjoyable evenings he could recall. The food was delicious, cementing Emily's reputation as a fine cook, and the conversation was surprisingly entertaining. It began with Beulah recounting what she'd learned at school, then turned to Greta, whose enthusiasm at being part of the tearoom was evident in the tone of her voice and the broad smile that accompanied her description of the various ladies' enjoyment of the scones and teacakes.

"I can't imagine a more perfect position for me," she said in conclusion. "I knew I missed serving people after my mother sold our family's restaurant, but I didn't realize just how much I missed it until today."

Mrs. Carmichael nodded before addressing Matt. "Now, young man, I want to hear why you're running for sheriff."

"That sounds as if you disapprove."

"Not at all. I simply want to understand your reasons."

He finished chewing one of the roasted carrots that accompanied the main course before he spoke. "There are two. Greta's not the only one who feels called to serve people. I do too, although in a different way. I may not be able to offer anyone scones or teacakes, but I believe I can keep the town safe."

Matt paused for a second, then added, "It's true that I have no experience, but neither does my opponent. I may not have served as sheriff, but until he moved to Houston, I spent a lot of time with one of Galveston's deputy sheriffs and count him as a good friend, so I understand what's involved."

Though Matt had been watching Mrs. Carmichael's reaction, his gaze turned toward Greta as it had so often during the meal. Instead of nodding as Mrs. Carmichael did, the blood had drained from her face, and she appeared frightened. Surely that couldn't be the case. There was nothing frightening about his intention of running for office. Besides, she already knew about that, because she'd been with him when Toby had announced it on Sunday.

"That's a reasonable enough first reason." Either Craig was oblivious to Greta's reaction or he'd decided the best way to handle it was to ignore it. "What's the second?"

"I think voters should have a choice. I know it's been a while since that's happened here, but that doesn't make it right."

Emily nodded vigorously. "I agree. I wish women could vote here the way they do in Wyoming. I'd cast my vote for you, and I'm sure my sisters would too."

"I certainly would," Mrs. Carmichael said as she took a second helping of chicken.

"Thank you all for your support." Matt knew that even though women couldn't vote, they wielded influence over their husbands, brothers, and occasionally their fathers. With the three sisters and Mrs. Carmichael on his side, his chances of becoming Sweetwater Crossing's next sheriff had improved.

When the meal was over, Mrs. Carmichael took Noah and Beulah to the parlor to read them a story and Craig carried Otto up to his bed before returning to the kitchen to help Emily with the dishes, leaving Matt and Greta in the dining room. Though Matt was curious about her reaction to what he'd said about his qualifications for sheriff, he was unwilling to ask questions that might make her uncomfortable, and so he said, "I'm happy to see that your brother is so much better."

Her relieved smile told Matt he'd been wise to choose a safe subject. "So am I," she said. "I was more worried than I wanted to admit, even to myself. Even though he tires easily, Otto is feeling well enough that he'll read a book for an hour before he goes to sleep and he hardly coughs at all." She leaned forward ever so slightly, as if to emphasize her words. "Now that I'm working at Porter's I'll be able to repay you for Blackie's care, but I wish there were a way I could thank you for being there when Otto and I needed you most."

This was the opportunity he'd sought, a way to address his part of the bargain with Toby. "There is." When Greta's eyes widened, as if she was surprised by his words, Matt nodded. "You mentioned meeting Rose Hannon today. What did you think of her?"

"I liked her. She seems like a genuinely nice girl, but I don't understand how my opinion is a way of thanking you. Why did you ask about Rose?"

"Two reasons."

Greta's lips turned up in a wry smile. "Do you have two reasons for everything?"

"I hadn't thought of that, but maybe. As far as Rose is concerned, I wanted to see if your opinion matched mine."

"Does it?"

"Yes, and since it does, we come to the second reason. My brother wants to court Rose, but since it's not an official courtship yet, there aren't many things he can do. I wondered whether you'd be willing to take nightly walks with me and them. That would give Toby a chance to spend more time with Rose." And Matt would have more time with Greta to discover whether the attraction he felt for her would fade with greater familiarity.

She was silent, and though he didn't see fear reflected in her eyes, something was causing her to hesitate. It was probably only a few seconds but it seemed like forever before she nodded. "I'd be happy to help you help them."

"Good. Toby will be happy."

And so would Matt.

» ·◆· «

"Am I a terrible mother and hostess to admit that I'm happy everyone's gone for a couple hours and I have the house to myself?" Emily asked the next morning as she rinsed the soap from a bowl and handed it to Greta to dry. Though she'd refused Greta's offer of help cooking meals, she'd readily agreed to accept assistance with washing breakfast dishes.

"But you don't have the house to yourself," Greta said as she placed the bowl in the cupboard. "I'm here." And would be for a while longer, since she didn't need to be at the tearoom until ten. Though he had protested mightily, Otto was in his room, waiting for Louisa to check on him.

Emily slid the last of the oatmeal bowls into the soapy water, then turned to face Greta. "I'm glad you are, because I want to get to know you better."

Before Greta could react, Emily continued. "I hope you know that you can tell me anything—anything at all—and I won't repeat it, not even to Craig if that's what you want."

Greta wasn't sure whether this was leading up to a probing question or was simply Emily's way of extending a friendly offer. It didn't matter, because Greta had the same desire Emily did: getting to know each other better. "I appreciate that. I had wonderful parents and I love Otto dearly, but I often wished I had a sister. Even though I could talk to my mother about almost anything, I thought it would be different with a sister."

Perhaps it was foolish. Greta had known Emily for only a few days and she wouldn't be staying in Sweetwater Crossing permanently, but she'd felt an immediate connection to the oldest Vaughn sister.

"It is different." Emily returned to washing the dishes. "As much as I loved my mother, there were things I wouldn't discuss with her because I didn't think she'd understand. Joanna always did."

"Not Louisa?"

"Not always. She and I are very different women."

"But you're best of friends now."

"That's because we're adults. When we were children ..." Emily's voice trailed off. "Let's just say that we didn't necessarily appreciate each other then. But Louisa's not what I wanted to talk about. I didn't have a chance to say anything last night, but I hope you didn't mind that Craig invited Matt to join us for supper."

"Of course not. It's your house. You can invite anyone you choose."

"Maybe so, but I don't want you to feel uncomfortable here, and you seemed that way when Matt talked about running for sheriff."

Greta pursed her lips, trying to decide how to respond. "I hadn't realized it was obvious."

"Probably not to anyone else, but I was surprised by your reaction. Matt's a good man."

"I know that, but ..." Greta paused, weighing her words. Should she tell Emily what she feared and why? Remembering Emily's promise of confidentiality, she decided that this might be the time to share her experiences. Perhaps Emily would have good advice for her.

"I'm afraid of the power a sheriff wields," she said softly.

"Do you want to tell me why?" Once again, Emily was exerting no pressure, simply offering a sympathetic ear.

Greta laid the last bowl on the counter, not wanting to possibly drop it. "I haven't told anyone, but I trust you. Besides, you should know what happened in case my past catches up to me. I don't think he'll follow me, but you never know."

Emily wrapped her arm around Greta's shoulders and led her to the table. "I think we both need to sit down for this story. Are you on the run from the law?"

"No. Not really, but the son of my employer in Houston is good friends with a man in the sheriff's office who used to live in Galveston."

"And you think that might be the same man Matt knew."

"It's possible, and that worries me."

"Who is it you fear—the son or the sheriff?" Emily asked as she took the chair next to Greta.

"Both."

Though she nodded, Emily said nothing, merely waited for Greta to continue.

"At first everything seemed fine when Nigel came home after a couple years in Europe. More than fine. My mother had just died, and I was grieving. Nigel seemed to understand that. He was kind to me. He even dried my tears once." That tenderness had touched Greta in ways she hadn't expected, helping her accept her mother's death and realize that she needed to be strong for Otto.

"Then things changed. His words of comfort became compliments. Looking back, I should have realized what was happening, but I was flattered by the compliments. After all, he was the heir to a fortune; I was only a servant."

This time Emily responded. "Don't denigrate yourself, Greta. Who you are is what's important, not what you do to earn a living."

"Maybe so. I don't know what would have happened if Otto hadn't become so ill. The doctor said there was nothing he could do and told Nigel and me that Otto would die within a few months."

"Oh, Greta. How horrible." Emily's eyes radiated sympathy.

"I was devastated. Otto was the only family I had left. How could I lose him? Nigel said he'd help me, but there was a price." Greta swallowed, not wanting to continue but knowing she needed to.

"When I wouldn't do what he wanted, Nigel told me I had a choice: I could agree to share his bed or he'd have his friend in the sheriff's office send Otto to the poor farm to die." Greta shuddered at the thought of her brother in that place. "I couldn't let that happen."

"Of course you couldn't." Emily reached over and grasped Greta's hand between both of hers, the warmth as comforting as her words. "That's why you left Houston, isn't it?"

"Yes. I couldn't save him, but I decided that if Otto was going to die soon, I wanted him to have a chance to see Pikes Peak. That had been one of his dreams." She swallowed deeply, trying to control the anguish that accompanied thoughts of her brother's death.

"Otto's dream wasn't the only reason I thought we should go there. I didn't tell him, but I'd heard that the climate in Colorado Springs was good for healing lungs. I thought that might give him another chance, but Louisa said it wasn't good for what's wrong with Otto. Still, I want him to see the mountain, and I don't ever, ever want to see Nigel again."

Emily tightened her grip on Greta's hand. "You did the right thing. You're safe here. There are no poor farms in this county, and even if there were, I can't imagine either Matt or Byron Winslow agreeing to send Otto to one. And if Nigel or the deputy tries to take Otto from you, they have no jurisdiction here." Emily's voice deepened with emotion. "I'll say it again. You're safe here."

"I hope so."

Chapter Nine

"Your brother is not happy with me," Louisa told Greta as she entered the parlor after her daily visit to Otto.

"What's the problem?" When she'd finished helping Emily with the breakfast dishes, Greta had gone to the parlor to reflect on all that Emily had said. She wanted to believe that Emily was correct and that Nigel had no power over her, but she couldn't help wondering if something else would go wrong. First there'd been Otto's new illness. Then the wagon's collapse. What would happen next?

As if she sensed Greta's worries, Louisa shook her head. "It's nothing to be concerned about. It's simply that he wants to go to school today."

Greta wasn't surprised, since Otto had expressed the same wish when she escorted him downstairs for breakfast. Though he no longer had to be carried, she still insisted on accompanying him while he negotiated the stairs. A fall would only complicate his recovery.

"I'm not a doctor," she said, "but he seems stronger each day."

"He is." Louisa laid her medical bag on the floor and touched her midsection. "Your brother isn't the only one who's growing stronger. So is this baby. That was quite a kick." She paused, perhaps waiting for another kick. "Otto's recovery has been remarkably fast, but even though he feels better, he's not completely healed. I'm glad you're staying here until at least January and not only because it helps Josh. If Otto does too much too soon, he could have a relapse."

Louisa's mention of Josh reminded Greta that she wanted to go to the mercantile this morning to buy some crochet thread. The more she thought about making angels, the more she liked the idea. But before she could go shopping, she needed to hear whatever else Louisa had to say about Otto.

"I assume you told him the consequences of not listening to you."

"I did, but he didn't want to hear it." Louisa looked as if she'd expected that. "He's a determined boy."

"A stubborn one."

"I was trying to be diplomatic." A chuckle accompanied Louisa's words.

"And you were. I'll talk to him. When do you think he'll be ready to go to school?"

Louisa tipped her head to one side, considering. "Possibly Monday. That'll give him five more days to recuperate."

"And that will be perfect."

Though Greta had seen Emily approaching, Louisa turned, apparently startled by her sister's voice. "I didn't know you were here."

Emily shrugged. "You should remember how voices carry in this house. I was dusting the dining room."

Greta was more interested in the reason for Emily's declaration than in what she'd been doing. "What's perfect about Monday?"

"That's the day Joanna gives Beulah piano lessons. I saw how excited Otto was about learning to play. Maybe if you tell him that if he listens to Louisa and rests most of the day until Monday, not only can he go to school, but he'll have his first piano lesson that afternoon." She paused for a second, letting Greta absorb the suggestion. "What do you think about that?"

"I think it's a brilliant plan." Otto wasn't a naturally patient person, but given the right incentive—and playing the piano was definitely the right incentive—he would agree to the stipulations.

"What did I ever do without you two?" Greta turned toward Louisa. "I told Emily I've always wanted a sister."

"And now you have three." Louisa exchanged a significant look with Emily.

"Are you adopting me?"

"Why not?" Perhaps asserting her role as the eldest, Emily replied. "I'm sure both Louisa and Joanna will agree with me that if having two sisters is good, three can only be better."

⊷ ·•· ⊶

Greta was still reveling in the idea of being part of a large family even if it was only for a few months when the tearoom opened at two. Though she'd had to rush a bit, she'd gotten to the mercantile before she had to come here and had found the crochet thread she wanted.

"There's no need to mention this to Louisa or Emily," she'd told Josh when she'd paid him for it.

"Of course not." He'd winked. "My wife may not be the best at keeping secrets, but I am. Surprises are good."

Greta hoped the angels would be a good surprise for the women who'd claimed they were adopting her. But first she had to make them, and right now she had a tearoom to manage.

The first customers were two women of a similar age—Greta estimated them to be between thirty-five and forty—but that was the only similarity other than their surnames. The one who introduced herself as Mrs. Jake Winslow was short and plump with bright red hair, green eyes, and the freckles so common to redheads. Her companion, Mrs. Byron Winslow, was a tall, thin brunette with chocolate brown eyes and a pale complexion.

When she'd seen their names on the reservation list, Greta had wondered whether the postmaster's wife and the wife of the man

75

who was running for sheriff against Matt would discuss the upcoming election. She hoped they wouldn't, because the subject was a contentious one and could make other customers' tea less enjoyable, but she suspected that one of the reasons the two Mrs. Winslows were here was to make their opinions known. They did, and in voices so loud that the women at the other tables as well as Greta and her servers had no difficulty hearing them.

"Jake and I aren't happy about the latest developments," the postmaster's wife said when she'd ordered China black tea and extra peach preserves for her scones.

"That's how Byron and I feel." The brunette tapped her fingers on the table as she waited for the food to be served. "My husband deserves to be sheriff."

"Then we'll have to ensure that it happens. Matt Nelson doesn't know Sweetwater Crossing the way Byron does. He's a newcomer from a city hundreds of miles away. What does he know about what's important for us? Nothing. He has no business running for sheriff."

Everyone was entitled to an opinion, but Greta wished these women were less vocal about theirs. When she greeted the next customers and led them to their table, she tried to keep their attention focused on her and her description of the foods they'd be served, hoping they would not be disturbed by the Winslow women.

Unfortunately, the postmaster's wife's voice overpowered Greta's. "Tradition dictates that once a man applies for a job, he gets it. There's no unpleasantness that way."

But there was unpleasantness, Greta wanted to say. It was unpleasant to listen to the two Winslow wives' conversation.

"Tradition is important," Byron's wife said.

Her sister-in-law paused long enough for the waitress to place the tiered serving dish with the scones and little sandwiches in front of her. "You don't have to convince me. Matt Nelson is the one who's bucking tradition. Maybe we can convince him to withdraw his candidacy."

As Greta passed by the women's table on her way back to the kitchen, she heard the postmaster's wife say, "Jake can't be the one to suggest it, but there has to be someone who'll do it."

"What about Mayor Alcott?"

"That's a good idea. I'll talk to his wife." She leaned forward and placed her hand on her sister-in-law's. "Don't worry. By this time next month, you'll be the sheriff's wife. Matt Nelson will realize he has no chance of winning and that he might as well give up now."

Greta hoped that wouldn't be the case. Having seen how determined Matt was to become sheriff, she doubted anyone could dissuade him. Perhaps he was as stubborn as Otto. If so, having the mayor try to convince him to abandon the race would only strengthen his resolve. And when that happened, his chances of winning increased.

Greta smiled at the thought of how interesting life in Sweetwater Crossing had become.

⋅≫⋅⋅◆⋅⋅≪⋅

"Aren't you too tired to walk after working all day?"

To Greta's surprise, Rose drew her aside as they left the Albrights' house, while Matt and Toby exchanged a few words with the two older couples. "I was afraid you wouldn't be willing to come," Rose continued, "but this will be so much better than sitting in the parlor with my parents and the Albrights watching every move Toby and I make."

"I'm not tired," Greta assured the woman who couldn't be more than a few years younger than she but who seemed almost childlike at this moment. "I'm looking forward to exploring more of the town."

"What I'm looking forward to is spending time with Toby." Rose glanced back, as if to determine whether she would be overheard, then said, "My mother wouldn't let us go out by ourselves, but after she met you at Porter's, she said you were sensible and could be trusted."

It was the first time Greta had heard herself described that way. Was she sensible? She supposed she was. Could she be trusted? She might not trust her own judgment where men were concerned, but she could be trusted to ensure that Rose and Toby adhered to the conventions that etiquette demanded.

"Mama said that any woman who could get Matt off the ranch had to be a good one. According to Mrs. Albright, folks figured he was a confirmed bachelor. Then you came, and suddenly he's willing to go out walking. I think Mrs. Albright and Mama want me to figure out what you did to change his mind, but I promise I won't ask."

That was good, because Greta knew Rose wouldn't believe her when she said she'd done nothing, that the only reason Matt was here tonight was to help his brother. It had nothing to do with Greta, nothing at all.

⇢ ⋅ ✦ ⋅ ⇠

"Thank you again for agreeing to do this." Matt smiled at Greta as they walked slowly south on East Street. When he and Toby had discussed tonight's itinerary, they'd decided to make a circuit, taking East to Main, then continuing to West and back on Creek. That way they'd pass all the major stores and establishments in Sweetwater Crossing, increasing the likelihood that they'd be observed. If Pa heard that Matt had been seen in the company of an eligible young woman—and the odds were high that he would—he could draw the conclusion that his elder son had finally listened to him.

"I'm glad to help." Greta tipped her head forward. "It appears you were right. Your brother and Rose want time alone."

Matt and Toby had come to Finley House to collect Greta. Then the three of them had crossed the street to the Albrights' where Rose was waiting eagerly, or so it seemed to Matt. She'd said a few words to Greta, then had placed her hand on Toby's bent arm, gazing up at him with what Matt could only call a besotted expression. The two of them had begun walking along the route Matt and Toby had chosen, leaving Matt and Greta to follow. And, though they did follow, he and Greta left enough distance between them and the other couple that they could not overhear their conversation.

"It's the first time I've been a chaperone." The idea made Matt chuckle, since part of the reason for their excursion was to convince his parents that he was also in need of a chaperone, even though he wasn't. After all, all he sought from Greta was friendship.

"Me too. I'm not sure what we're supposed to do."

"According to what my mother told Toby, all we have to do is keep them in sight. That'll ensure that their reputations aren't sullied."

Though she might not have been aware of it, Greta's grip on his arm tightened as she said, "It takes so little to sully a woman's reputation."

The tighter grip and the emotion in her voice told Matt she felt strongly about this, but why?

"I always thought it was wrong that men aren't held accountable for their actions more often," he told her. "I saw women shunned in Galveston while the men who'd been involved in the same supposedly scandalous behavior escaped scot-free."

When Greta let out a little gasp, as if she were surprised by his opinion, Matt knew it was time to change the subject. Unfair treatment of anyone, men or women, wasn't what he wanted to discuss tonight. This was supposed to be a time to enjoy Greta's company and learn more about her.

"Let's talk about something happier," he suggested. "Are you enjoying working at the tearoom?" Even though this was only her second day, he imagined she would have formed an opinion by now.

"Very much." She paused as they turned right onto Main Street and studied the front window of Josh Porter's mercantile. "Josh's stores are as memorable as the tearoom. I think it was a great idea to have the teashop next to the tearoom and not sell anything there that he does here."

She gestured toward one corner of the window. "There was a set of dishes here this morning, and now it's gone." She leaned forward, trying to see farther into the store. "I wonder whether Josh sold it or simply changed the display. Either way, it was a good move. Seeing new things here will keep customers interested."

Matt had never paid much attention to the mercantile's window display, but he'd occasionally heard his mother mention something she'd seen in it, so it must play an important role in Josh's success.

"When I was in here this morning," Greta continued, "I was impressed with how much merchandise Josh has, yet it doesn't feel crowded."

"He told me he learned that from his grandfather. Porter & Sons has a reputation for knowing what customers want."

Greta laughed. "I think it's more a case of showing customers what they ought to want."

"You could be right."

"Of course I'm right." The saucy note in Greta's voice was one Matt hadn't heard before but one he found oddly endearing.

"To answer your question about the tearoom," she said as they resumed their walk, "it's different from my parents' restaurant where we served some of the same people every day. From what Caroline said, the most frequent customers come to the tearoom once a month. That means that I'm getting to meet new people every day." A hint of humor colored Greta's voice as she said, "Today your opponent's wife and her sister-in-law were customers."

"Let me guess. They made no bones about being unhappy that I'm running for sheriff."

"That's true. I wasn't eavesdropping—they both spoke so loudly that there was no way to avoid hearing them—but how did you know?"

"Because Mayor Alcott came out to the ranch this afternoon to advise me that it would be in the town's best interest if I withdrew my candidacy." It was almost ironic that they were having this conversation in front of the mayor's office and home. Though Matt doubted that Alcott would come out and confront them, he quickened his pace, not wanting to risk any unpleasantness.

"And you refused."

"I did. I don't like bullies, so his visit made me even more determined to win."

This time there was no question about her mirth, for Greta laughed out loud. "That's what I expected. After you won your father over to your side, you're not about to let anyone dissuade you."

Once again, Greta surprised him by her insights. "You're right."

"Now it's my turn to ask questions," she told him. "What brought your family to Sweetwater Crossing? A small town and ranch life in the Hill Country must be a big change after living in Galveston."

"It is, but it's what my father has dreamt of his whole life. He was a successful haberdasher, but he always wanted to be a rancher, and now he is, thanks to Craig."

"Craig?"

"You haven't been here long enough to hear all the stories, but Craig used to live in Galveston. He and I met when we were boys and remained friends. Good friends. I was the best man at his first wedding." Matt paused, remembering how happy Craig had been that day and how Rachel's death had devastated him.

"I was shocked when he decided to move here, even though he told me it was the best thing for him and Noah. Seeing him with Emily, I know it was, but I missed him."

"And now you and your family are here."

Matt nodded, thinking of how much his life had changed in less than a year. "When Craig wrote that the Albrights were selling their ranch, I encouraged my parents to buy it, because I knew it would be good for Pa."

Matt and Greta stopped at the corner of Center Street to let a wagon pass, then increased their pace to catch up to Toby and Rose.

"You said the move was good for your father. What about you? You sound as if you don't enjoy ranching."

Matt wasn't sure how she did it, but Greta seemed to understand how he felt without his saying anything. "I don't," he admitted. "Toby and Pa love being outdoors with the cattle. Their favorite topics of conversation revolve around how many steers they have and the best time to take them to market. That's important, but it's not what makes me happy."

"You need to be with other people and serve them."

Again Greta voiced his thoughts before he could. "I'd have been happy to stay and run the haberdashery in Galveston, but if I did that, my parents wouldn't have come here. They felt strongly that the family should not be separated. I couldn't let Pa's dream die, not when I owe him and Ma so much."

Greta nodded. "I think we all owe our parents a lot."

"That's true, but Toby and I would probably have died if it weren't for ours." When Greta gasped, Matt laid a comforting hand on top of hers and began the explanation. "Our parents died of typhoid soon after Toby was born. If the Nelsons hadn't adopted us, I'm not sure we would have survived." The orphanages were overcrowded and more children perished than should have due to neglect.

"Now I understand why there's no resemblance between you and Toby and your parents. I was a bit puzzled when I saw you with them at church." Greta's expression was somber. "I'm sorry you were orphaned, but I'm glad that the Nelsons took you in."

Matt had been part of the family for so long that he no longer noticed that he didn't look like either parent, but Greta—observant Greta—had.

"Toby and I couldn't have asked for better parents," Matt told her. "Ma and Pa gave us everything a child could want—love, support, an example of what being a good person means. There's no way I can repay them for that."

As the sound of Rose's laughter drifted back toward them, Matt wished he hadn't told Greta about his parents. He'd meant this to be a lighthearted evening, not one colored by sad stories.

Apparently less concerned by the gravity of the discussion than he was, Greta said, "I can't speak for your parents, but I doubt they expect to be repaid. If they're like my parents, everything they did was out of love. I didn't agree with my mother's decision to sell our restaurant, but I understood that she believed it would make life easier for Otto and me. As it turned out, she was wrong, but I know she acted out of love, just as your telling your parents about the Albright ranch and helping them move here was done out of love. That's what families do for each other. That's why I ..."

Greta stopped abruptly, as if she'd said more than she intended.

"Left Houston?" Matt tried to complete her sentence.

"Yes. It was Otto's dream to spend Christmas near Pikes Peak, and I was determined to make that dream come true."

"But now you won't be able to do that."

She took a deep breath before she spoke. "We may not get there by Christmas, but I won't let that dream die. Otto *will* see Pikes Peak, and in the meantime I'll find a way to make this a happy Christmas for him."

Another woman might have wept; another woman might have railed at the way her circumstances had changed, but Greta was not another woman. She was strong and determined, and that made her the most unusual woman Matt had met.

"You talked about Otto, but what are your dreams?" he asked.

Greta was silent for a moment, making him wonder whether she would answer. Finally she said, "A home of my own." She stared into the distance, then turned back to him. "That's something I've never had. First I lived with my parents. Then my mother, Otto, and I moved to the Channings'. Now I'm at Finley House." The way Greta tightened her grip on Matt's arm told him this was important to her.

"I'm grateful for the welcome Emily and Craig have given us, but someday I want to live in my own house. With Otto, of course.

It doesn't have to be a big house. It could even be an apartment over a restaurant if that's where I wind up working. I just want it to be ours alone."

Matt tried but failed to dismiss the disappointment that surged through him when Greta made no mention of a husband. Why not? Didn't most women want to be married? He wouldn't ask her, not tonight. Instead he said, "I can't help you with your dream." At least not until he became sheriff and had an apartment to offer her. "But I agree that your brother deserves a special Christmas. Let me know what I can do to help. I'll do anything I can."

Greta looked up at him, her eyes filled with gratitude. "You're a good man, Matt Nelson."

Chapter Ten

"Did you enjoy your walk last night?" Emily asked as she handed Greta a bowl to dry. The only thing that surprised Greta about the question was that Emily had waited so long to pose it. She'd expected her or perhaps Mrs. Carmichael to mention the walk during breakfast, but no one had.

"I did," she said with a small smile that probably told Emily as much as her response. "The town looks different after dark, and the almost full moon was beautiful." It had been a clear night, with the moon providing a measure of illumination. Unlike the part of Houston where the Channings lived, Sweetwater Crossing had no street lights. "No one thought they were necessary," Matt had explained when Greta commented on their absence.

"And, of course, you had the chance to spend more time with one of the town's most eligible bachelors."

That had been pleasant, but Greta didn't want Emily to get the wrong impression. There had been nothing romantic about the evening. Even if Greta had been interested in a romance—and how could she be when she was here only temporarily and when caring for Otto took all her spare time?—a man like Matt wouldn't be interested in her. Nigel had made that clear.

"Matt and I were serving as chaperones so that his brother and Rose could spend time together." And while they'd done that, they'd shared stories of their past. That was what people did when they were getting to know each other. That was what friends did.

"Is that the story Matt told you when he invited you to go for a stroll?" The skeptical tone of voice told Greta that Emily didn't believe it.

"Yes."

Emily regarded a dried-on bit of egg on a plate, her face a study in concentration that Greta was certain had little to do with the dish. "It's a plausible story, but I'd say that was a secondary reason. The man looks at you the way Josh looked at Louisa before they became engaged." When Greta shook her head, Emily continued. "You have an admirer."

It was a ridiculous idea. More than that, it was preposterous. In an attempt to distract Emily, Greta said, "We need to see if Louisa has a remedy for your over-active imagination."

But Emily would not be distracted. "I know what I saw. The question is whether you reciprocate his feelings."

"I'm not looking for a husband," Greta said firmly. She'd learned her lesson about men and romance. "Don't forget that I'm here for no more than a couple months. Besides, the only man in my life is Otto."

As she began to scrub the oatmeal pan, Emily frowned at Greta. "That's hardly the same thing. A grown man—the right one—will bring more joy to your life than you dreamt possible."

Greta didn't doubt that, for she'd seen the happiness her parents had shared. What she doubted was her ability to recognize the man God intended for her. "How do you know whether he's the right one? Nigel seemed like a good man at first." What girl wouldn't be impressed with the compliments he'd lavished on her or the romantic notes he'd left in unexpected places?

"Some men are like that. It's as if they wear masks to hide their real selves. The important thing is to learn everything you can about a man. Don't be swayed by a handsome face or flattery. You need to know the person beneath the surface."

Greta was silent for a moment, absorbing Emily's advice. "You've made me realize that I didn't know Nigel. I saw what I wanted to see, not who he really was."

"I can tell you that Matt is a good man—and he is—but you have to discover that for yourself."

A good man. Greta chuckled. "Do you know what I said last night? I told Matt he was a good man."

Handing the oatmeal pan to Greta, Emily smiled. "That means you're on your way to learning whether or not he's the right man for you."

The right man to be a friend.

⋙ ⋆ ⋆ ⋆ ⋘

Greta was happy to see that although Otto wasn't sleeping, he was at least resting when she returned to Finley House after the tearoom closed on Friday. Louisa had insisted that he take a nap each afternoon, and although he'd protested mightily, he'd acquiesced, persuaded by the promise of a piano lesson on Monday.

"We have guests coming for supper tonight," Greta told her brother.

"I know." Otto swung his legs over the side of the bed. "Mrs. Carmichael said the minister and his wife are coming, but Beulah won't be there because she goes home for the weekend."

"That's right. It's important that she spends time with her parents." Emily had explained that they normally came into town to shop on Saturday and again for church services on Sunday, but Beulah spent Friday through Sunday nights at their ranch. It was an unusual arrangement, at least for Sweetwater Crossing, but according to Emily, Beulah was thriving under it.

Otto frowned. "I wish Beulah could stay here all the time. I like reading stories to her."

Greta was grateful that Otto had found something to occupy him after his naps, because she knew boredom weighed heavily on him. Mrs. Carmichael said he played with Noah occasionally, but Noah was an active little boy and it frustrated Otto that he couldn't run with him.

"Beulah told me she likes your stories. She says they're better than the ones her mother reads to her."

Otto's frown turned into a smirk. "That's cuz they're adventure stories. She liked *Treasure Island*. I told her about *Robinson Crusoe*. Do you think I could read it?"

That was one of the books Greta had read to Otto a year ago, because while the story was designed for children, the writing was considered too difficult for most of them. "Let's see if the library downstairs has a copy." The book might be challenging, but it would give Otto something to do and could alleviate his boredom. "We can check the library on our way to supper."

"Can't we go now? If they have it, I could start reading it."

It was difficult to fault Otto's logic. "All right."

As she'd expected, the Finley House library contained a copy of Daniel Defoe's adventure novel, and within minutes Otto was settled in a comfortable chair with the book in front of him.

When she heard Louisa and realized she was in the kitchen with Emily, Greta joined them, wanting to report that Otto was coughing less frequently. Louisa had missed her morning checkup with him because Caroline was in labor. Both women were standing next to the counter where Emily had been rolling out biscuits.

"The coffee's almost ready," Emily told Greta. "I hope you'll join us."

She nodded, then turned her attention to Louisa. "I probably shouldn't say this"—Greta softened her words with a smile—"but you look tired."

Louisa returned the smile and sank onto one of the chairs as if her legs would no longer support her. "I'm not as tired as Caroline. She had a difficult delivery, but both she and Junior are fine."

"So she was right in saying she was having a boy." That was one of the things Caroline had confided to Greta the day she'd shown her around the tearoom.

"His official name is Raymond after his father, but they've already started calling him Junior." Louisa reached for one of the cookies Emily had placed on a plate, perhaps anticipating her sister's hunger. "I can't recall when I've seen a happier set of parents."

"Your memory is failing you, sister dear." Emily slid the pan of biscuits into the oven. "You said that about Craig and me when Prudence was born and about Joanna and Burke when Curtis arrived. I think you say that about all your patients." She poured herself a cup of coffee, then joined Greta and Louisa at the table.

"I probably do say that." Louisa looked down at her expanding abdomen. "Imagine what I'll be like when I hold my baby for the first time."

Greta had no trouble imagining it. "You'll probably look like my mother did when Otto was born, like you've witnessed a miracle." That was what Mama had called Otto, her tiny miracle. "She was exhausted when I handed him to her, but I'd never seen her so happy."

"You were there? You assisted with the birth?" Louisa's surprise was evident.

"I did more than assist. The midwife was with another patient when Mama went into labor, so I delivered Otto."

Both Emily and Louisa stared at Greta, Emily with curiosity, while Louisa's eyes registered her shock. "How old were you?"

"Thirteen. It was the most frightening thing I've ever done." Even now, ten years later, the memory made Greta shudder. "I was so afraid I'd do something wrong."

"But obviously you didn't." Louisa gave Greta an approving smile. "I'm impressed. Very impressed. Josh and Burke keep telling me I should have an assistant. Would you be interested?"

"Have you forgotten that I'm here only temporarily?"

Louisa and Emily exchanged conspiratorial grins. "Have you forgotten that we adopted you?" Louisa countered. "We want you to stay permanently, and now that I know you've successfully delivered a baby without any training, I hope you'll consider becoming my assistant. Josh can find someone else for the tearoom."

Greta shook her head. "I did what I had to the day Mama was in labor, but I couldn't deliver babies on a regular basis." What would she do if she failed, if despite her best efforts either the mother or the baby or both died? She wouldn't ask the question, because Louisa had probably had to deal with losses like that. Instead she said firmly, "I'm better suited to working in the tearoom."

As if she sensed how desperately Greta wanted to change the subject, Emily asked, "Did you have any memorable guests today?"

"Mrs. Nelson and Mrs. Lindstrom."

"Matt's mother. How interesting." Emily gave Louisa a look that Greta could not decipher.

"It was a bit awkward. It was probably my imagination, but I felt as if I was being inspected." And that brought back memories of Nigel's mother's appraisal and subsequent rejection of her.

Louisa shrugged and helped herself to another cookie. "You probably were. The grapevine says you and Matt were seen walking two consecutive nights. That started speculation that you'll be Sweetwater Crossing's next bride."

But she wouldn't.

"You know why we go out each evening," Greta told the sisters. "Toby wants Rose to be the next bride."

Undeterred by Greta's declaration, Emily tipped her head to the side, as if considering something. "I don't believe there's ever been a double wedding in Sweetwater Crossing. That might be nice."

Mrs. Lindstrom—Della, she'd urged Greta to call her—entered the kitchen. "Are you talking about Greta and Matt?"

Louisa nodded. "Plus Toby and Rose."

"Mary Nelson's not convinced that Rose is the right woman for Toby. She thinks they're both too young, but she was impressed with you, Greta."

Shaking her head, Greta tried to discourage the minister's wife from continuing the discussion. "The speculation is silly. I'm only here temporarily."

A wide grin was Della's initial response. "That's what I thought when I arrived. I was going to be here for no more than two weeks, but temporary turned into permanent. That's what happens when you meet the right man."

"I know what Greta's going to say, so instead of listening to her protests, let's take these dishes into the dining room." Emily rose and gestured toward the bowls and platters she'd arranged on the counter. "It's time for supper."

⇥ ·•· ⇤

"Sit down, son." Pa pointed to the chair across from him after Saturday supper. When Matt was seated, he continued. "I reckon you know why I want to talk to you."

Though Matt had strong suspicions, he refused to take the bait. When he'd heard that Ma had invited the preacher's wife to have tea with her at Porter's yesterday, Matt had expected one or both of his parents to initiate what he and Toby called a "serious conversation" with him. Since Ma did not like tea—she called it a weak substitute for coffee—he knew there was only one reason she'd gone to the tearoom.

"If it's about running for sheriff, the mayor already tried to convince me I was making a mistake. I told him no one could persuade me to abandon my campaign."

"It wasn't about that. I won't pretend to understand why ranching isn't good enough for you, but your mother convinced me that we should let you try your hand at being a lawman. She reminded me that you could always quit if it wasn't what you expected."

But Matt wouldn't do that. Even if he disliked being sheriff, which he strongly doubted would happen, he would serve his full term. "The first step is to win the election."

"Agreed, but that's not what I wanted to talk about. I heard you and Toby have been stepping out with two young ladies. Toby fancies himself in love with the Hannon girl. I'm not worried about him, because I expect his feelings for her to fizzle out the way all the others did, but I must say that I'm surprised and more than a little disappointed in you."

This wasn't turning out the way either Matt or Toby had expected. They'd both thought Pa would be pleased that Matt was showing interest in a woman.

"Why are you disappointed that I'm spending time with Greta? Everyone needs a friend."

"A friend? Is that what you're calling it?" Pa scoffed. "I saw the way you looked at her after church last Sunday, like you were infatuated. I thought you had more sense than Toby."

Matt started to protest, but before he could speak, Pa continued. "You're a grown man now. You don't need to take my advice, but I'm concerned about both you and your brother. You're moving too fast. Both of the girls are visiting Sweetwater Crossing. Do you think you can convince them to make this their home?" Pa shook his head, answering the question he'd raised. "You just met them and you're already thinking about getting hitched without considering everything. That worries me, son. I'm afraid you're being swayed by a pretty face."

"But, Pa ..." Greta was more than a pretty face, and while it was true that he found her attractive, Matt was far from thinking of marriage. Unless he won the election, he had no future to offer her, and even if he did win, as Pa pointed out, there was no guarantee that Greta would remain in Sweetwater Crossing. She'd promised to take Otto to Pikes Peak, and if there was one thing Matt was certain of, it was that Greta kept her promises.

"Hear me out." Pa was in no mood to listen to Matt. That much was clear. "Marriage is about more than physical attraction. It's a lifetime commitment. There's a reason the vows include 'for better, for worse.' There are hard times in every marriage, and it takes strength to go through those hard times. That's why you've gotta be sure you have the right partner." Pa leaned forward, as if to emphasize his fears. "Your ma says she's a nice enough girl, but I'm worried that you and Toby are making a mistake."

It was time for Matt to speak, to let his father know that he was the one who was making a mistake by not trusting his sons' judgment. "I don't believe either of us is making a mistake. Greta's not like any woman I've ever met. Yes, it's true that I've only known her for a week, but she's a strong, caring woman. She's the first woman I've met who makes me think about marriage."

As the words echoed through the room, Matt realized they'd surprised him as much as they had his father. The question was what he was going to do about it.

Chapter Eleven

"So this is the young man who wants to play the piano." Joanna smiled at Otto as her husband helped her remove her cloak, then carried their son into the dining room. The three Finleys were the last to arrive for what Emily had said had become a weekly tradition with the three sisters and their husbands sharing the Sunday midday meal at Finley House.

Though the others had gathered in the dining room, when Otto had heard that Joanna was coming, he'd insisted on sitting on the stairs to wait for the front door to open, and though her mother would have scolded her, saying it wasn't seemly for a woman of her age to do so, Greta had joined him, relishing the time with him.

The one thing she regretted about working at the tearoom was that she did not see her brother at all during the day. When they'd lived at the Channings', she'd found excuses to slip into the stable and spend a few minutes with him. Since that was no longer possible, she'd resolved that Sundays would be their time together.

Today Otto had little interest in what Greta was saying. Instead, he had kept his eyes fixed on the door, willing it to open. As soon as it did, he jumped to his feet and hurried to greet Joanna.

"Yes, ma'am," he said in response to her question, his eyes shining with excitement. "I hope someday I can play like you."

It was a lofty goal, for few pianists were as talented as Joanna. This was the second Sunday Greta had heard her play the church piano, and she'd been even more impressed than last week. Though Joanna's music had soothed Otto while he was in the infirmary, today had been his first day in church, and he'd spent the walk back to Finley House telling Greta how beautiful the hymns had been.

He looked up at Joanna, admiration shining from his eyes. "I wish people hadn't sung the hymns today. They were trying to drown you out."

Joanna's smile turned into a full-fledged laugh. "That's the first time anyone's said that. I'll take it as a compliment."

"That's what it was, ma'am."

Amazement and pride warred for dominance inside Greta. Amazement that Otto was speaking so freely with an adult, pride that he had conquered what she'd believed to be shyness. When they lived with the Channings, he rarely spoke to anyone other than Greta and their mother. She hadn't been greatly surprised when he'd formed friendships with Noah and Beulah, because they were children, but the way he appeared so relaxed around adults here was something new and very welcome.

"I don't know how to thank you, Joanna." Greta gave her a warm smile as they made their way into the dining room. "My brother is rarely this excited. I hope you don't regret agreeing to teach him."

Joanna shook her head. "The truth is, I never intended to give lessons. I knew I'd never be as good a teacher as Craig, but I've found it unexpectedly rewarding to help Beulah. If Otto turns out to be equally teachable, I may reconsider and offer lessons to others."

Emily, who'd obviously overheard her sister's last sentence, nodded. "Our parents would be happy to hear that. You know how often they told us that God meant us to use the talents he gave us to benefit others."

Greta agreed that it was good advice. The question was, what talents had she been given? How could running a tearoom benefit anyone? The women who came enjoyed the food and the chance to relax, but that wasn't the same as playing hymns to worship God, healing the sick and injured, or giving people a home the way Joanna, Louisa, and Emily did.

Greta gave herself a mental shake. What she did was different from what the sisters did, but that didn't mean it was of no value. Didn't the Bible say there was a reason everyone had different talents? The Vaughn sisters had found their callings, and as she reflected on it, Greta realized she might have as well.

The day she'd refused his ultimatum, Nigel had told her she had no talents, but he was wrong. She did have talents. Hadn't Jesus admonished Simon Peter to feed his lambs? Greta was doing that. She was preparing food for others and, based on the compliments she'd received, she was doing it well. Perhaps brewing tea, preparing scones and teacakes, and creating a peaceful space for women to enjoy each other's company was what she was meant to do, both here and in Colorado Springs when she and Otto reached it. Perhaps the serving part was the reason she'd felt so bereft when Mama had sold the restaurant, why even though she was still cooking at the Channings' she'd felt as if a part of her was missing.

"Giving lessons is a good idea." Louisa's words brought Greta back to the present. The youngest Vaughn sister looked stern as she faced Joanna. "Just don't forget that Burke and I need you to play for our patients."

Joanna shook her head as she took her place at the table. "I won't, but aren't you worried that some of your patients might be reluctant to consult you after you were so outspoken today?"

"Let's all sit down." Craig used his schoolmaster voice to get everyone's attention. "We can continue this discussion while we eat. I don't want the food my wife worked so hard to prepare to get cold."

After Josh offered a blessing for the meal and everyone served themselves from the platter of fried chicken and the bowls of mashed potatoes and green beans, the conversation returned to what had happened after church. As Craig had predicted at breakfast, the residents of Sweetwater Crossing had strong opinions about the upcoming election for sheriff and the fact that for the first time in some of their memories, it was a contested race.

Some were supportive of Matt's candidacy, but others were vocal in their disapproval. When she'd heard members of the congregation repeating the same concerns about Matt's lack of qualifications that both of the Winslow women had raised at the tearoom, Louisa had attempted to refute their arguments. Even though she'd spoken calmly, not everyone had exercised the same restraint but had shouted their objections. It had taken Pastor Lindstrom's intervention to break up what had become a contentious scene.

"One far greater than I declared, 'Blessed are the peacemakers, for they shall be called the children of God,'" the minister had said as he made his way into the center of the group. "Since we're all children of God, surely we can be peaceful even when we disagree."

His words had defused the situation, but before the crowd had dispersed, Greta had seen several women glare at Louisa.

"I only spoke the truth." Louisa reached for a roll. "It's hypocritical of them to say Matt shouldn't be sheriff because he's a newcomer when they didn't trust me to treat their injuries simply because I've always lived here."

"I hadn't realized you'd faced that problem." If she'd been asked, Greta would have said that residents' hesitation to consult Louisa would have been because she was a woman, not because she'd been born here. "That sounds like the story of a prophet in his own country."

Emily turned from watching her daughter attempt to stuff three green beans into her mouth. "It's Matthew 13:57. That's one verse I can't recall Father ever using for his sermon." She looked from Louisa to Joanna. "Can either of you?"

They both shook their heads, but it was Louisa who responded. "That's probably because he had no need of it. Father wasn't born and raised here, so the town accepted him."

"You may be right about that, but you've overcome their misgivings. I don't think what you said today will keep people away from our office." Burke gave his partner a reassuring smile. "You were right to say what you did."

Craig nodded. "I agree. Does everyone agree with me that Matt's response was a good one?"

A round of yeses followed. Greta didn't see how anyone could have disagreed with Matt when he said it was up to everyone in Sweetwater Crossing, not just a few, to decide whether he deserved to be sheriff. That was the American way. The only question was whether enough people would see that Matt was the right man to become Sweetwater Crossing's next sheriff.

⇥ ⋯ ◆ ⋯ ⇤

Matt hated the feeling of disappointment that welled up inside him as he knocked on the front door of Finley House. Even if the rain stopped, which was unlikely, it would not be a good night for a stroll around town. Puddles and mud were hardly conducive to a pleasant evening.

"I'm afraid we won't be able to walk tonight," he told Greta as she ushered him into the impressive hallway. "Toby's disappointed, and so am I."

She appeared startled by the water dripping off his hat. "I hadn't realized it was raining," she said, "but that's no reason why we can't all spend time together. I know Emily and Craig won't mind if we use the parlor. They may even join us."

When he started to smile at the thought of not having to abandon his plans, Greta continued, "It won't be as private as our walks, but change might be good."

"It's amazing the way you always find something positive, even on a night like this. Being warm and dry sounds like a great idea, but will it be all right with Craig and Emily?"

"I'm sure it will, but I'll ask them. Craig's helping Emily wash dishes."

98

Matt grinned at the idea of his friend in the kitchen. "I thought he'd gotten enough of that when he was a widower in Galveston." The few times Matt had joined Craig and Noah for supper, his friend had groused—good naturedly, of course—about the trials of cooking, cleaning, and washing dishes.

"Maybe he views it as a way to spend more time with Emily," Greta said as she headed for the kitchen.

Would he be searching for ways to spend more time with his wife if he were married? To the best of his knowledge, Pa had never helped Ma with the dishes, but they'd been married far longer than Craig and Emily. The thought of marriage was so new that Matt wasn't certain how he'd react, but he suspected Greta's assessment of Craig's motives was accurate.

When she returned two minutes later accompanied by both Craig and Emily, all three were smiling. His friend clapped him on the shoulder. "Of course it's all right for the four of you to meet here, but I hope you don't mind if we join you tonight." Craig wrapped his arm around Emily's waist and gave her a quick hug. "My wife and I were just talking about how important it is that you win the election. We want to hear how you plan to do that."

Still smiling at the pride he'd heard in Craig's voice when he'd said "my wife," Matt retrieved his hat and headed across the street to tell Toby and Rose the good news. While he was confident that the Albrights would have allowed them to use their parlor, the idea of being under the watchful eye of both Rose's parents and the two Albrights had not set well with Matt. Finley House was a better solution.

Rose agreed. As she entered the hallway, Matt heard her gasp, then quickly recover to say, "Thank you for inviting me, Mrs. Ferguson. I've wanted to see the inside of Finley House ever since my parents and I arrived." Her smile broadened. "It's even more beautiful than I expected."

"I wish I'd known. You could have come any time, but please call me Emily. We're not formal here."

Craig gestured toward the parlor. "Let's get down to business," he said as they all took seats. "What are we going to do to help Matt win?"

Matt shouldn't have been surprised by Craig's direct manner. While this was not like the casual get-to-know-you conversations he and Greta had had, it was in keeping with his friend's determination to be in control of every situation.

Toby, who'd settled on the settee next to Rose, leaving the rest to choose chairs, wrinkled his nose. "You've probably heard about the flyers I created for the businesses."

"They weren't well received, or so I heard." Like her husband, Emily did not believe in sugarcoating an unpleasant fact. "No one wanted to possibly offend a customer by hanging a flyer for one candidate. Even Josh thought that was a bad idea, and you know he supports you, Matt."

Greta nodded. "I wish I could help you, but Josh is right—that's not the right way to run a business."

"I agree that it was asking too much." Matt turned his gaze to his brother. "I warned Toby about that."

"And I told you I knew what I was doing. I didn't expect many if any of the people I approached to actually post the flyers in their windows. What I wanted to do was get folks talking about Matt."

"You definitely accomplished that." Seemingly more relaxed, Craig leaned back in his chair.

Toby nodded. "That's why I went to each business when I thought it would be the busiest. I wanted to reach the maximum number of people, because I knew I'd have only one chance."

Rose, who'd been sitting silently, turned to smile at Toby. "We haven't been here that long, so I don't know whether it's happened before, but folks seemed more animated than usual after services today, and the only thing they wanted to talk about was the election."

While that was true, Matt hadn't considered that his brother's flyers might have contributed to the discussions. It appeared that Toby was wiser than he'd realized.

"Even though some of them were a bit loud, the fact that they were talking is good." Greta's smile underscored her words. "There's nothing worse than apathy."

Though Toby hadn't phrased it that way, Matt knew he agreed. "Toby's planning to talk to all the ranchers and encourage them to vote. We heard they rarely come into town on Election Day."

"Why would they bother if there's no contest?" Greta's question was a valid one.

"Exactly." Perhaps it was his imagination, but Matt thought his brother moved an inch or two closer to Rose as he said that. "But this year there is a contest, so their votes are important."

Both Emily and Craig seemed to approve Toby's plan. What would they say when they heard what he intended to do?

"Before Toby does that, I intend to visit every family both in town and on the ranches."

"To sell yourself?" For the first time, Craig appeared wary.

"No. I'm going to ask them what they're looking for from their sheriff. I want to be certain I can meet their expectations."

"So you're going to listen rather than talk." Greta's tone said she approved. "My parents used to say that was the best way to ensure that customers returned. I imagine the same approach would work for you. You're a good listener, and people like to know that they're being heard."

When Rose and Emily nodded their agreement, Greta continued. "I wish I could campaign for you, but I'm a newcomer like you. I doubt anyone would listen to me."

The fact that she would even consider doing that made Matt's pulse race for a second. "I'm glad you have faith in me."

Rose turned to his brother, who had indeed continued to move closer to her. "I have faith in Toby. He'll do everything he can to help you."

Toby's smile was so broad Matt wondered if his cheeks would crack. "You're a fortunate man, Matt. With these two lovely ladies on your side, how can you lose?"

As Toby had undoubtedly intended, everyone laughed.

"Good morning, Greta." Josh made no attempt to hide his surprise that she was visiting the mercantile early on Monday morning. "If you've come to check on the supplies you ordered on Friday, I received confirmation that they'll arrive by the end of this week."

"That's good news, but it's not the reason I'm here. Even though it's only the beginning of November, I've been thinking about Christmas and wondering how you celebrated it at the tearoom last year."

While she'd crocheted a second angel last night, Greta's thoughts had turned to Christmas. Even though it would likely be the only one she and Otto spent in Sweetwater Crossing, she wanted it to be a memorable one, not only for him but for all the townspeople. That was why she'd decided to approach Josh with her ideas.

"We didn't do anything different," he told her. "I never even thought about making any changes, probably because while the store part of Porter & Sons had Christmas merchandise, the tearoom was the same year-round." Josh paused for a second. "Your expression says we should have done something special."

Greta fingered the bolt of dark blue cotton Josh had laid on the counter, wondering whether she would have enough time between now and Christmas to make a shirt for Otto. When he'd dressed for school this morning, she'd noticed that the one he was wearing no longer covered his wrists.

Wrenching her thoughts back to Josh and the reason she'd come to the mercantile, she said, "Not necessarily. The tearoom was new and as such attracted a lot of people, but now that it's an established part of the town, you might want to do something extra this year."

A smile crossed Josh's face. "You've only been here for a week, but that's long enough for me to know that you have some ideas. What would you suggest?"

Pleased that he hadn't dismissed her summarily, Greta said, "I have three things in mind. Blue is lovely, but it's not a Christmas color. What do you think about ordering different linens and china? That will change the room's appearance enough to tell people that we're celebrating." When Josh said nothing, Greta continued. "There's another reason to have different linens and dishes. I can't guarantee it, but I expect at least some of the customers will like the idea well enough to order some for their homes."

The sparkle in Josh's eyes told Greta he approved even before he said, "That's a good idea. As soon as you tell me the other two, we'll look through my catalogs to see what's available."

"Since the décor will be Christmasy, I thought we might make all the December teas Christmas teas by adding a few items like cookies and possibly slices of fruitcake. We might also offer spiced tea."

"Another excellent idea."

Greta's heart leapt with pleasure. Nigel was wrong. She did have talents. Josh Porter, who'd been part of a highly successful business, liked her suggestions. That proved she was not useless.

While Greta exulted over his praise, Josh stared into the distance for a moment, obviously considering something. "The only problem I foresee is that those teas may be so popular that they sell out. I'd hate to disappoint anyone."

When Greta had envisioned December at the tearoom, that was something she hadn't anticipated. Her parents hadn't changed the restaurant's décor or its menu, and so she had not faced that potential problem. "You're right. That could happen."

"I think it probably will, so I'd like to be prepared." Josh was nothing if not the consummate businessman. "Would you be willing to extend the hours? Instead of serving tea from two to four, maybe we should be open from one to five to accommodate everyone. If you agree, I'll double your pay and that of the servers for December."

It was a generous offer but one Greta could not accept. "You don't need to pay me anything more. Your family is already doing so much for Otto and me, but I can't imagine that the girls will refuse." The additional money would make their holidays easier, allowing them to buy more gifts for their families.

Josh frowned, obviously not happy with her refusal. "Don't you think these very good ideas for increasing my profits at both the tearoom and here at the mercantile will help me? I believe in rewarding good ideas and hard work, but I'm not going to argue with you today. We'll discuss payment later. You said you had three ideas. What's the third?"

Greta wouldn't tell Josh that this was the most important one for her, something she wanted to do to help Otto recapture one of his childhood memories. "For me, Christmas carols are an important part of the season." Joining a group of carolers and going from house to house had been something she and Otto had done together from the time he'd been old enough to walk the distance until Mama had sold the restaurant and moved them to the Channings'. "I asked Emily whether the town had caroling, but she said they've never done that."

Josh nodded, confirming that he hadn't heard of it happening here.

"When my parents owned a restaurant, they organized a night of caroling through the neighborhood, then invited everyone back to the restaurant for hot chocolate and cookies. They called it a thank-you for all the business they'd been given during the year. What do you think?"

As the bell over the front door tinkled, announcing the arrival of a customer, Josh's helper emerged from the back. Josh greeted the woman, then returned his attention to Greta.

"I think it's a great idea. If you're willing to oversee the refreshments, Craig and I can organize the caroling itself." He appeared almost as excited by the prospect as Otto had when he'd been five years old. "Three for three. Greta, you're amazing. What did I do without you?"

Greta was still glowing from Josh's praise when she returned to Finley House that afternoon. Though she'd expected the house to be as quiet as it normally was at this time of the day, the discordant sounds of wrong piano keys being pressed greeted her as she opened the front door.

"That's wrong, Otto." Beulah's voice carried clearly into the hallway.

To Greta's surprise, her brother laughed at the criticism. "But it's fun. I'll get better. I promise."

Curious to see the scene in the parlor, Greta peeked into the room, then smiled when Joanna beckoned to her. "Come in, Greta. I want you to see what your brother has learned."

When she'd taken a position at the end of the piano bench, Otto pointed to a key. "This is middle C." He placed his thumb on it and extended his hand over the neighboring keys. "Listen." Slowly and deliberately, he pressed middle C, then the next four keys. After his pinkie hit the final note, he pressed the same keys in descending order, his forehead furrowed with obvious concentration. When he finished, he looked up at Greta, his face as radiant as if he'd played an entire sonata.

"That's wonderful, Otto. I'm proud of you."

Beulah nodded. "Me too. I helped him." She nudged Otto, and as the two of them burst into giggles, Greta felt as if her heart would burst from sheer joy. Try though she might, she could not recall the last time she'd seen her brother so happy. His dream might have had to be postponed, but he'd found something to fill the void. What a blessing.

Chapter Twelve

Matt knocked on the front door of the house across the street from the tearoom. Some might think he was wasting his time here, because Mrs. Sanders was a widow. Not only could she not vote, but she didn't have a husband or an adult son to influence. No matter what others thought, he knew he wasn't wasting his time. He was following through on his plan to visit everyone in Sweetwater Crossing, and the woman who managed Josh Porter's teashop was as deserving of his attention as anyone.

"Matt Nelson. What brings you here?" The woman, whom Matt guessed to be in her mid-thirties, had hair as dark a brown as his and hazel eyes. Right now, those eyes were filled with concern. "I hope it's not something my boy did."

"This has nothing to do with Mitch." Craig had mentioned that Mitch Sanders was one of two boys who'd been involved in more than their share of mischief when he'd first come to Sweetwater Crossing but that they'd settled down. "Matured a bit" had been Craig's term. "As you know, I'm running for sheriff and wanted to ask your opinion of a few things."

"You're asking me when I can't vote?" Mrs. Sanders didn't bother to hide her skepticism, although she ushered him into the small but immaculate house and gestured toward one of the two comfortable chairs in the parlor.

"You may not be able to vote, but you live here and you pay taxes," Matt said when he'd taken the seat she'd indicated. "You have every right to expect the sheriff to serve you."

"Serve me?" Her eyebrows rose in surprise. "I never thought of it that way. The only times I saw Sheriff Granger were when Mitch got into some kind of trouble."

"That's unfortunate." But it wasn't totally unexpected. Craig had told him that Sheriff Granger had insisted on severe punishments for every infraction, no matter how small. "What do you think the sheriff should do?"

"I think he should keep us safe." Mrs. Sanders closed her eyes for a moment, making Matt suspect she was saying a silent prayer. "I'm not sure the sheriff could have done anything to stop them, but there've been too many deaths in this town."

Matt had heard what had happened to the previous minister and a number of elderly residents as well as the Albrights' daughter and son-in-law.

"You're right about that. Even one unnatural death is too many."

"Even if he can't stop people from killing other people, the sheriff should let folks know they can call him if they're worried about something, and he shouldn't laugh at them if it turns out to be nothing serious."

Matt was getting a better picture of the former sheriff, and he didn't like it. "If you're worried about something, it's serious."

"That's what I thought, but Sheriff Granger said it wasn't a crime—not a serious crime—for people to pick my flowers." Mrs. Sanders gestured toward the front of the house. "They're not much to look at now that we're past the main blooming season, but I like having pretty things growing in my yard."

"I noticed your flowers the first time I came down this street. They make this block the most colorful one in town." When Mrs. Sanders started to smile, Matt continued. "My mother said they were a gift to everyone who came this way."

The widow's smile blossomed like her flowers. "I hope you'll thank your mother for me. I've thought about moving the flowers to the back of the house, but now I won't."

Missing flowers didn't constitute a serious crime, but Mrs. Sanders's distress was real, and that made Matt determined to do what he could to stop the thefts.

"I'll talk to Miss Engel about keeping an eye on your yard. She has a better view from the tearoom than you do from the teashop."

"I don't want to impose on her." The hesitant note in her voice told Matt that Mrs. Sanders wasn't accustomed to others helping her.

"I'm certain Greta won't view it as an imposition."

Mrs. Sanders nodded. "If you can find out who's been stealing the flowers, I'd be grateful. Whoever it is takes only one or two, but they're always the best ones."

Interesting. This wasn't random vandalism but a deliberate act.

"I can't make any promises, but I'll make it a point to come this way more often." And if he happened to see Greta while he was passing by, that would be no hardship.

"Thank you. You've got a nice way about you. I reckon folks will see that at the debate."

"The what?" Matt was certain he'd misunderstood what Mrs. Sanders had said.

"Didn't the mayor tell you? He decided the town should have a chance to compare you and Byron Winslow, so he's going to have you debate each other. I heard he said it would be kind of like the Lincoln and Douglas debates back before the War Between the States." Mrs. Sanders paused, then shook her head. "The way you look tells me he hasn't said anything to you."

"Not yet." The fact that he'd learned about it through the grapevine rather than directly from the mayor told Matt that Alcott was doing whatever he could to make Matt's life more difficult. Little did he know that the very idea of a debate made Matt's blood run cold.

"It'll be Saturday the 22nd in the afternoon," Mrs. Sanders told Matt. "There'll be a church social afterwards, so almost everyone will come."

That was what Matt feared. He had no problem talking to one person or even a small group, but the idea of standing in front of a room full of people filled him with dread. He knew what would happen. He'd be tongue-tied, and if he spoke, the words would come out as gibberish. Whatever goodwill or support he'd garnered would vanish. No one would vote for him when they saw his ineptitude. Thanks to the debate, his dream of becoming the town's sheriff would never come true.

◆◆ ·◆· ◆◆

"Good morning, Miss Engel. What can I do for you?" Sweetwater Crossing's dressmaker gave Greta a look that made her think she was assessing more than her clothing. It was almost as if she was questioning Greta's presence not simply in her shop but in Sweetwater Crossing.

Since it wasn't the first time Greta had experienced such scrutiny, she merely smiled and said, "I'd like a new gown. Something fancier than this." She gestured to her navy skirt and white shirtwaist. After Josh had agreed to the expanded menu and the new linens and china for the December teas, Greta had decided that she needed to look as festive as the tearoom. The dark skirts and white shirtwaists that she'd been wearing each day were suitable for ordinary teas, but she wanted everything about the December teas to be special, including her clothing. And, thanks to the generous salary Josh was paying her, she would be able to afford a new dress.

"For church?" The expression in Thelma Scott's light blue eyes said she didn't think that was the reason Greta had come. She was correct.

"I don't know whether you've heard, but we're going to have Christmas teas throughout December."

"And you want something different for them. Do you see anything here that you like?"

Though Greta wished she could say yes, the dresses she saw draped over cabinets and hanging from hooks weren't what she had in mind. She wouldn't tell Miss Scott that she considered them ordinary, but that was the only word Greta could find to describe them, and so she shook her head.

The dressmaker gave Greta another of her penetrating looks, then nodded. "I finished a dress yesterday that might be suitable. Just a moment." She disappeared behind a door in the back of the shop, then returned carrying a dark green dress. "What do you think?" Miss Scott held the gown so that Greta could study it from every angle.

Greta almost sighed with pleasure. This was a garment that surpassed anything Mrs. Channing had worn, and she'd had several gowns sent from Paris.

"I've never seen anything like it," she told the dressmaker. The lines were simple but elegant, with long sleeves, a high collar, and a skirt that was gathered rather than relying on a bustle. The fabric had a sheen that reminded Greta of silk, although she doubted that this was made from such costly yard goods, but what made it extraordinary was the lace that trimmed the bodice and the delicate ruching that highlighted the waistline. "This is the most beautiful gown I've ever seen."

Miss Scott's cheeks flushed, perhaps from Greta's praise. "I saw something similar in a French magazine and wanted to try my hand at it. At the time, I thought Louisa might want it, but now that I've met you, I know it was meant for you. Do you want to try it on?"

"Oh, yes."

Five minutes later, Greta stared at her reflection in the long mirror, astonished at how perfectly the dress fit. "It's gorgeous," she said. "This is even more beautiful than anything I could have imagined."

The dressmaker pursed her lips. "I'll sell it to you on one condition."

That was something Greta hadn't expected. "What is that?"

"You need to let your hair down. You have lovely hair, but you hide it with that dreadful style."

Greta touched the braids she'd wrapped around her head. When they'd arrived at the Channings' house, Mrs. Channing had insisted that both Mama and Greta wear their hair that way rather than in chignons. "That is more suitable for a servant," she had declared.

After Mrs. Channing had left, Mama had chuckled. "She doesn't realize that that style is called a coronet. A crown. We're royalty." And for the next week as they'd braided their hair and pinned the braids into place, Greta and Mama had curtseyed to each other.

There was no reason to continue wearing a coronet. Mrs. Channing no longer had power over her, and the truth was, there were times when the braids and the pins required to keep them in place made Greta's head ache.

"What do you suggest?"

Miss Scott unpinned Greta's braids and unplaited her hair, then gathered it into a single loose braid that she left hanging down her back. "There you go." She turned Greta so she could see how the less formal style complimented the dress. "No more prim and proper spinster. Now you look like a sheriff's wife."

As the blood drained from her face, Greta stared at the dressmaker. "What do you mean?"

Miss Scott shrugged. "I probably shouldn't repeat gossip, but some of my customers don't think it's coincidence that Matt Nelson started courting you the day he decided to run for sheriff. He's smart enough to know that folks will be more likely to vote for him if he's a married man."

"But ... but ..." Unable to form a coherent sentence, Greta simply shook her head. The very idea was ludicrous. Matt was an honorable man, not a calculating one. He wasn't courting her, but if he were courting a woman, it would be for only one reason: he loved her.

"Do you know what Mrs. Joanna told me?"

When Greta entered Otto's room after Porter's closed on Wednesday, her brother laid *Robinson Crusoe* on the bed next to him, then gave her his most winsome smile. It was clear that rather than complain about the rest Louisa had insisted was essential, he'd chosen a different tactic and wanted to play the "Can You Guess?" game that Mama had taught them. That would be better than letting Miss Scott's words continue to echo through her brain. Greta had tried her best to dismiss them, telling herself that it was likely that either the postmaster's wife or Byron Winslow's wife had started the rumor, but still they lingered.

Determined to let nothing spoil her time with Otto, she posed a question that was almost as ridiculous as the rumor.

"Did Mrs. Joanna say you needed to eat all your peas?"

"No."

"Did she say she'd read *Robinson Crusoe?*"

"No."

"Did she say you were going to be a good pianist?" The rules of the game were that each person had only three chances to guess, and that was the most likely reason for Otto's smile.

"No."

"Then what did she say?"

Otto gloated over Greta's inability to have guessed correctly. "She's seen snow. And mountains. She said that snow is soft, but you can make it hard by rolling it in your hands. That's called a snowball. You can play with it."

Greta wouldn't spoil her brother's mood by telling him she'd heard about snowball fights, and so she feigned ignorance. "That sounds like fun."

"It will be. When are we going to Colorado?"

Although Greta had hoped that attending school here and learning to play the piano would make the delay in heading west easier for Otto, it appeared she'd been wrong.

"The earliest we can leave is in January. You know that I promised to run the tearoom until then. Besides, we need to make sure that you're fully recovered before we travel again."

Otto took a deep breath, then exhaled slowly, following Louisa's admonition to count to four as he let out his breath. When he finished, he fixed his gaze back on Greta. "You don't have to worry anymore. I'm not going to die."

For a second, shock kept her from responding. "What made you think you were going to die?"

Her brother looked at her as if the answer should be obvious. "I heard the doctor tell Mr. Channing it was a matter of a couple months. He said the best thing was to send me to the poor house, because they'd know what to do with me."

And the Channings wouldn't be bothered by a boy whose wheezing kept him from doing much work. "Oh, Otto, where did you hear that?" Surely no one, not even Nigel, would have knowingly inflicted that knowledge on a boy of Otto's age.

"I was cleaning the stable when the doctor left. Mr. Channing came out with him and asked him what was wrong with me. I don't remember the long word he used, but he said I didn't have long to live."

Greta shuddered at the thought of how her brother would have reacted to that announcement. He must have been frightened, even devastated, and yet he had said nothing to her. Had Otto been trying to protect her just as she'd tried to protect him?

"I wish you hadn't heard that. One of us worrying is enough. And you're much better since we came here." Otto didn't need to know that until they discovered what had caused the attacks he'd had in Houston Louisa and Burke wouldn't make any promises that his current remission would continue. Prevention, they'd told her, was essential, but in order to prevent recurrences, they had to find the origin of the problem.

"I know I'm better. But if we have to stay here, you can marry Mr. Matt."

For the second time in less than two minutes, Greta recoiled in shock. Had Otto heard the same rumors that the dressmaker had? "Wait a minute, young man. I'm not going to marry anyone." And even if she were, it wouldn't be a man she'd known for less than two weeks.

"Why not? I like him better than Mr. Channing."

"So do I, but that doesn't mean I want to marry him or that he wants to marry me." It was true that she enjoyed Matt's company and that he appeared to enjoy hers, but it was a long way from that to wedding vows. She had no intention of repeating her mistake and believing that a man meant one thing when he had something very different in mind.

Greta took a deep breath, mimicking the ones Otto took, before she spoke. When she'd entered his room, she'd looked forward to telling her brother what Matt had suggested today. Now she hesitated, worried that it might put more ideas in his mind. Still, she couldn't deprive Otto of what promised to be an exciting outing.

"We will not talk about marriage anymore. Do you understand? You need to promise me that you will never mention anything about it to Matt."

There was a long moment of silence before, his reluctance obvious, Otto nodded. "All right, but I still think it's a good idea. He's a good man."

Yes, he was. Or at least he appeared to be. "One of the reasons I wanted to talk to you before supper is that I saw Matt this afternoon, and he gave me an invitation for you. Would you like to spend Saturday with him? He thought you might like to see his ranch."

Matt had pointed out that as someone who'd lived his whole life in a city, Otto had no knowledge of ranching and might enjoy learning a bit about it. "You needn't worry," he'd assured her. "I won't let him overexert himself."

This time Otto's response was immediate. "Can I round up cattle?" Excitement shone from his eyes.

"I'm not sure it's round-up season, but I imagine Matt will show you some of their cattle. Do you want to go?" The question was perfunctory.

"Yes!"

It was what Greta had expected, but she had to issue a caveat. "It all depends on how you're feeling. You need to keep resting each day if you're going to be ready to go to the ranch."

"I keep telling you that I'm"—a coughing spasm interrupted him—"all better."

Greta waited until the coughs had subsided before she shook her head. "Not quite, but if you do everything Louisa tells you, you should be able to go." As she'd told Matt, this would give Otto an additional inducement to follow Louisa's orders.

Holding up his hand, Otto started counting on his fingers. "Thursday, Friday, Saturday. Three days. No, two and a half." He sighed. "I wish tomorrow was Saturday."

⋅≫⋅⋅◆⋅⋅≪⋅

Had he and Toby ever been so excited? Matt couldn't help smiling at Otto as he bounced up and down on the wagon seat, peppering him with questions about the ranch. He'd arranged to arrive at Finley House after breakfast but before Greta left for Porter's to give her a chance to say goodbye to Otto and wish him well on his big adventure, because according to Greta, Otto considered this the most thrilling day of his life, something he was certain would equal Robinson Crusoe's exploits or playing in the snow. Fortunately, the weather had cooperated, and the day was bright, sunny, and warmer than usual for mid-November.

"I wish I could have ridden a horse." So far that had been the boy's sole complaint, one Matt had anticipated.

"Maybe next time." He dangled the carrot of another visit to help mitigate Otto's disappointment. "We don't have any horses

115

that are the right size for you, but if you grow a couple inches, Daisy will be a good choice."

He could have shortened the stirrups and put Otto on Daisy today, but when Matt had asked Louisa what Otto should and shouldn't do, she'd cautioned him against letting him try to control a horse. And since Matt doubted Otto would want to ride double with him, he'd brought the wagon.

"You get to see more this way, because you don't have to concentrate on the horse," he said, hoping Otto would take the cue and look around. The rolling hills with their occasional limestone outcroppings never failed to boost Matt's spirits.

"I suppose you're right."

"I'm always right. Just ask my brother."

As Matt had hoped, that provoked a laugh. "You're just like Greta. She always thinks she's right."

"Your sister is pretty smart." As well as being selfless, putting Otto's wants and needs ahead of her own. "You should listen to her."

"I do." Otto wrinkled his nose and added, "Most of the time."

Matt stifled the laughter that threatened to erupt at the way Otto qualified his statement. "I wish Toby would listen to me."

"I could tell him he oughta do that. You're smart too."

The boy's faith in him warmed Matt's heart at the same time that it made him wonder whether his son—if he had one—would feel the same way. He hoped so. Even though there were times when he'd chafed over Pa's restrictions when he was younger and even though he disagreed with his insistence that he marry before Toby, Matt had never doubted that his father loved him and had only his best interests at heart.

As he'd expected, the morning passed quickly. After a brief introduction to his parents, Matt had taken Otto to the section of the ranch where the largest herd of cattle was grazing. The boy had been fascinated by the animals, marveling at the length of their horns and laughing at the way they walked single-file, following the leader.

"I want to be a rancher," Otto announced when they'd reached the spot where Matt had planned a picnic lunch.

"That's what my father wanted too. That's why we moved here."

Otto stuffed another piece of roll into his mouth, waiting until he'd chewed it carefully before he spoke. "You're lucky your parents are still alive. Mine died."

"I am fortunate." Even if Ma and Pa were his second set of parents, they were good ones. "I'm sure you miss your ma and pa."

Otto nodded solemnly. "Sometimes I can't remember what Papa looked like. I hate that!" His voice was gruff, as if he were trying to hold back tears. "If he hadn't died, we wouldn't have had to live with the Channings. I hated that."

It appeared there were many things Otto hated. In an attempt to keep him from dwelling on them, Matt asked, "What's your happiest memory of your father?"

A smile lit the boy's face. "He used to lift me up so I could put the angel on the top of the Christmas tree."

That was a good tradition. Matt promised himself that he would do that if he had a child. "We always had a star on our trees."

Otto reached for another of the hardboiled eggs Ma had included in their lunch. "Greta said some families do that, but we had an angel, cuz Engel means angel in German." His smile broadened. "It was a special angel. My grandpa made it in Germany." Otto continued speaking though his mouth was still half full of food, something Matt was certain Greta would not have allowed. "He made lots and lots of angels. Greta says folks wanted one like ours, but he wouldn't do that. Theirs had to be different. Greta says that means ours is priceless."

It sounded as if the elder Engel had been an accomplished artist. "I'm sure there'll be a tree at Finley House this year. Maybe Craig will let you put your angel on it."

His smile disappearing as quickly as it had appeared, Otto shook his head. "We don't have it anymore."

Had he broken it? Matt couldn't imagine any other reason why Greta wouldn't have brought what was obviously a cherished heirloom with them.

"What happened?"

"Greta had to sell it so we could leave Houston and the mean man."

>> —•+•— <<

"You're even smarter than I realized." Toby clapped Matt on the shoulder as they washed up for supper. "Getting the boy's trust is a good ploy. Maybe he'll give up the idea of going to Colorado and convince his sister they should stay here. Josh Porter would be happy about that, and so would you."

Matt wouldn't attempt to refute that statement, because it was true. He would be happy if Greta became a permanent Sweetwater Crossing resident, and after the time he'd spent with Otto, he'd be happy to have the boy around too.

"Yep. You're definitely smart." Toby inspected his fingernails the way Ma had taught them, ensuring that they were clean. "If Otto sings your praises—and I imagine he will after today—you'll have a better chance at winning his sister's approval. Who knows, you might even win her hand."

Though the prospect was more appealing than Matt would admit, it was so far in the future and so dependent on too many ifs that he refused to consider it.

"Who'd have thought that a herd of cattle would fascinate a boy?" Toby mused. "You and I were more interested in horses."

This was a neutral enough subject, and so Matt responded. "That's probably because there weren't herds of cattle in Galveston." He hadn't planned to say anything more, but he couldn't let Toby continue to harbor mistaken ideas. "You're wrong about my motive in bringing Otto here. It wasn't a ploy. The boy's been through a lot, so I wanted to give him a chance to be outside for a while. A bit of sunshine goes a long way to making a person feel better."

And Otto had definitely felt better by the time they returned to Finley House. His perpetual grin and the continued bouncing on the wagon seat attested to that. It was only Matt whose mood was somber as he wondered exactly what the person Otto had referred to as the mean man had done to make Greta flee her home.

Chapter Thirteen

"Is something wrong?" Greta hadn't expected to see Louisa waiting on the porch when she closed the tearoom Saturday afternoon, her smile less confident than usual. "Is Otto all right?" Though she shouldn't have worried, because Matt had assured her that he wouldn't let Otto do anything that might hurt him, Greta's thoughts had turned to her brother frequently during the day. Most of the time she'd tried to imagine what he was doing on what he claimed would be a great adventure, but occasional concerns that he might have had a relapse intruded.

"He's more than all right." Louisa's smile broadened. "I ran into him and Matt on their way back and can't recall when I've seen such an excited boy. He told me he plans to be a rancher when he grows up."

As her fears dissipated, Greta took a deep breath, then returned Louisa's smile. "I'm not surprised. Otto's dreams change depending on what he's been doing. When he started working in the stable in Houston, he wanted to be a farrier." The one dream that hadn't faded quickly had been seeing Pikes Peak.

"Otto must like animals." Though Louisa glanced toward her home, she made no move to leave the tearoom's porch.

"That he does. He keeps nagging me to take him to the livery to see our horse." Greta had stopped in several times to reassure both herself and Otto that Blackie was doing well, and he was. The enforced rest as well as ample food had given the horse what the livery owner called a new lease on life.

"Boys and their animals." A chuckle accompanied Louisa's words. "But that's not the reason I came. I had a checkup appointment with Caroline today and what I thought would happen has. She told me she won't return to Porter's. Both she and Raymond believe she should stay home with Junior." Louisa paused for a second before saying, "Josh and I hope you'll consider staying here permanently. Will you?"

The prospect of returning here and making Sweetwater Crossing their home after they visited Pikes Peak had popped into Greta's mind occasionally, and yet she hesitated. "The thought is very appealing," she told Louisa, "but until I'm sure Otto's fully healed and that he doesn't have a recurrence of what happened in Houston, I can't make any promises. I still need to take him to Colorado. I know you said the altitude might not be good for him, but he wants to see the mountains, and if he likes Pikes Peak, we may stay there."

Louisa nodded. "I understand. Burke and I will do everything we can to ensure that Otto is healthy. He's still healing from the bronchitis, but you're right—it's too soon to know whether the problem he had in Houston will recur. Neither of us believes it was consumption, but we don't know what it might have been."

Though she kept her gaze fixed on Greta, Louisa touched her midsection as she did so often these days, perhaps reassuring her unborn child that she would care for him or her the way she did for her patients.

"We're praying there won't be a recurrence," she continued, "but if there is, don't underestimate Burke. He's determined to ensure that your brother is as healthy as possible, and when Burke's determined to do something, he won't accept failure."

"Neither will you." Greta squeezed her friend's hand. "Thank you." With both Louisa and Burke caring for Otto, surely there was no need for her to worry.

"Nelson, I've been wanting to talk to you."

Matt kept a smile fixed on his face as the mayor strode toward him. He'd wondered when the man would tell him about the debate. When he'd seen Matt after he'd left Otto at Finley House yesterday, the mayor had turned his head the opposite direction. The almost childish reaction would have amused Matt if he hadn't known the man was playing games. Perhaps he'd chosen to wait until after the church service concluded to make the announcement so that he would have an audience.

"What can I do for you, Mr. Mayor?" Formality was the best way to deal with a man like Alcott.

"Folks here want to know more about you, seeing as how you think you ought to be sheriff. That's why we're gonna let you plead your case to them." The mayor raised his voice slightly, though Matt had no trouble hearing him. "I figure the best way is to have you and Byron address them. That's why we're gonna have a debate on Saturday."

"I heard rumors about that," Matt said as peacefully as he could. The mayor's use of the word "address" concerned him. "Will you be preparing the questions, or will they come from the audience?"

"Both, but first each of you will have two minutes to make a speech. The way I figure it, that's the most important part."

A speech. Responding to questions would be difficult enough, but standing in front of everyone and trying to convince them of his merits would be close to impossible.

"Do you understand?"

Matt nodded. What he understood was that the situation was worse than he'd feared.

"This has been the best week ever." Though Greta tried to restrain him, Otto skipped at her side, obviously wanting to demonstrate that he was fully recovered from his bronchitis, even though Louisa had told them that the healing was still incomplete. "I got to visit the ranch, and now I'm gonna see Blackie."

When his breathing became labored, Greta placed a hand on her brother's shoulder. "Careful, or we'll have to go back." Both Louisa and Burke had said that a relapse was unlikely, but she was taking no chances. Otto had sat quietly at church and ate a healthy serving of the turnips Emily had made, even though Greta knew he disliked the root vegetable, but now that they were on their way to the livery, his excitement overruled his common sense.

She couldn't blame him. It was another beautiful day with a few puffy cumulus clouds drifting across the vivid blue sky and the slightest of breezes reminding them that it was autumn. The words of Psalm 118:24 echoed through Greta's mind. This was indeed the day the Lord had made, a day to rejoice. And even though she had not had a chance to speak to Matt after church, because the mayor had cornered him, she had their walk to look forward to.

To Otto's annoyance, several people stopped to talk to them when they passed the park, and he tapped his foot impatiently while Greta exchanged pleasantries, but eventually they reached the livery. As they crossed the street, though Greta urged caution, Otto was unable to control his enthusiasm. He raced inside, leaving her to follow. When she found him, Otto was in Blackie's stall, rubbing the animal's flank.

"I missed you. Did you miss me?" The horse neighed in apparent response, causing Otto to turn toward Greta, a grin splitting his face. "He did, Greta. I knew he would." When Blackie whinnied, Otto reached into his pocket and withdrew the carrot Emily had given him. "This is for you, because you've been a good boy." He placed the carrot on his hand and extended it, giggling when the horse's tongue tickled him.

Otto was happy. More than that, he was ecstatic, and that made Greta happy. Perhaps everything would work out. Perhaps they would return here after visiting Pikes Peak.

"I wish we could take Blackie back with us," Otto said ten minutes later when Greta told him it was time to leave. Even though he wasn't exerting himself, she was mindful of Louisa's order that he not do too much, and they still had to walk back.

"You know there's no room in the stable," she reminded her brother, "but once Mrs. Louisa says you're fully recovered, you'll be able to visit Blackie after school every day."

Otto shook his head. "Not the days Mrs. Joanna teaches me. I can't miss my piano lessons."

If Otto's enthusiasm for music continued, that would be another reason to make Sweetwater Crossing their home. They'd been gone from Houston for more than two weeks, and there'd been no sign that Nigel was looking for her. That reassured Greta. So did Emily's assurance that even if Nigel found her, she and Otto had nothing to fear from him.

There was much to like about Sweetwater Crossing, including the way the sisters had welcomed her and Otto into their family. And then there were the friends Greta had made. Friends like Matt.

⋅⋗⋅⋅⋆⋅⋅⋖⋅

"Are you worried about something?"

Matt should have realized that Greta would notice his preoccupation. He'd thought that the moonless night would have hidden it, but he'd been wrong. She must have heard something in his voice.

"I hope it's not Mrs. Sanders's flowers. I check on them frequently, but I haven't seen anyone walking on that side of the street. Everyone seems more interested in the tearoom and the teashop."

"It's not the flowers." Perhaps it was cowardly of him, but when Matt told Greta about his conversation with Mrs. Sanders, he'd mentioned the theft but not his concerns over the debate.

"If not that, what is it? You look as if something's bothering you."

Rather than ask what had revealed his discomfort, Matt admitted the truth. "The debate."

"I don't understand." Greta stopped and looked up at him, her eyes searching his. "I think it's a good idea, and so do the ladies who came to Porter's the last couple days. They're excited about it, because they want to see how you compare to Byron Winslow."

That was the problem. "I can tell you what they'll say afterward. Even those who might have favored me before the debate will be convinced that Winslow is the better choice."

Greta tipped her head to one side the way she often did when she was considering something. "I have trouble believing that."

"Believe it, Greta."

She shook her head. "I can see that you believe it. What I don't know is why."

"Because I'll make a fool of myself standing in front of everyone. I'll either freeze or I'll stammer. What I won't be able to do is demonstrate that I deserve anyone's vote."

Matt hated admitting his weakness, especially to this woman who was so strong, but when he met her gaze, he saw not pity but understanding.

"I'm surprised," she said. Then when she noticed how far ahead of them Toby and Rose were, she added, "We'd better start walking again. We don't want to fail in our responsibilities as chaperones."

"The way I'll fail as a debater." He tried to inject a light note into his voice but failed.

"I'm surprised that you're uncomfortable in front of a group, because you're very good talking to people. I've seen the way you respond to them after church. Even when they're critical, you're always calm and reasonable."

"That's very different from standing in front of dozens of people and having to make a speech." Matt paused, wondering whether he should tell her the whole story, then decided he owed her that.

"When you were in school, did your teachers have you stand when you answered a question?"

Greta nodded.

"Did they make you stand in front of the classroom to answer?" This time she shook her head.

"Mine did. I was okay when all I had to do was stand by my desk, because the only person I was facing was the teacher, but when I had to go to the front and look at all my classmates, I froze. Even though I knew the answer, the words wouldn't come out. I knew everyone was going to ridicule me, and they did."

He and Greta were now only a few feet behind Toby and Rose, both of whom were laughing. Greta wasn't laughing. "That must have been horrible."

"It was. I was humiliated and angry."

"I'd have been angry at them too."

For once, she didn't understand. "I wasn't angry at the other kids. I was angry at myself. How could I have been so stupid?"

Greta squeezed his arm in what he guessed was an attempt to comfort him. "How old were you?"

"Eight."

"You were just a child, Matt. What you experienced was normal. It could have happened to anyone."

"Maybe so, but I'm not eight any longer, and I still can't do it. I might as well withdraw my candidacy."

"Don't do that. Don't even think about it." Her voice was fierce with emotion. "Sweetwater Crossing needs you. You'll be a good sheriff. An excellent sheriff."

"I appreciate your confidence in me, but that won't get me through the debate without embarrassing myself."

Greta was silent for a moment. When she spoke, he heard her excitement. "You're not the only one who's had that experience. I remember one of the men who used to eat at our restaurant talking about how he hated to address constituents. He was one of the town councilmen and from what my father said was well-regarded. Like you, he was comfortable talking to one or two people at a time, but he didn't like giving speeches."

While it was encouraging that he wasn't alone, that knowledge wouldn't help Matt on Saturday. But Greta wasn't finished.

"We'd seen him talking to a crowd outside our restaurant one day, and he appeared composed and assured, so my father asked him how he did it. He said that instead of thinking about everyone in the audience, he looked at one person in the back of the crowd and spoke to that person. That made him feel as if he was having a conversation rather than making a speech."

It was an unusual approach, one Matt had never considered, but it might work. He laid his hand on top of Greta's and waited until she looked at him before he said, "Will you be my one person?"

"Of course."

For the first time since he'd heard about the debate, Matt thought he had a chance of succeeding, and it was thanks to Greta.

Chapter Fourteen

In her dream, the wind was whistling, but the trees weren't moving and the flag hung limply. Greta turned on her side, trying to block out the sound, but it only grew louder.

"Help! Help me, Greta!" The words came out in small bursts, dispelling the vestiges of her sleep, replacing the vaguely disturbing dream with unbridled terror. As she recognized the source of the cries, Greta sprang to her feet and raced into Otto's room. The oil lamp they kept burning all night revealed what she'd feared. Her brother was wheezing, his face almost as pale as the sheet, his lips turning purple. This was what had happened in Houston, but it was worse, far worse. She hadn't wanted to believe Dr. Fletcher when he said Otto was close to death that day, but now she could no longer deny the possibility. It was evident that her brother was having extreme difficulty breathing.

She reached Otto's side and laid her hand on his shoulder, wanting to assure him that he wasn't alone.

"I'm scared."

It was little more than a whisper, but the expression in his eyes said more clearly than words that Otto was frightened. So was Greta, though she wouldn't admit it to him, lest that cause him even more distress. "I know you're scared. Can you take a deep breath?" That was what the doctor in Houston had advised.

Otto shook his head as he reached out to grip her hand. "It hurts too much."

Though she hated to leave Otto, even for a minute, Greta knew she had no choice. He needed help, and he needed it immediately.

"I'm going to fetch Dr. Burke," she told her brother. "He'll know what to do." Louisa's house was slightly closer, but Burke was the one Greta wanted. Not only was he an expert on lung ailments, but she didn't want to disturb Louisa in the middle of the night when she was so close to her confinement.

"Try to relax," she said. "I'll be back as soon as I can."

Releasing her hand from Otto's grip, Greta headed toward Emily's room and knocked on the door. "Emily and Craig, I need you."

Only seconds later a still sleepy Emily opened the door. "What's wrong?"

"It's Otto. He can't breathe. Can you stay with him while I get Burke?"

Craig joined them at the doorway, shaking his head. "I'll go for him. Your place is here with Otto."

Even though she hated inconveniencing him, Greta knew Craig was right. She returned to Otto's bedside, holding his hand and murmuring reassurances that help was on the way, but all the while, her heart pounded with fear that Burke would be unable to restore Otto's normal breathing.

It seemed like hours but was only minutes before Burke arrived, slightly out of breath from having climbed the stairs two at a time. He gave Otto a quick appraising look, his expression inscrutable. If he was concerned, Burke gave no sign of it, and that encouraged Greta. So did Emily and Craig's presence. Emily wrapped her arm around Greta's waist and Craig stood at her other side, a bulwark of strength.

Burke laid his medical bag on the floor next to the bed and smiled at Otto. "I hear you're having a bad night. Let's see what the problem is."

He turned to Greta. "Is this what happened in Houston?"

"Yes, but it wasn't this bad."

Nodding, Burke fitted his stethoscope to his ears and listened to Otto's lungs, then urged him into a sitting position. When he was finished, he patted Otto's shoulder. "Your lungs are sick, but you already knew that, didn't you? I'm going to do my best to heal them."

The fear Greta had seen in Otto's eyes lessened as he listened to Burke. The man was not only an accomplished physician; unlike Dr. Fletcher, he was also one who knew how to reassure his patients.

Burke turned to Emily. "We need strong coffee."

If the request surprised her, she gave no sign. "I have some left from today. All I have to do is heat it."

To Otto, Burke said, "Don't try to talk. That only strains your lungs more."

While they waited for Emily to return, Greta fixed a smile on her face, trying to reassure her brother, whose wheezing seemed to have increased. "You're getting your wish, Otto. Remember all those times you asked Mama to let you drink coffee and she said you had to be older? Dr. Burke says you're old enough."

The doctor in Houston had never recommended coffee or, for that matter, anything else. He'd told Greta there was nothing to be done, that Otto was destined for an early death.

"Thanks, Emily." Burke took the cup she offered and held it to Otto's lips, nodding when she and Craig left the room as if they knew that the fewer people in a sickroom, the better.

Now that Burke had completed his examination and was treating Otto, Greta's fears began to subside. Otto wasn't the only one Burke had reassured.

"Drink slowly," he cautioned Otto.

Otto took a sip, then grimaced. "Bitter."

A brief chuckle was Burke's first response. He waited while Otto took another sip, then said, "I thought so too the first time I drank it. You'll get used to it. I know your sister likes it."

"I do." While Greta enjoyed a cup of coffee, nothing compared to the way Otto was relaxing thanks to Burke. She had no doubt that what ailed her brother was serious, even life-threatening, but Burke was doing his best to calm him.

When Otto had drained the cup, Burke carefully lowered him to the pillow. "I'm going to give you something to help you sleep." He rose, pulled a green bottle from his medical bag, saturated a cloth with its contents, then placed the cloth over Otto's nose and mouth. Within minutes, Otto appeared to be sleeping peacefully.

"That smells like chloroform," Greta said as Burke returned the green bottle to his bag.

"That's what it is." He laid a finger on Otto's wrist to check his pulse. "Some doctors use conium and belladonna, but I consider them too dangerous. Chloroform sedates him, but his pulse is still healthy."

"When I heard Otto wheezing, I thought you'd put him in another steam tent. That worked the last time."

Burke shook his head. "I would have done that if it had been a recurrence of capillary bronchitis, but this is different. I know the doctor in Houston claimed Otto was suffering from consumption, but I believe your brother has bronchial asthma."

"Asthma?" Though Greta had heard of it, she had no idea what the symptoms were.

"Asthma affects the same portion of the lungs as capillary bronchitis, but instead of being caused by an infection, what's happening is an extreme contraction of the bronchial muscles. That means that Otto can inhale normally, but exhaling is extremely difficult and painful. That's what causes the wheezing."

"Then he's not contagious? Dr. Fletcher said Otto had an infection that was going to kill him and that he had to be kept away from others. He only let him keep working in the stable, because horses were immune."

Burke muttered something under his breath that sounded like "fool" but said only, "Fletcher was wrong. Bronchial asthma is a serious ailment, but it is not contagious."

And that was wonderful news, especially if Burke could prevent another attack. "What causes it?"

Now that Otto was sleeping, Burke led Greta into the hallway. "That's what we have to determine. It could be a number of different things or possibly a combination. Did Otto do anything unusual today?"

Greta tried to recall the day's events. "We went to the livery. That was the first time Otto had been there since we arrived. He was eager to see Blackie, but I don't think he overexerted himself." Greta hated the idea that she might have done something to provoke this attack.

"Hmmm." Burke stared into the distance for a moment, the lines between his eyes telling Greta he was thinking. Turning his attention back to her, he said, "I believe you mentioned that Otto worked in the stable in Houston. Is that correct?"

"Yes. He used to help my mother and me in the kitchen, but when she died, he was assigned to the stable."

Burke nodded at Greta's confirmation. "Did he have these attacks before he worked there?"

She thought back, then shook her head. "No. They started soon after Mama died."

Burke appeared satisfied by Greta's response. "I think we may have found the cause of Otto's asthma. From what you've said and what happened today, there's a strong likelihood that your brother has a sensitivity to horses."

Greta didn't want to disagree with Burke—after all, he was a doctor and, more than that, he was a doctor who specialized in lung disorders—but he needed to know everything she'd observed.

"Otto was close to Blackie when we were traveling, and that didn't seem to affect him. He was much better after we left Houston until the day before we arrived here. That's when the coughing started, but you said that wasn't asthma."

"No, it wasn't. That was definitely capillary bronchitis. My suspicion is that Otto doesn't have problems with horses when he's outside, but being in a confined space like a stable or livery concentrates whatever it is about horses that irritates his lungs."

If that was true, it was good news. "Do you think that if Otto avoids being near horses in confined spaces he won't have any more attacks?"

Burke nodded. "That's exactly what I think. Only time will prove whether I'm right or not, but I believe that as long as he stays away from horses, he'll be fine."

"And he won't die?"

"Asthma is serious, but if your brother takes the precautions I've outlined, there's no reason to believe it will kill him."

Relief flowed through Greta, almost overwhelming her with its intensity. This might not have been the miracle she'd prayed for the day she and Otto arrived in Sweetwater Crossing, but it was close. "Thank you, Burke. This is the best news I've had in months." As frightening as the attack had been, it had given Burke what he sought, a strong indication of its cause.

His eyes serious, Burke said, "I don't think Otto should go to school tomorrow. His attack has weakened him, so he should remain in bed for at least a day."

"What about his piano lesson? He'll be disappointed about school but devastated if he misses that."

"That should be safe enough. I'll check on him around noon to be sure." Burke rose and walked to the stairway. "Meanwhile, try to get some sleep yourself and don't worry."

Thanks to Burke, that might be possible.

⇢⋯⋅⋆⋅⋯⇠

"I'm happy your brother is feeling better." Matt was even happier that Greta was walking by his side, her hand resting on his arm as they made their way toward the town's one restaurant. When Toby had announced that it was time to do more than simply walk around town with Rose, Matt had suggested they invite the women to have supper at Ma's Kitchen. While there'd be speculation about the two couples, it was a public place and a perfectly acceptable way for them to spend an hour or so.

133

It would also be a small way for him to thank Greta for the advice she'd given him on Sunday. It would be an exaggeration to say he was looking forward to the debate, but the thought no longer filled him with dread. He could—and he would—focus on her during his opening speech. That prospect gave him the courage he knew he would need to stand in front of everyone else.

"You may be happy," Greta said, "but you can't possibly be as happy as I am. Happy, relieved, and grateful. Sunday night was frightening, but by yesterday afternoon Otto seemed to have recovered." She let out a little chuckle. "He was determined to be well enough for his piano lesson, and he was, but he paid the price later. He was exhausted before supper time. Even though Burke tells me not to worry so much, I was afraid Otto would have a relapse. That's why I couldn't go out last night."

Though he understood her reasons, Matt had found the evening without her tedious. He'd joined Toby and Rose but had had to walk with them rather than strolling a few yards behind. And while Toby seemed to find Rose's conversation scintillating, Matt had not.

"I understand worrying about brothers." He lowered his voice lest the couple walking ahead of them overhear. "I worry about Toby. He says he's cap over boots in love with Rose, but he's said that many times before; then he loses interest. Adelaide, the last lady he fancied in Galveston, lasted longer than most—almost a month—but this seems different. I think Toby's really in love, not simply infatuated. Now I'm worried that Rose might not feel the same way."

Greta gave Matt's arm a little squeeze, perhaps to reassure him. "I don't think you need to worry. She seems equally—dare I say?—besotted."

"That's a good word. I wonder whether Toby and Rose will taste anything or simply spend the evening staring at each other."

"The polite way to phrase that is to say they gaze into each other's eyes." Though Greta's words were chiding, the mirth in her voice told Matt she was joking.

"I stand corrected. Maybe I should have you write my opening speech for Saturday's debate. I want to be sure I say the right thing."

"You will." This time her voice was infused with confidence. "Just be yourself. Don't use any fancy words."

Matt laughed. "I don't know any fancy words."

"Good. Then you'll be a success. I'm as sure of that as I am that we'll enjoy the evening."

Her second prediction proved true. When they reached the restaurant, Mrs. Tabor gave them a warm greeting before showing them to their table and explaining the menu choices. The heavyset woman with the snub nose was the consummate hostess, making them feel as if they were honored guests, not customers. Though the restaurant was full, she spent more time than many proprietors would at each of the tables, coming back after she served the meals to ensure that everything met her customers' expectations.

It met Matt's. The food was delicious, his pot roast so tender he barely had to chew it. And, according to Greta, the fried chicken surpassed her mother's recipe. He'd been concerned about Greta's reaction to the restaurant. As someone who'd grown up in one and who now managed the tearoom, she was likely to be more critical of Ma's than the average customer. As it turned out, he need not have worried.

"This reminds me of my parents' restaurant," Greta said as she forked a green bean. "Good food and a warm welcome. Papa used to say those were the recipe for success."

Toby and Rose seemed equally satisfied with their meals. That alone would have made the evening a success in Matt's estimation, but even though there was indeed some gazing into each other's eyes, his brother and Rose were active participants in the conversation. Rose seemed genuinely interested in Greta's work at the tearoom, and Toby regaled them with stories of the recalcitrant steers that made rounding them up so difficult.

The one thing Matt hadn't counted on was the fact that other customers might want to talk to him, but half a dozen men approached their table one after another to discuss the upcoming election. While Matt fielded most of the questions, Toby chimed in when one man appeared unconvinced by Matt's qualifications.

"Even if he wasn't my brother, I'd vote for Matt. He'll uphold the law but will never railroad anyone."

Though he should have focused on the man who'd posed the question, Matt glanced at Greta. She nodded as if in agreement with Toby, then when her eyes met Matt's, she gave him a conspiratorial smile similar to the ones Rose and Toby had been exchanging, and as she did, Matt's heart leapt. He couldn't explain it. It made no sense, and yet winning Greta's approval seemed more important than winning the race.

It was too soon—much too soon—to have moved beyond friendship. Until he had a secure future and until Greta decided where she would make her home, there was no point in harboring tender thoughts for her. But he did.

Chapter Fifteen

"You look happy this morning," Mrs. Sanders said as she stepped out of the teashop, a sure sign there were no customers there. Although Greta knew she looked out the window whenever she could to check on her flowerbeds, she would not leave customers to fend for themselves. "You seem even happier than usual."

Though Greta hadn't realized it was obvious, there was no reason to deny it. "I am. My brother continues to improve, and Burke thinks he may be able to avoid future attacks if he's careful." Otto had pouted when Greta told him he couldn't visit Blackie, but when she'd asked whether he wanted to be sick again, he'd agreed that he didn't.

The teashop's manager pushed a stray lock back into her chignon. "That's welcome news, but I suspect your smile has more to do with the man who took you to Ma's last night."

Of course the news had spread. Emily had warned Greta that few things remained secret in a small town like Sweetwater Crossing. And given the number of people who'd been in the restaurant and who'd spoken to Matt, it was no surprise that Mrs. Sanders had learned about the meal Greta and Rose had shared with the Nelson brothers.

"It was a very enjoyable evening. Mrs. Tabor's chicken is delicious."

"I imagine the company was even better."

Mrs. Sanders was right. "It was."

The teashop manager waved to two women who strolled by, their arms filled with packages from Josh's mercantile. "We'll be back later," one promised. "We need to take all this home."

When they were out of earshot, Mrs. Sanders turned back to Greta. "No one's ever accused me of being a matchmaker, but I can't help saying that you and Matt are the perfect couple."

"We're friends," Greta insisted.

"Friends can become more." Mrs. Sanders studied Greta's face, then chuckled. "You can deny it if you wish, but your blush says you agree with me."

They were friends. Friends who shared their hopes and fears with each other. Friends who helped each other. Just friends. Not once had Matt said or done anything to make her believe he regarded her in any other way, and that was fine with Greta. She wasn't looking for a husband, at least not until Otto was older. She'd learned her lesson with Nigel. And yet, if she were looking for a husband, he would be a man like Matt. A man who made her heart skip a beat when she saw him. A man whose smile warmed her more than the August sun. A man whose gentle touch sent shivers of delight down her spine.

But though she told herself it was nonsense to be thinking about Matt that way, Greta was still pondering Mrs. Sanders's words hours later when the doorbell tinkled. Greta rose to greet her customer, then stopped, surprised by the sight of a man in what was normally a feminine domain. A second later the blood drained from her face. It couldn't be. She didn't want to believe it, but her eyes had not deceived her. Though she had thought she and Otto were safe, somehow Nigel's closest friend had found her.

Mustering every bit of courage she possessed, Greta walked toward him. "Good afternoon, Mr. Powell." She wouldn't call him Francis, not when the ladies who'd been quietly conversing among themselves had become silent, clearly curious about the stranger. "What can I do for you?"

An inch or so taller than Nigel, Francis had medium brown rather than blond hair, light brown rather than gray eyes, a round rather than an angular face. There was no physical resemblance between the two men, and yet both had the same almost predatory gleam in their eyes when they looked at Greta.

"We need to talk." Francis pitched his voice low enough that the customers would have difficulty hearing him.

Greta had no desire to talk to him or anyone connected to Nigel. "As you can see, I'm busy."

"I'm not leaving until you listen to me." As if he realized how threatening that sounded, Francis plastered a placating smile on his face. "It won't take long."

"All right." There was no point in prolonging this, especially since the customers were watching avidly. "Let's go outside." Greta opened the door, knowing Francis would follow her. Though the porch that connected the tearoom and teashop had two benches, she remained standing in an attempt to make this as short a conversation as possible. "Why are you here?" She could ask how Francis had found her, but that was irrelevant at this point.

Another smile that attempted but failed to be ingratiating lifted Francis's lips. "Nigel misses you. He wants you to come back to Houston."

The words sounded as rehearsed as his smile. Greta doubted Nigel missed *her*. What he wanted was a girl who'd agree to clandestine meetings, a girl who was so infatuated with him that she would allow him liberties that should have been reserved for a husband. Greta was not that girl.

"There's nothing for me in Houston."

Francis shook his head, his expression cajoling. "You're wrong about that, Greta. There is something for you in Houston. There's Nigel. He asked me to find you and give you this." Pulling a sealed envelope from his pocket, Francis extended it toward Greta. "He said it would explain everything."

Greta stared at the ivory envelope that bore her name in bold script and remembered all the times Nigel had left her notes—Mama would have called them billets-doux—in similar envelopes. She'd found one in the china cabinet, another in the silverware drawer, one in the pocket of her apron. He'd even placed one on her pillow. Each was filled with declarations of his love for her and his plans for their future together. They'd been designed to woo her, but they'd all been false, as false as this one would prove to be.

"Aren't you going to read it?"

Greta shook her head. "Nothing Nigel can say would convince me to return."

"You can't be sure of that. After all, Nigel cared enough to send me to deliver it. Open it. I won't leave until you do."

Reluctantly, Greta broke the seal and withdrew the single sheet of paper.

My darling.

Like his other notes, this one didn't address her by name; only her name on the envelopes had indicated that the missives were meant for her. At the time, that hadn't bothered her. Now Greta wondered if he made copies of the notes and gave them to anyone he was trying to charm.

Houston is unbearable without you. The sun still shines, but I feel as if I'm in a fog. Nothing brings me pleasure without you here to share it as we shared so many wonderful moments.

What had they shared? There'd been brief walks in the garden, stolen moments when she was cleaning a room, times when he'd kissed her hand, and then the final day when Nigel had tried to do more than kiss her.

Mother now realizes that you're the woman for me. Come back. Give me a reason to live.

Yours always, Nigel.

He wasn't hers. What he was was overly dramatic, dispensing flowery words, acting the role of an ardent swain when in reality he was nothing more than a spoiled child who expected the world to satisfy his every whim. That was Nigel. He was the same as he'd always been, only now Greta saw the truth.

"Well?" Francis raised a questioning brow.

"Nothing he wrote has changed my mind." A month ago her answer might have been different, but Greta no longer believed anything Nigel said. She doubted his mother had changed her mind about Greta's suitability. Georgina Channing had very definite criteria for her future daughter-in-law, and Greta did not meet them.

Furthermore, Nigel had not mentioned marriage in his letter. As she thought about everything he'd said and written when she'd been in Houston, Greta realized that was one word he'd never used. He'd spoken of being together and she—foolish, naïve Greta—had believed that he'd meant marriage. But he hadn't. The afternoon when he'd cornered her had made his intentions clear. Marriage was not part of them. And now ... Even if by some small miracle Nigel's mother had agreed to accept Greta, she no longer wanted Nigel. Being here had shown Greta that her life could be far better than anything Nigel could offer.

Though she neither liked nor trusted the man, Greta felt a moment of sympathy for Francis. He'd traveled halfway across the state, expecting her to capitulate to Nigel's request. Instead, he'd return to Houston having failed at the task, and Nigel being Nigel would place all the blame on Francis.

"I'm afraid you've wasted your time. As I said before, there's nothing in Houston for me."

Francis fidgeted as if envisioning Nigel's reaction when he told him Greta had refused to accept him. "Nigel won't be happy."

"But I am. Goodbye, Mr. Powell."

Greta spun on her heel and reentered the tearoom, a smile on her face as she headed to the kitchen to toss the letter into the stove. There was no longer any reason to fear Nigel, no reason even to think of him. He was part of her past, a past that as dreadful as it had been had taught her a lesson. She would not repeat that mistake.

"I expect the church will be crowded," Emily told Greta as they walked toward the site of the debate.

"Curiosity is a strong motivator." Craig, who'd paused briefly to greet Louisa and Josh as they left their house, rejoined Greta and Emily.

His wife laughed. "So is food. That's why the mayor scheduled the debate on the same day as our autumn church social." Emily had explained that they'd meet in the church for the debate itself, then move to the parsonage annex for the meal that would follow it.

A crowded church was what Matt feared, but Greta was hopeful that now that he'd practiced his opening speech he'd be able to deliver it without the freezing or stammering he'd experienced as a boy.

"What do you think the questions will be like?" she asked. There had been no way to rehearse answers.

"I imagine the mayor will ask most of them, but a few could come from the audience." A wry smile accompanied Craig's words. "Having seen the way the town reacted to some of my teaching techniques and the way they confronted me after church one day, I suspect there will be some loud and possibly hostile questions."

"Matt will be able to handle them." At least Greta hoped he would. She'd advised him to focus on the person who asked the question and try to ignore everyone else. If he could do that, she knew he would succeed, for she'd seen the way he'd responded to questions at Ma's, always calm, always polite, but also always firm in his answers.

Craig nodded. "I'm sure you're right. I've never seen him at a loss for words." But Craig didn't know what had happened in Matt's past.

As Emily had predicted, the church was full. Though Emily looked askance when Greta declined to sit with her and her family in the fourth pew from the front, she chose a seat in the back of the church. After leaving their son with Mrs. Carmichael, who'd volunteered to stay with all the children, Joanna and Burke had arrived early to save seats for the others. "We want to be close to the speakers," Joanna had said. They were, and Greta was where she'd promised Matt she would be.

At precisely eleven a.m. Mayor Alcott strode down the aisle. Rather than using the pulpit, he stood at the end of the aisle.

"Good morning. I'm glad to see such a good turnout." His booming voice echoed through the church. "Y'all know why we're here, so I'll say only that our purpose is to learn more about the two men who would like to become Sweetwater Crossing's next sheriff. I advise you to listen carefully so you can make the right choice on Election Day."

His expression solemn, he gestured toward the back of the sanctuary where Matt and Byron Winslow stood waiting to be summoned. Other than a quick glance and a nod, Matt had not acknowledged Greta's presence, but she'd seen the tension in his shoulders and prayed that he would relax enough to show the town's residents his qualifications.

"Gentlemen, please join me." When Matt and Byron Winslow reached him, the mayor smiled. "I don't believe introductions are necessary. Y'all know Byron. He's been part of Sweetwater Crossing his whole life. I imagine y'all also know that Matt Nelson and his family arrived here earlier this year to become ranchers."

Greta took a deep breath, trying to control her anger at the mayor's obvious bias. While she wanted to protest that it was unfair that he was trying to influence people, Greta sensed that would only hurt Matt, and that was something she'd never do.

Beaming with approval, Mayor Alcott turned toward Byron. "We'll begin with you. You have two minutes to state your case."

Matt's opponent straightened his shoulders, then smiled. "Good morning, gentlemen." He paused for a second. "As the mayor said, I'm the best candidate because I've lived here all my life. I'm older than my opponent and, I'd like to believe, wiser than him. I know what you expect from a sheriff, and I promise that I will give you that. I will carry on the fine tradition that Sheriff Granger started."

Though he continued speaking for more than the allotted two minutes, the mayor made no effort to stop him. Eventually, he said, "I look forward to serving this fine town as its next sheriff."

After the applause died down, Mayor Alcott turned toward Matt. "And now we'll hear from Matt Nelson."

"Thank you, Mr. Mayor." Matt's voice was infused with warmth, even though the mayor had extended none to him. He turned from addressing Mayor Alcott and faced the audience, his gaze searching for Greta. When she gave him a smile that was meant to encourage him, he began to speak. "It's true that I have not lived here as long as Mr. Winslow. Before we moved to Sweetwater Crossing, my family owned a haberdashery in Galveston."

If Matt was nervous, he gave no sign of it. He spoke clearly and confidently, and as he did, Greta began to relax. Matt was doing well. Very well.

"You may not think that has any relevance, but I believe that working at the haberdashery helped prepare me to be your sheriff, because it showed me the problems a business can have, problems like thievery and vandalism. I saw how lawmen can make a difference, how they can do more than punish wrongdoers. They can help prevent those crimes."

The murmurs that followed his final words told Greta the town hadn't considered prevention to be the sheriff's role.

When the room was once more silent, Matt continued. "Living in Sweetwater Crossing has given me a different perspective. I now understand the challenges that ranchers and farmers face. They're similar and yet different from those of businesses. Because I've had both of those experiences, I believe that I am well qualified to serve all of Sweetwater Crossing, those of you who have businesses in town as well as those who ranch or farm."

His expression forbidding, the mayor looked at his watch. "Your two minutes are up."

They weren't, but Matt made no move to contradict him. "Thank you for this opportunity to address my fellow residents."

"Now it's time for questions." Mayor Alcott looked around the room, nodding when Earl Dodd raised his hand.

The town's livery owner and blacksmith stood. "I want to know how you're going to enforce the law."

"I intend to ensure that every letter of the law is enforced. Only the threat of severe punishment will deter crime." Byron's frown left no doubt that his punishments would be harsh. "Sheriff Granger did not tolerate any infractions, and I won't either. The Bible is clear: an eye for an eye."

Nodding his approval, the mayor turned to Matt. "Do you agree?"

Though the mayor had asked the question, Matt looked directly at Earl Dodd. "I agree that the law is important and will do my best to ensure that those who break it suffer consequences. Unlike my opponent, I believe there are multiple ways to deter crime. Making people responsible for restitution is one."

Confusion clouded the livery owner's face. "What do you mean?" The low murmurs from others in the audience confirmed that he wasn't the only one who didn't understand Matt's position.

"If someone damaged your anvil, what do you believe should be done?" Matt asked.

Before Earl Dodd could respond, Byron shouted, "Lock the culprit up!"

Ignoring his opponent's outburst, Matt kept his gaze fixed on Earl. "But that wouldn't help you make horseshoes, would it? I would propose that the person who was responsible for the damages work for you for however long it took to pay for repairs or replacement of your anvil."

A wry smile was Earl's first response. "Few folks want to work in a forge. It's hot, dangerous work."

Matt inclined his head, acknowledging the difficulty involved in being a blacksmith. "It's my belief that knowing that vandalism might result in having to work like that might deter someone from committing vandalism in the first place."

Earl wrinkled his nose, then nodded. "You could be right."

Others did not agree. Several men jumped to their feet and shouted their disapproval. Others accused Matt of not being a true lawman. Throughout it all, he maintained his composure, responding calmly to the attacks. And as he did, Greta's esteem for him grew.

She thought about the way Nigel had pretended to court her and the letter she'd received from him. Matt would never do anything like that. Matt was a man of firm principles. He was an honorable man, one who would never make false promises or mislead anyone. Matt was a real man.

Chapter Sixteen

Would Greta agree? Matt hoped so. He'd been surprised when his mother had mentioned it. Last night all anyone had discussed was the debate and how well Matt had done. It might be prideful, but he'd been pleased with his performance, thanks to Greta. Her advice had been invaluable. With her smiling at him from the rear of the sanctuary, Matt had gained the confidence he needed to speak clearly. It remained to be seen whether the townspeople approved of what he'd said, but at least they wouldn't dismiss him because of how he'd spoken.

He'd expected a fairly quiet morning, but then Ma had announced her intent, surprising Matt and making him wonder about both the timing and her motive. Even though Toby had told both parents he planned to marry Rose, the most Ma had done was have tea with Rose and her mother at Porter's. She had never invited the Hannons to the ranch, but now she was planning to have Greta and Otto as dinner guests.

Though Ma claimed that it was Pa's idea, that he wanted to give Otto a chance to see more of the ranch, the gleam in Ma's eyes when she said she was looking forward to spending time with Greta made Matt suspect that was the real reason for the invitation. His mother was on a mission, and that mission was learning more about the woman whose name was being coupled with her older son's. He could say he had no interest in Greta beyond friendship, but that would be a lie, and Matt would not lie. The truth was, the more time he spent with Greta, the more his attraction to her grew, but it was still too soon to take the next step and ask to court her.

He'd sat with his family through the church service, rising to sing hymns at the appropriate times, joining in the common prayers, listening to Pastor Lindstrom preach about brotherly love, but all the while he'd wondered what the rest of the day held in store for him.

"I know it's very short notice," Ma said as she and Pa approached Greta, who stood in front of the church watching Otto join two other young boys, "but Daniel and I were hoping you and your brother would join us for lunch today." Toby, who'd been privy to the plan since it was announced at breakfast, had headed toward Rose and her family as soon as they left the church, leaving Matt with their parents.

For a second, Matt thought Greta would refuse. She appeared startled and a bit wary, but then a smile curved her lips, and those pretty blue eyes sparkled. She was wearing a dark blue dress today that complimented her pale hair and the eyes that were shades lighter than the bluebonnets that carpeted the fields near Sweetwater Crossing each spring.

"We'd be happy to come." She glanced at her brother who, if the enthusiasm with which he was chasing another boy was any indication, had recovered from his asthma attack. "I have to warn you, though, that Otto will probably beg to see the cattle. He can't stop talking about the size of their horns."

Matt's father returned Greta's smile. "I have something else to show him. We have a small herd of goats that I thought he might enjoy watching."

"I know he will." Greta looked at Otto again. "My brother loves most animals, and this will be a treat. There were no goats in Houston." She paused, a frown threatening to mar her lovely face. "Looking is fine, but he can't go too close to them. I don't know if they're like horses and might affect his breathing, but I can't take any chances."

Ma laid a comforting hand on Greta's arm. "Matt warned us about your brother's illness, so you can be assured that we'll be careful. You can trust Daniel to keep Otto a good distance from the goats. It'll be like when our boys were small and I told them they could look but not touch."

"It's always good to be cautious around our goats." Matt gave Greta a conspiratorial smile. "Unfortunately, they like to eat everything." He gestured toward the light blue shawl she had wrapped around her shoulders. "If I were a goat, I might consider that a tasty morsel."

She raised her eyebrows as if she doubted him. "Tasty? I would have said soft and warm, but I'm not a goat." With another smile, this one for Matt, Greta said, "I'll make sure Otto isn't wearing a scarf."

"That's a good idea. It never hurts to be careful." He'd be careful not to let Otto get too close to his horse. "I know you don't have a wagon anymore, so I brought our wagon to take you and Otto to the ranch if you agreed."

"Thank you. Could you meet us at Finley House? I don't want Otto to walk too much, but I need to tell Emily to set two fewer places at the table."

Matt looked around. Though Craig and Emily often lingered to speak with others after church, they were no longer here.

"I hope that won't be a problem for Emily." Ma sounded concerned, as if she hadn't realized that her last-minute invitation might affect others.

"I'm sure it won't be. She and Craig might enjoy some relative quiet." Greta tipped her head toward the trio of boys who were chasing each other around the large live oak. "I think Otto was the instigator."

"I remember when my boys were Otto's age." Ma punctuated her sentence with a laugh. "Quiet and calm weren't words I used very often. Daniel and I will head back home, but you don't need to rush. We'll plan to eat in an hour."

Once again Greta smiled. "Thank you, Mrs. Nelson. I'm looking forward to it."

And so was Matt.

⇒⟩ ⋯•⋯⟨⇐

Greta took a deep breath as Matt helped her out of the wagon, trying to convince herself she hadn't made a mistake. Otto had said that Mrs. Nelson was kind, and what she'd observed at the tearoom and again this morning confirmed that, but she was still wary. Was Matt's mother going to pass judgment on her and find her wanting the way Mrs. Channing had? Oh, how she hoped that wasn't the case.

It wasn't that she fancied herself in love or that she entertained dreams of marrying Matt. She didn't. Of course she didn't. As she'd told Mrs. Sanders, she and Matt were simply friends, and she didn't want anything to interfere with that friendship. Their nightly walks had become the highlight of her days, something Greta did not want to end. And while her heart did beat faster each time she saw Matt and she'd once dreamt of them standing arm in arm watching two children playing in a yard, one of whom was Otto, the other a toddler with a strong resemblance to Matt, that wasn't love, was it?

In an attempt to settle her nerves, Greta studied the Nelsons' home. Emily had told her that while it wasn't as large as Finley House, it was the largest ranch-style home in the county. Though it was only one story high, it was a sprawling building, perhaps the result of multiple additions over the years. A wide front porch with half a dozen rocking chairs seemed to welcome visitors, a welcome that was seconded when Mrs. Nelson opened the front door and stepped out to greet her guests.

"I'm so glad you could join us." There was no doubting the sincerity in her voice.

150

Otto, who'd insisted on jumping down from the wagon rather than waiting for Matt's assistance, looked around. "I want to see the goats."

Greta put a restraining hand on his shoulder. "Where did you leave your manners? That's no way to greet Mrs. Nelson."

Unabashed, Otto shook his head. "She knows I like animals. We talked about that the last time I was here."

"That's no excuse. What do you say to your hostess?"

Greta's brother wrinkled his nose, then grinned. "Thank you for inviting me." He punctuated his words with a bow like the one he'd seen in a picture book, making Matt chuckle, though his mother maintained a sober mien.

"You're most welcome," she said.

Greta's last reservations vanished. Her impression had been accurate. Mrs. Nelson was a genuinely kind person.

"Where are the goats?" Otto looked in all directions, searching for the animals that Matt had described as mischievous. There were no animals in sight other than the horse still hitched to the wagon Matt had driven. His parents' carriage must have been put in one of the outbuildings that, like the house itself, were well cared for.

"I hate to disappoint you, Otto, but I'm afraid you'll have to wait until after we eat to see the goats." Mrs. Nelson ushered them through the front door. "There'll be plenty of time later, but you wouldn't want my chicken to dry out, would you?"

Though Otto shook his head in apparent agreement, Greta knew that he'd gladly forego a perfectly cooked meal for the chance to meet a new breed of animal.

When her eyes adjusted to the relative darkness, Greta saw that the interior, while not as elaborate as Finley House, was still more elegant than she would have expected of a ranch house. A center hallway divided the parlor and dining room, its walls covered with what Greta knew to be expensive wallpaper. A Persian rug muffled footsteps, while crystal sconces promised a rainbow of light when the candles were lit. If Mrs. Channing were here, she would be envious of the décor, for unlike the Channings' home, this one was beautiful without being pretentious.

Chiding herself for allowing thoughts of the Channings to intrude on what was supposed to be an enjoyable afternoon, Greta addressed her hostess. "Can I help you with anything?"

Though Greta had expected her to refuse the offer, Mrs. Nelson nodded. "Would you mind mashing the potatoes? Daniel and Toby are taking care of our horses, and I suspect Matt has more goat tales for Otto."

Sensing that Matt's mother sought a private conversation with her, Greta nodded. "Otto can tell you that I'm an expert at mashing potatoes." It had been the first thing her parents had taught her to do.

When they reached the kitchen, Mrs. Nelson pulled an apron from one of the cabinet drawers and handed it to Greta. "You probably guessed that the potatoes were an excuse to give me a chance to talk to you without my son overhearing." When Greta had donned the apron, she pointed toward the pan of boiled potatoes and waited until Greta had drained them.

"Here's the masher." It was a wooden utensil similar to the ones Mama had used in their restaurant.

As Greta began to mash the potatoes, Mrs. Nelson continued. "I wanted to tell you how much I appreciate what you've done for Matt. I've never seen him so relaxed talking to a group. He said you helped him."

"All I did was tell him what I heard a customer say helped him. It was just a suggestion. The rest was up to Matt." When Mrs. Nelson appeared skeptical, Greta decided there was no point in trying to convince her, and so she changed tactics. "I thought Matt did well, and I'm glad about that, because he deserves to be sheriff."

Greta looked at the row of spice jars but did not see what she wanted. "Do you have any dried parsley?"

Although her expression was dubious, leading Greta to assume she'd never added the herb to her potatoes, Matt's mother nodded and retrieved a jar from a cabinet. "He said you did more than show him how to relax."

"What do you mean?"

"He told me you advised him about what he should say in his opening speech."

Matt had given her more credit than she deserved. "I simply suggested he be frank. I've heard too many people make promises they have no intention of keeping. I know Matt wouldn't do that—he's an honorable man who's determined to have a positive influence on the town—so I urged him to let everyone see that."

"And he did." Mrs. Nelson glanced at the potatoes but said nothing about the green flecks that now colored them. "I'm glad you see the true Matt. Too many people—especially the ladies—see only his handsome face. My son is much more than that."

"Yes, he is."

Ten minutes later after everyone was seated in the dining room and Mr. Nelson had given thanks for the food and the company, Mrs. Nelson began passing platters and bowls of food.

Toby stared at the bowl of potatoes. "What did you do to the potatoes, Ma? What's that green stuff?"

Though she knew him to be in his mid-twenties, Matt's brother sounded so much like Otto when he was annoyed that Greta was tempted to laugh. Instead, she kept her expression neutral.

"It's parsley. Greta always puts it in potatoes." Otto practically crowed with perceived superiority. "Try them, Mr. Toby. They're good."

"I can't be outdone by a guest." Toby spooned a medium-sized serving onto his plate, then took a taste. "You're right, Otto. These are good potatoes, even if they look a bit strange."

Once everyone had served themselves, the discussion turned to the debate and Matt's chances of winning.

"I'll say it again, son. You did a good job yesterday. I think you'll make a fine sheriff."

Though Matt was visibly pleased by his father's praise, it was Toby who spoke. "That's what I told you, Pa. He'll be better as a lawman than he was selling hats."

"What do you mean?" Greta couldn't decide whether Matt's umbrage was real or feigned. "I was good at selling hats. Don't forget that I convinced Mr. Berger to buy seven, telling him he needed one for each day of the week."

Toby's eyes sparkled with mirth. "I didn't say you were bad at selling hats. I said you'd be even better as sheriff. Besides, the way I recall that day, it was Mrs. Berger you convinced."

Otto, who'd been shoveling mashed potatoes into his mouth with apparent disregard for the manners Mama had taught him, looked up. "That's a lot of hats."

"It was indeed." Mr. Nelson gave Otto an approving smile. "But Mr. Berger could afford them. He's a man who likes to impress others."

Greta could have said the same thing about Mrs. Channing. *Stop it,* she told herself. *There's no reason to be thinking about Nigel's mother.* She shouldn't let unpleasant memories of the past taint her present.

"Do you want more potatoes?" When Otto reached for the bowl, Mrs. Nelson continued. "Speaking of the Bergers, the Galveston paper had the announcement of Adelaide's engagement. It seems she's going to marry a rich man from Houston."

Adelaide, Greta remembered, was Toby's last infatuation. Though Matt had said that he'd forgotten her as soon as he met Rose, Toby's surprise at the news indicated he had at least some feelings for her.

"Adelaide's getting married?"

Toby's father shrugged. "You didn't think she'd pine away just because you left Galveston, did you?"

"Well, no, but she said she'd never leave Galveston, and now it seems like she plans to move to Houston."

"It must be true love." Matt's ironic tone belied the words.

There were dozens of rich men in Houston. Greta knew that, but still she felt compelled to ask. "Who's the groom-to-be?"

"Nigel Channing."

Greta tried not to frown at the thought that of all the men in Houston, Adelaide Berger had somehow become engaged to Nigel.

Her brother made no effort to control his reaction. "He's a mean man." Otto's lips twisted into a scowl.

Nigel was a mean man. He was also one who didn't deserve a good woman. He may have been honest when he said he wanted Greta to return to Houston, but Greta was certain he hadn't told Adelaide that he'd sent Francis to bring Greta back with him. Perhaps he believed his wife wouldn't care if he had a dalliance with another woman, for that was the relationship Nigel had intended for him and Greta, a dalliance, nothing permanent or honorable.

Poor Adelaide. Had Nigel turned her head with flattery, soothing her wounded pride after Toby left Galveston? Greta wished she could warn her that Nigel was not to be trusted, but Adelaide would probably dismiss anything Greta said. Still, there had to be a way. She looked at Matt. Perhaps there was.

"That sounds like you know him."

Greta nodded in response to Matt's statement. "Otto and I worked for the Channings when we lived in Houston, but I'd rather not talk about it now. It wasn't the happiest of times for either of us."

"I understand. No one wants to relive unpleasant experiences." Matt lowered his voice so that only Greta heard him. "If you ever do want to talk, someone told me I'm a good listener."

He was, and it was time to tell him what had happened.

⟫ ·•· ⟪

She wasn't going to confide in him. Matt took a deep breath, wishing it didn't hurt so much that Greta didn't trust him. He'd seen what he thought was indecision on her face and had hoped it meant that she would consider telling him about whatever had happened in Houston, but so far, even though they were walking far enough behind Toby and Rose that she wouldn't be overheard, Greta remained silent.

"The half moon is beautiful, isn't it?" And if that wasn't an inane question, Matt didn't know what was. He should have said nothing, but the silence was grating on his nerves.

"It is, but I doubt you really care about the moon." Greta slowed her pace, perhaps wanting to put even more distance between them and his brother and Rose. "You're wondering why I didn't want to talk about life with the Channings and why Otto called Nigel a mean man. It's not a pretty story."

"I didn't imagine it was." He'd known something was wrong when Otto had first mentioned a mean man, and that feeling had been intensified by Greta's expression when she'd heard Nigel Channing's name.

"I keep telling myself that it's all in the past and that there's no reason to talk about what happened, but now I'm afraid that if I remain silent another woman will be hurt—not the way I was, but still hurt."

"And you can't let that happen." Greta was compassionate, wanting to help everyone. Look at the way she'd help him prepare for the debate.

"I don't want Adelaide to suffer."

"Adelaide Berger? How do you know her?"

Greta shook her head. "I don't know her, but I imagine that if Toby was interested in her, even if only briefly, she's a good woman."

"She is."

"Then she needs to know what Nigel's like before she marries him."

"Your brother called him a mean man."

When Greta closed her eyes for a moment, Matt wondered whether she was praying. "Most people would describe Nigel as charming, and he could be. He was the Channings' only child."

Greta began the explanation. "From what I heard, after Mr. Channing died, his mother doted on him. He could do no wrong in her eyes."

"Some parents are like that." Matt had seen evidence of similar behavior among his schoolmates. The results were rarely pleasant.

"When he returned from Europe, Nigel began to woo me." Greta's laugh held no mirth. "At least that's what I thought he was doing. He'd leave me flowery notes and talk about what life would be like when we were together. I thought he meant he wanted to marry me."

His fists clenched, Matt struggled to control his temper. He already knew there was no happy ending to this story, but the picture his imagination conjured filled him with fury. No woman deserved such treatment. Especially not Greta.

"But he didn't." Matt completed the sentence.

She shook her head. "Everything he said were lies. He had no intention of marrying me. When I realized that and tried to avoid him, he persisted, claiming that I was the only woman for him. He admitted his mother didn't approve of me, but that didn't mean we couldn't ..." Her voice trailed off, as if she was unwilling or perhaps unable to admit what Nigel had suggested.

"You didn't agree with his plan."

"How could I when it went against all that I believe? I thought Nigel would accept my rejection, but then Otto became so ill and everything was more complicated. The doctor said he was going to die and that Nigel should put him in the poor house so he could die there."

Matt's anger, which had turned into fury, was now directed at both the doctor and Nigel Channing. "You couldn't let that happen."

"I didn't know what to do. All I knew was that I couldn't let anyone take Otto away from me. If he was going to die, I didn't want him to be alone."

Matt heard the anguish in her voice as she remembered the fear that had encompassed her. Greta had been more than Otto's sister;

she'd served as his parent after their mother died. Of course she couldn't abandon him to strangers.

"What happened?" Though Matt wasn't certain he wanted to hear the answer, he had to ask.

Her eyes glistening with unshed tears, Greta said, "Nigel told me the only way he'd let Otto stay at their house was if I agreed to his terms."

Violence solved nothing. Matt knew that, and yet his anger was such that he was considering it. "I never met him, but if I did, I would be hard pressed not to knock some sense into him. How could he—how could anyone—try to take advantage of you like that? Otto was wrong. Nigel isn't a mean man. He's an evil one."

Greta gave a little nod, as if she agreed. "You know what happened next. I sold what I could to buy the wagon and Blackie so I could take Otto away. If he was going to die, I wanted him to have a chance to see Pikes Peak. You know that was his dream and that that's where we were headed when he took ill again."

"But fortunately you came here, and Burke and Louisa were able to help Otto." Matt paused, giving thanks that Greta and Otto had reached Sweetwater Crossing before it was too late. "You're safe here. Nigel will never bother you again."

Greta shook her head. "That's where you're wrong. He sent one of his friends to find me and give me a letter, begging me to return to him. Francis arrived on Wednesday."

"This past Wednesday?" When she nodded, Matt asked, "Why didn't you mention it?"

"Because I didn't want to think about Nigel again. I told Francis I would not return, and I burned the letter. Now I wish I hadn't. If I hadn't, I could have sent it to Adelaide to warn her about the kind of man she planned to marry. Nigel has no intention of being faithful to her."

Matt was silent for a moment. "I knew Adelaide wasn't the right woman for Toby, but I don't want her to make a mistake like this. We need to do whatever we can to stop the wedding." As the plural pronouns echoed in the night air, Matt realized how much he wanted to help Greta. She was strong and determined, but that didn't mean that she couldn't use help. The question was whether she would accept it.

To Matt's relief, Greta squeezed his arm and gave him a small smile. "I was hoping you'd say that. I doubt Adelaide would listen to me—I'm a complete stranger, and Nigel would tell her I can't be trusted—but from what Toby said, her family respects you."

"I believe they do. I'll send Adelaide's father a letter, suggesting he look into his future son-in-law's behavior and recommending he have a conversation with the man Nigel sent here. It may not do any good, but at least we'll have tried."

"Thank you, Matt. I knew I could count on you."

Matt's heart swelled at her praise. "Thank you for trusting me with your story. It's a horrible one, and I'm sorry you had to go through it, but I can't regret that it brought you here." Matt saw the softening of Greta's expression as he spoke. Hadn't she known how much joy she'd brought to his life? Perhaps not.

"A few months ago Pastor Lindstrom used a verse from Romans for his sermon, the one that says God makes even bad things work for the good."

"Romans 8:28."

He nodded. "That's the one. What you told me tonight is proof of that verse. If it hadn't been for Nigel, you wouldn't have left Houston, but you did. You came here, and you made my life better. God turned bad into something good."

Though it was breaking the rules of etiquette his mother had taught him, Matt couldn't resist, and so he touched Greta's cheek, savoring the softness he could feel even through his glove. This woman, this sweet, caring woman, had changed his life. It may have started as a way to help his brother woo the woman he wanted to marry, but the time Matt had spent with Greta had dispelled his worry that he was prone to fleeting infatuations like Toby and given him hope that he might have found the kind of love his parents shared.

Greta had been part of his life for less than a month, but that was enough to show him that love hadn't eluded him. And now that he'd met her, Matt didn't want to think about life without her.

Chapter Seventeen

"Why did Mr. Matt's family do bad things?"

Greta blinked in surprise at Beulah's question. The girl's face was scrunched up in confusion, and though she normally ate everything she'd put on her plate, tonight the chicken with mashed potatoes and gravy sat virtually untouched.

"They didn't do anything bad." Otto tapped his fork on his plate to emphasize his words. "They're good people. They have goats."

If the subject hadn't been so serious, Greta might have laughed at her brother's reasoning, but she needed to learn why Beulah had posed the question in the first place. A quick glance at Emily and Craig told her they were as puzzled as she.

"Why do you think they've done something wrong?" Greta kept her voice neutral, not wanting to do anything that might discourage Beulah from speaking. She hoped—oh, how she hoped—Beulah wouldn't say what she feared.

Beulah shrugged, as if the answer should be apparent. "I heard it at recess. Two girls said they're cheaters."

Greta's fears were confirmed. She'd overheard similar comments at the tearoom this afternoon, but this was more concerning. It was one thing for the adults to spread gossip, quite another for them to do it where their children could overhear and repeat the lies.

"It's not true, Beulah." Craig's voice was calm but firm, probably the same tone he used to maintain order in the schoolroom. "I've known the Nelsons all my life, and I assure you that they're honest people."

"Good." Apparently satisfied with the answer she'd received, Beulah turned her attention back to her dinner. "This is good chicken, Mrs. Emily."

The remainder of the meal passed uneventfully, but when Mrs. Carmichael took Beulah, Noah, and Otto out for a walk along the creek, Craig suggested that Greta join him and Emily in the kitchen.

When Greta had taken a seat at the table, Craig spoke. "Emily's lived here her whole life, so she's used to it, but I'm still surprised at how quick the rumor mill is."

"It's unfortunate," Emily agreed. "Father used to say we would have no need for a newspaper if the gossips could content themselves with the truth."

"Unfortunately, they don't. I heard several of the children whispering today, but when I asked them, they said it was a secret." Craig began to dry the dishes his wife was washing.

Greta nodded. "I imagine what Beulah overheard was similar to the conversations in the tearoom this afternoon. Almost all the ladies were talking about the debate. Several said they believed Matt would win, but others said he had no right. They claimed his family took advantage of the Albrights' grief after their daughter and son-in-law's deaths and offered them less than the ranch was worth. According to them, you can't trust anyone in the Nelson family."

Emily hissed her disapproval, leaving Craig to respond. "Those are lies—out and out lies. I know how much the Albrights valued the ranch for. There was no haggling. Matt's family paid the full amount the Albrights asked."

Emily turned, a plate in her hand. "Obviously, someone wants to discredit Matt. The question is who."

"It's hard to believe it's Byron. I don't agree with many of the things he says, but I don't think he'd stoop so low."

Craig might be right, but there were other Winslows in Sweetwater Crossing, and Greta knew that neither Mrs. Winslow wanted Matt to win. "What about his brother or even his wife and sister-in-law? I know all of them are as determined to see Byron win as we are convinced that Matt would be the better sheriff."

"That's possible," Craig admitted, "but without proof, there's nothing anyone can do." And finding the source of rumors was notoriously difficult.

"Do you think I should tell Matt what's being said?" It was almost time for them to walk, and although Greta hated to spoil their evening together, she didn't want him to be unaware of the vicious rumors.

Craig shook his head. "I don't think there's any need to say anything. I imagine he's already heard."

⁂

"You've got to do something."

Toby's frustration was evident by the way he stomped his boot on the wagon floor, making Matt wonder whether he'd seen Otto do something similar. The truth was, he was surprised at how long it had taken Toby to demand he take action to squash the rumors that had started flowing on Monday. It appeared he'd been foolish in believing they would die a natural death, because they'd increased as the days passed. Now it was Friday, and the election was only four days away.

"I can't stop people from gossiping." As much as Matt hated the lies that were being spread, he knew that denying them would only fan the fire. Folks would claim that he'd say anything to convince them to vote for him.

His brother did not agree. "This is more than idle gossip. It's slander, and it hurts."

In a few minutes they would reach town, where they both had multiple errands to run. Matt needed to settle this before then. It had been easy enough to send Mr. Berger the letter he'd promised Greta he would write, but this problem was anything but easy to resolve.

"It's Ma and Pa who are being accused, and they don't want to do anything. They know it's all lies." Matt had spoken to his parents as soon as he'd heard about the malicious stories, and they'd been insistent that he do or say nothing to refute them.

"But those lies are hurting you ..." Toby turned to glare at Matt. "And me."

The almost plaintive tone in his brother's voice drew Matt's attention more than Toby's angry words had. "What do you mean? How are you being hurt?"

"Rose's parents don't want me to see her any more. Even though the Albrights said the stories are false, the Hannons are not convinced. They claim if there's smoke, there must be fire."

And that changed everything. While Matt wouldn't respond to the scurrilous gossip for his own benefit, he couldn't—and he wouldn't—let his brother suffer.

"I didn't realize my running for sheriff would cause problems for you. Let me see what I can do."

His plan to speak to men at the livery this morning would have to be postponed or eliminated, because as much as he hated the idea of confronting Byron, he needed to get to the source of the rumors.

Ten minutes later, Matt knocked on the front door of the Winslows' home. Byron's wife opened the door, her smile turning to a scowl when she recognized him. "What are you doing here?"

"I'd like to speak to your husband."

"About what?" There was no mistaking the tall, thin brunette's hostility. She crossed her arms and blocked the entrance to her home.

"That's between him and me."

For a long moment, Matt wondered whether Mrs. Winslow would continue to refuse him admission, but eventually she nodded, her reluctance evident as she turned and shouted, "Byron, Matt Nelson is here. He says he wants to see you."

Heavy footsteps marked Matt's rival's approach. While Byron's expression was cautious, it held curiosity rather than hostility. "Nelson, I didn't expect this."

"I didn't expect to have to come." Matt looked around. "Is there somewhere private we can talk?" While he had no doubt that Byron would relate their conversation to his wife, he did not want her to be part of it.

A quick nod said the other man understood. "It's time for me to feed my horse. There won't be anyone else in the barn."

He stepped outside and led the way around the small house to the backyard. Once they were inside the barn, rather than begin feeding his horse, he turned to Matt. "So, what's on your mind?"

"I thought you should know that someone's been spreading lies about my family."

Byron's shock could have been feigned, but Matt doubted it. "What kind of lies?"

"They're saying my parents cheated the Albrights when they bought the ranch. They didn't, but the inference is that my family cannot be trusted."

Though Byron said nothing, he listened intently, his shock turning to what appeared to be concern. If he wasn't involved, he was a good actor.

Matt waited for a second before he spoke again. "That probably hurt my chances of becoming the next sheriff, but that's not as important as what the lies are doing to my brother. Folks know that Toby fancies Rose Hannon. Because of everything that's being said, the Hannons are questioning whether Rose should have anything to do with him. I can't let that continue."

His eyes narrowing, Byron took a step toward Matt. Though his posture could be interpreted as intimidating, Matt thought he saw a hint of vulnerability in the other man's expression. "And you think I'm responsible?"

Half an hour ago, Matt would have said yes, that Byron had either started the rumors or given his consent to whoever had, but that was before he'd spoken to him. "I don't want to believe that. The problem is you're the one who has the most to gain."

Byron looked at Matt, his gaze unflinching. "It's no secret that I want to win and that I believe I'd be a better sheriff than you, but I give you my word that I had nothing to do with this. When I win—and I still intend to—I want it to be honestly. The people of Sweetwater Crossing deserve an honest, honorable sheriff." Byron's words rang with sincerity. "Do you believe me?"

Matt looked at the man he wanted to defeat at the polls. He might not like Byron's approach to enforcing the law, but he couldn't deny that his declaration seemed honest. "I do."

Unfortunately, the damage had already been done.

After Pastor Lindstrom finished the benediction, instead of walking to the rear of the sanctuary to greet parishioners, he remained in front of the altar. "Before we leave today, Byron Winslow has asked for an opportunity to speak to you." He directed his gaze to the middle of the church. "Byron …"

Matt's contender in the race for sheriff walked slowly up the aisle, his face more solemn than Matt had ever seen it, his shoulders bent as if he were carrying a heavy weight on them. Though he would have thought it impossible, Byron seemed to have aged years in the two days since their confrontation in his barn.

When he reached the front, Byron turned to face the congregation. "I'm sure you're wondering what I have to say. It's been only a little more than a week since I stood here urging you to choose me as your next sheriff." He paused for a second. "Since then someone has been spreading lies about my opponent and his family. I've heard the stories, and I can assure you that they are false, but there's no undoing what has been said."

A low murmur greeted his words, mirroring the surprise that Matt felt in hearing Byron's declaration.

"I've tried to find out who was responsible, but no one will admit it. All I can do is tell you that I had no hand in it."

The murmur grew as people registered Byron's humility, so different from the almost arrogant demeanor he'd demonstrated last week.

He held up a hand to urge silence. "I can't erase what you've heard, but I can make sure that no more innocent people are hurt." Once again, Byron paused. "I have no desire to become sheriff as a result of unfair tactics, and so I withdraw my candidacy. Matt Nelson will be Sweetwater Crossing's next sheriff."

Before anyone could react, Jake Winslow jumped to his feet. "You can't do that, Byron. I won't let you. I was only trying to help. You're my big brother. I want you to succeed."

The murmur became an uproar as the congregation recognized both the source of the lies and their own gullibility. As postmaster, Jake had the opportunity to speak to almost everyone in town. And as postmaster, he was well respected. In all likelihood, nothing like this had ever occurred, and so people had believed his allegations rather than questioning them.

Now everything was in question, even Jake Winslow's future as postmaster, because a few voices called for his resignation. Matt couldn't let the situation stand. Jake was the guilty one, not Byron. He rose and strode to the front to stand at Byron's side.

After Pastor Lindstrom quieted his parishioners, Matt spoke to Byron, pitching his voice to carry throughout the church. "I hope you'll reconsider your decision and will remain a candidate. Let's let the voters of Sweetwater Crossing decide who should be their next sheriff."

The gasps from several women matched the surprise Matt saw on Byron's face.

Turning to face the congregation, Matt said firmly, "Byron and I may disagree about many things, but I admire his honesty, and so should you."

Chapter Eighteen

"This is beautiful." Louisa smiled as she fingered the edge of a tablecloth. Though Josh had visited the tearoom earlier this morning and had seen the Christmas decorations, this was the first time Louisa had been here in weeks, and even though she had known of her plans, Greta had been anxious, waiting for her friend's opinion. After all, Porter's was Louisa's company as much as it was Josh's. Furthermore, Louisa had chosen the original china and linens, making Greta concerned that she might feel she'd overstepped her authority by changing them, even if only for a month.

"I'm so glad you're running the tearoom." The sincerity in Louisa's voice bolstered Greta's confidence. "I would never have thought to have seasonal linens and china, but they'll make this a special Christmas season for everyone who comes to tea."

That had been Greta's goal. Whether she remained in Sweetwater Crossing permanently, she hoped the holiday décor and foods would become a tradition along with the night of caroling. "I'm sure Josh told you that we're hoping that the décor encourages some women to buy similar things for their homes. I don't know how many would want to have a patterned tablecloth like these, but the china would be equally striking on plain linens."

Louisa nodded, although whether that was because Josh had mentioned the possibility of more sales in the mercantile or whether she agreed with Greta's assessment of the china on a neutral tablecloth wasn't clear. "I predict everything will be a huge success."

"We'll know more tonight." Today was the first day of both the new décor and the extended tearoom hours.

"And by tomorrow evening, we'll have a new sheriff."

The nervous butterflies that invaded her stomach every time Greta thought about the election returned in full force. "I'm more concerned about that than the ladies' reaction to our Christmas theme. I don't know what Matt will do if he doesn't win."

"I imagine he'll continue working on the ranch."

"Probably, but that's not what he wants to do. He told me he believes serving the town is what he's meant to do."

"Just as making women feel welcomed and pampered here is what you're meant to do." Louisa winced and cupped her abdomen. "This baby is anxious to make his appearance."

"So you think you're having a boy?"

A shrug was Louisa's first response. "Today I do. Yesterday I was convinced she would be a girl, but the truth is, Josh and I'll be happy with either just so long as the baby is healthy."

"That's what every parent wants, isn't it?" Greta's mother had said the same thing while she was carrying Otto.

"Of course." Louisa nodded when Greta asked if she wanted to sample one of the Christmas cookies she'd made. She took a bite, then gave a little moan of delight. "These are delicious. Even Emily can't match them, but don't you dare tell her I said that."

When she'd finished the last bite and washed it down with a cup of the holiday spiced tea, Louisa hoisted herself to her feet, laughing at the effort required. "I'd best be heading back to my office. Burke said he'd handle everything and I know he will, but I don't want to take advantage of him. Once the baby arrives, I won't be ready to work for a couple weeks."

"You'll miss your patients, won't you?" Greta knew she would miss what she'd begun calling her regulars, the women who had started coming for tea every week instead of their former once-a-month schedule, when she left Sweetwater Crossing.

"I will, but fortunately none of my patients' babies are due for at least a month." Louisa stopped when she reached the door, her hand on the knob. "I'm so thankful that Emily and Mrs. Carmichael love children as much as they do. I won't have a single worry about leaving my baby with them."

"Not one?" Greta teased.

Louisa shrugged. "I'm sure I'll miss the baby when I'm in the office or with patients, but Emily and Mrs. Carmichael will take good care of him." She started to open the door, then paused. "I haven't asked them, but I'm sure they'd be happy to have your baby join the nursery."

"My baby?" Shock made Greta's voice higher than normal.

"Yours and Matt's. We've all seen the way you two look at each other. It's only a matter of time before you're walking down the aisle."

"But ... but ..." Though she was rarely speechless, Greta had trouble forming a complete sentence. While she'd entertained thoughts of more than friendship with Matt, she had never, ever said the words aloud. Hearing Louisa voice her deepest feelings made Greta's heart pound.

She swallowed deeply, trying to find a way to speak, to refute Louisa's claim. "Matt has never said anything that makes me think he views me that way." And though Miss Scott had claimed that he was looking for a bride to increase his chances of becoming sheriff, as far as Greta could tell, that rumor had died.

"He will. Trust me, he will."

Louisa's words continued to echo through Greta's mind for the rest of the day, though she tried to push them away. It was true there'd been times when she'd thought Matt regarded her as more than a friend, and he'd told her she'd made his life better, but that wasn't the same as declaring his love and asking to court her. Louisa must be mistaken about that.

One thing she wasn't mistaken about was the customers' reaction to the holiday décor and food. The approval was unanimous. After they complimented Greta on her new gown and hairstyle, the ladies praised the spiced tea and shortbread cookies cut in the shapes of stars and angels.

"These make me feel as if Christmas is only a few days away," one woman told her.

Another asked whether the mercantile stocked the cookie cutters, confessing that she wanted to surprise her children with not only cookies but also fudge cut in the festive shapes. "It'll make it a special Christmas for them," she said, her face beaming with happiness when Greta assured her that Josh had ordered several sets of the cutters.

Greta was pleased—no, she was more than pleased; she was thrilled—by the reception her holiday decorations were receiving. The sole discordant note was sounded when she overheard two women discussing the best topper for a tree, with one arguing for a star, the other insisting that an angel was preferable.

Pangs of regret tore through Greta as she thought of the porcelain angel that had graced her family's tree for so many years. Though she told herself it was only a possession, a piece of clay that was of no importance when compared to saving Otto's life, she wished she hadn't been forced to sell it.

Telling herself she wouldn't think about that anymore, just as she wouldn't think about Louisa's mistaken opinion of Matt's feelings, Greta resolved to focus on the success of today's Christmas teas. Today was a good day, and if Matt won the election, tomorrow would be even better.

⊷ ⋅⋅◆⋅⋅ ⊶

Matt waited until the last of the children left before he climbed the two steps and entered the schoolhouse. Whether or not Craig agreed with his suggestion, he did not want any of the pupils to overhear their conversation.

Alerted by the sound of footsteps, Craig turned from the blackboard he'd been washing. "If you came to convince me to vote for you, you're wasting your time. You know you have my vote."

"I would hope so," Matt said as he walked to the front of the room and perched on the edge of Craig's desk, "since you were the first to urge me to run for sheriff, but that's not why I'm here. I've been thinking about Christmas."

The idea had lodged in his brain the day Greta and Otto had come to the ranch for lunch. Though Otto had been excited about the prospect of seeing the goats, when he and Matt had been alone in the parlor, he'd grumbled that the special Christmas activities were designed for the adults, not children his age.

"Caroling's okay," he'd conceded, "but the grownups take us everywhere. I wish there was something we could do by ourselves."

It had taken a while, but as he remembered his own childhood, Matt realized there was something the children could do. While it would require assistance from the adults, it would give the children a chance to demonstrate their talents. Now Matt needed to convince Craig.

Craig let out a chuckle and sank into his chair, clearly anticipating more than a casual conversation. "I'm not surprised you have Christmas on your mind. So does everyone else in Sweetwater Crossing. The women are excited about the holiday teas, and my pupils can't wait to go caroling."

"Is the attraction the caroling or the cocoa and cookies?"

Holding his hands up in mock surrender, Craig said, "You've got me there. It's the food."

"That's what I thought, and that's why I wanted to talk to you. The teas and the caroling are good ideas, but they're mostly for the adults. I think we need something that's centered on the children."

Craig's nod encouraged Matt. "I don't disagree with you," he said. "The question is what that something should be. Since you're here, I assume you have a suggestion."

"I do. You and I attended different churches in Galveston, so you may not be aware of it, but my church had a Christmas pageant for a couple years. The children enacted the nativity—shepherds, wise men, angels, and of course the Holy Family. Toby and I were the best shepherds anyone ever saw."

As Matt had hoped, Craig laughed. "Humble too. I can see why you enjoyed it, but you said it lasted only a couple years. Why did it stop?"

That was the troubling part. "No one would say, but in retrospect, I think it involved more work than the ladies wanted to do."

A slow, thoughtful nod was Craig's first response. Then he said, "It would be a big undertaking. We'd need costumes and sets, not to mention having to write a script and then teach the children their parts."

Matt took heart that Craig hadn't dismissed the idea completely. "The first year is the hardest, but once you have the costumes, sets, and script, the following years should be easy."

"Easy?" Craig laughed. "You obviously have no experience teaching youngsters to memorize anything."

Matt tried not to let his disappointment show. It seemed that his optimism had been misplaced. "I was afraid you wouldn't like the idea."

"Who said I didn't like it?" Craig grabbed a piece of paper and a pen. "I think it's a great idea. Let's figure out how we're going to do it."

❯❯ ·◆· ❮❮

"You're going to win." Toby clapped his hand on Matt's shoulder when he joined him in front of the mayor's office.

Even though they were in the middle of a lull with no one in line to vote, Matt kept a smile fixed on his face. "I wish I were as sure as you." The only thing he was sure of today was that Sweetwater Crossing would have a children's Christmas pageant this year.

When he'd made a brief stop at the schoolhouse this morning, Craig had confirmed that plans were going forward. "Emily's enthusiastic, and when my wife is enthusiastic, there's no stopping her."

That was good news. Now if only the day would end with equally good news.

"Folks aren't talking too much," Matt told his brother, "but I know that a lot of people like the Winslows."

Toby shook his head. "*Liked*. Past tense. When I was at the livery, I heard several men say that anyone who'd break a Commandment like that can't be trusted."

As hurtful as the lies had been for his family, Matt hated the idea that they were affecting the election in a different way. "It wasn't Byron who bore false witness. It was Jake. Byron had nothing to do with it. I don't believe he should be punished for his brother's mistake." Matt wouldn't call it a sin. That was passing judgment, and the Bible cautioned against that.

"You're right. We'll know how the rest of the town feels in a few hours." Toby looked around. Other than two women who'd just emerged from the mercantile, their arms filled with packages, this block of Main Street was deserted. "I'm surprised Byron isn't here."

It had been Greta's suggestion that Matt spend most of the day in front of the mayor's office, greeting men as they came to vote, and both he and Toby had thought it a good suggestion.

"I'm surprised too," Matt admitted. "Jake has seen me." With the post office directly across the street from the mayor's office, it would have been difficult for him not to realize what Matt and Toby were doing. "I thought Jake would have asked someone to tell Byron to come here, unless they're not speaking." Byron's anger when he'd learned what Jake had done had been unmistakable. "I hate to see brothers estranged."

Toby gave Matt's shoulder a playful punch, reminding him of the games they'd played as boys. "That won't happen to us. We've been helping each other, and it's working. Once you make your courtship of Greta official, I expect Pa to agree that I can marry Rose." Toby's expression softened. "If everything goes the way I hope it will, I want to propose to her on Christmas Eve like Pa did. Ma said the memory of their engagement night makes every Christmas even more special."

Matt nodded. At least once a year, their mother told the story of how Pa had surprised her with a ring as they walked home after Christmas Eve services. "It was the perfect ending to a perfect day," she would say, her eyes filling with happy tears as she recalled that night so many years ago.

"I hope Rose is as happy as Ma."

"She will be," Matt assured his brother. "Anyone with eyes can see that she cares for you. Your courtship may be unofficial, but it's going well."

"It'll go even better once you make your intentions known. I don't understand why you've waited so long. It's plain as anything that you fancy Greta."

"I do, but I've been waiting for the right time." Matt had no intention of telling Toby that if he won the election, tonight would be the right time. With his future assured for at least the next three years, he would have a life he could offer to a wife. Not just any wife. Greta.

He hoped that once he made his feelings known, she would agree to make Sweetwater Crossing her home. Otto seemed comfortable here, and the way Greta talked about her days at the tearoom told Matt she was happy there. In his mind, the only question was whether she had the same feelings for him that he did for her.

He pulled out his pocket watch and glanced at it. "Six more hours." His future would be decided in six hours.

"Counting the hours?"

Matt turned at the sound of Craig's voice. Judging from the noise coming from the school playground, his friend had dismissed the pupils for lunch.

Before he could respond, Craig continued. "I should have mentioned this earlier, but Emily wanted me to tell you that we're hoping you'll join us for supper tonight. I heard rumors about a celebratory chocolate cake."

"You're that confident?" Matt wished he were.

His friend nodded vigorously. "It's called positive thinking. You're the better candidate, and I have faith that Sweetwater Crossing's voters will agree."

"I hope you're right."

⇒⇒ ·•· ⇐⇐

"It looks like the whole town is here," Greta said as she and Emily turned onto Main Street. Emily had come to the tearoom a few minutes before it closed and had helped Greta and the staff wash dishes so that they'd be able to reach the mayor's office when the outcome of the election was announced. The polls had been open from nine until five, and unless something unusual happened to delay them, the results were scheduled to be revealed at 5:30.

"I'm not surprised by the turnout," Emily said. "It's the first time we've had a real election. I imagine everyone's as curious about the winner as we are."

"There are even some children." Greta suspected that their parents hadn't been able to leave them home alone, but she felt a moment of regret that she'd refused Otto and Beulah's plea to come. "Maybe we should have brought Otto and Beulah with us. I've been surprised at how interested they are in the election."

"You shouldn't have been surprised." Emily's chiding was gentle. "Otto thinks the sun rises and sets in Matt, and he and Beulah talk about everything. I imagine the election is one of their main subjects."

"True, but Beulah seems particularly interested in the outcome." Greta shook her head. "Interest isn't the right word. I'd say she's worried about it, and that puzzles me."

"We'll know the results soon."

Greta studied the crowd, looking for Matt. There he was, at the other side of the gathering, standing with Craig, Toby, and his parents. "I'm thankful Pastor Lindstrom is counting votes along with the mayor." As much as she didn't want to believe the mayor would do anything dishonest, having a second person validating the results reassured her.

"So am I," Emily admitted. "Mayor Alcott hasn't given us any reason to doubt his integrity in the past, but he made his opinion that Byron would be the better sheriff known, and he wasn't completely fair during the debate. That's why Harold volunteered."

"And that offer was difficult to refuse."

"Exactly."

As they made their way through the crowd, Greta tried to quell her worries. Matt had done everything he could to persuade voters. He'd made compelling arguments during the debate, and he'd shown his true character when he'd urged Byron to remain in the race. In a few minutes, they would know whether that had been enough to convince Sweetwater Crossing's men to elect him.

When Greta and Emily reached Matt, though Matt's eyes lit with pleasure, Craig was the first to speak. "Greta, you look more nervous than our candidate."

She nodded, knowing there was no point in denying her concern. "I want him to win, because I know he'll be a good sheriff."

Matt moved to her side as he said, "Thanks for your vote of confidence."

"I wish it could be a real vote."

Emily, who'd linked her arm with her husband's, nodded. "Someday maybe the men will realize that we're just as smart and capable of making good decisions as they are."

As Craig smiled and said, "I already knew that," Greta's heart was warmed by the love that shone from his eyes. Emily was a fortunate woman.

At precisely half past five when the door to the mayor's office opened, the crowd's conversations ceased. Mayor Alcott stepped outside, followed closely by the minister.

"I'm pleased to see y'all here." The mayor's voice boomed across the street. "As Pastor Lindstrom can attest, we had the largest number of votes ever cast in an election."

Greta wasn't surprised. Why would people who lived outside the town limits have made the effort to come into town to vote in previous elections when the results were known in advance?

"Five hundred and thirty-seven of y'all chose to make your opinion known. That tells me ..." The mayor continued speaking, first extolling the previous sheriff's accomplishments, then pontificating on various subjects only remotely connected to the election, demonstrating why some called him a windbag.

Greta had no idea how long he would have digressed had not a man in the back of the crowd shouted, "Who won?"

"That was going to be my next announcement once I finished telling y'all my plans for the town, but never let it be said that I didn't listen to my constituents' wishes." Mayor Alcott paused, then pulled a sheet of paper from his pocket. "I counted every vote twice. Pastor Lindstrom did as well, because we wanted to ensure there were no mistakes."

Greta tried not to frown at the realization that the election must have been close if they'd needed a second counting.

"So, who won?" Another man demanded when the mayor did nothing more than gaze at the crowd.

"The result was decisive," he said, speaking as slowly as if he were addressing someone who had difficulty understanding simple words. "There is no question who the good men of Sweetwater Crossing believe should be their next sheriff." He turned to the man at his side. "Isn't that right, Pastor?"

"You're correct."

A third voice shouted, "Who won? We're tired of waiting."

His lips flattening as if he was annoyed by the interruptions, the mayor drew himself up to his full height and looked at the crowd, perhaps searching for the source of the demands for an answer.

"As I said, it was a decisive victory. Of the 537 votes, 502 were cast for one candidate."

A collective gasp greeted his words and left Greta wondering why, if the vote was so decisive, they had counted the ballots multiple times.

Mayor Alcott paused, waiting for the crowd to be quiet. "Byron and Matt, please come forward. The town owes both of you a round of applause for volunteering to become our next sheriff and for the spirited campaign you ran."

The clapping began even before the two candidates reached the mayor's side. When it subsided, the man who was obviously enjoying delaying the revelation of the new sheriff's name inclined his head slightly. "It is my opinion that either one of these gentlemen would serve the town well, but we have only one sheriff."

He glanced at Pastor Lindstrom, then looked out at the townspeople whose patience seemed to be waning. "Our citizens have spoken. Matt Nelson is the new sheriff of Sweetwater Crossing."

Yes, yes, yes! Greta felt as if her heart would burst with gratitude. Matt had won. Against difficult odds, he'd convinced the town that he would be a good and honorable lawman. What a glorious day this had become.

Chapter Nineteen

"I'm proud of you, son."

After Pa had clapped Matt on the shoulder, Ma drew him close for a big hug. Other congratulations followed his parents'. Men shook his hand; women smiled. Through it all though Matt was happy, his pleasure was incomplete because Greta wasn't here to share it with him. Before the mayor had emerged from his office to make the announcement, she'd told him that Otto and Beulah were waiting anxiously for the news and that as soon as she knew who'd won, she would return to Finley House to tell them. Now she was gone.

It felt like hours but was only a few minutes before the crowd dispersed, some going to Ma's Kitchen for supper, others like his parents and Toby heading home.

"Are you ready?" The three Vaughn sisters had left along with Burke and Josh, but Craig had remained at Matt's side until the last of the townspeople had offered their congratulations.

"More than ready."

When Matt set a brisk pace, Craig chuckled. "In a hurry?"

"You bet. And it's not for the chocolate cake."

Craig's chuckle turned into a full-fledged laugh. "I'll be a gentleman and won't ask what—or should I say who?—is the reason for this unseemly haste."

Even though supper should have been served by now, the sound of voices told Matt that the family had gathered in the parlor to wait for him and Craig. He doffed his hat and coat, leaving both on the coat tree, then entered the parlor with Craig close behind him.

"You won!" Otto jumped up from the chair where he'd been sitting and began to clap. "I'm glad!"

"So am I, Otto." Matt's gaze remained on the boy, even though it was Greta he wanted to watch. "I'm looking forward to serving as sheriff."

Beulah, who'd been sitting next to Otto, lifted her hand, as if seeking permission to speak. When Matt nodded, she asked, "Are you glad you won the bargain?"

"What bargain?" Otto demanded, swiveling his head to glare at Beulah. "You didn't tell me about any bargains."

The girl looked abashed. "I'm sorry, Otto. I shoulda told you." She kept her head turned toward her friend. "Mr. Toby said he'd help him win the election if Mr. Matt would court a girl. They shook hands."

Matt tried not to grimace at the memory of the day Toby had proposed the bargain. Even though he'd long since dismissed it, Beulah had overheard them and remembered what they'd said. At the time, it had seemed like a harmless agreement. Now ...

His heart filled with dread, Matt looked at Greta. Her face was unnaturally pale, her hands clenched.

"I see." Two words. Two simple words, but the way Greta pressed her lips together told Matt she was struggling to say nothing more.

"Did I do something wrong, Miss Greta?" Beulah's face crumpled, as if she were on the verge of tears.

"No, Beulah, you didn't. You were right to tell the truth."

Greta wasn't certain how she'd gotten through supper. She must have eaten, because when she looked down, her plate was empty, but she had no memory of tasting the roast beef and green beans. And though she'd accepted a slice of cake rather than offend Emily, she might as well have been eating dry toast for all the pleasure it gave her.

How could she have been so gullible? The question echoed through her brain while everyone else congratulated Matt, then turned to more ordinary topics of conversation. Hadn't she learned her lesson with Nigel? Apparently not, because she'd believed Matt truly cared for her.

Even though he'd never mentioned courtship or gone beyond the limits of simple friendship, she'd begun to believe that his feelings were as deep as hers. Even though Miss Scott had claimed that Matt saw courtship as a way to improve his chances of being elected sheriff, she hadn't believed he could be so calculating. And not once had Greta considered that Toby was involved, that the time Matt spent with her was because of an agreement with his brother, a bargain.

It seemed that Nigel was correct. She wasn't pretty enough, smart enough, or talented enough that a man would want to marry her. And she was a terrible, terrible judge of character.

At last the seemingly endless meal ended, and Louisa and Joanna and their husbands returned to their homes. If only Matt would leave, Greta could flee to her room and try to forget the way the day she'd found so glorious only a few hours ago had become a nightmare.

Leave, Matt. Leave. But when Mrs. Carmichael ushered Beulah, Noah, and Otto upstairs for their nightly story time, he turned toward Greta.

"We need to talk. I want to explain."

But Greta did not want to listen. Not tonight when she couldn't forget that Nigel had been full of explanations too.

"You don't owe me anything." The fault was hers. She'd been the one whose imagination had conjured thoughts of happily-ever-after. Foolish, foolish Greta.

"Please, Greta. It's important that you hear the whole story." Matt's voice was low but fervent, practically begging her to listen. "Let's go into the parlor."

If Greta knew one thing about Matt, it was that he was persistent. He wouldn't leave until he'd had his say, and so she inclined her head. "All right."

When they reached the parlor, Greta took a seat on one of the chairs rather than sitting on the settee. No matter what he had to say, she didn't want to be so close to Matt that she could smell his hair cream, so close that she could hear his breathing, so close that their hands might brush. She wouldn't put herself in that position again, because it would only lead to more heartbreak.

When Matt had settled onto the chair opposite her, she spoke. "If you're going to try to deny what Beulah said, I won't believe you. Your expression made it clear that she hadn't misunderstood you." Matt had appeared almost sheepish, as if he regretted either the bargain or the fact that he'd been overheard. Probably the latter.

"She wasn't mistaken, but that was only the beginning of the story."

"So you admit that you and Toby made a bargain." Oh, how it hurt to know that others in Sweetwater Crossing had realized that those nightly walks she'd enjoyed so much were designed to garner sympathy for Matt's candidacy. Gullible Greta. Even though Matt hadn't proposed an official courtship, she'd thought they were approaching that, just as she'd believed that Nigel's promises of a future together meant marriage.

"What Beulah heard took place the day you arrived, only minutes before you stopped in front of the doctor's office." Matt's eyes darkened, perhaps remembering how distraught she'd been.

"It started when I told Toby how much I wanted to become sheriff. He said he'd help me if I'd help him."

That was the part Greta didn't understand, what Toby had to gain from their agreement. "How could courting me or anyone help your brother?"

"I told you how Toby was always falling in and out of love when we lived in Galveston. My parents despaired of him settling down and hoped things would be different here." Matt crossed, then uncrossed his legs, a sign that he was less than comfortable with the story he was recounting. "At first things were different. Toby seemed to have lost interest in finding a wife, but then the Hannons came to town and he was once again smitten."

Though the way Matt had described Toby's romances in Galveston sounded like infatuation, that was not the way Greta would describe his feelings for Rose. "From what I've seen, I'd say that he and Rose love each other, that it's more than infatuation." She might have been mistaken about Matt's intentions toward her, but Toby and Rose looked like Emily and Craig, Louisa and Josh, and Joanna and Burke—happy and truly in love.

"I agree. Toby's different with Rose. The problem is, my father didn't believe that, so he told Toby the only way he'd approve his marriage was if I married first. Toby's like me—he knows how much we owe our parents—and so he wanted me to at least begin to court a woman so that he could marry Rose before her family returns to San Antonio."

This sounded like something from one of the dime novels Greta had read, almost too farfetched to be true. "I don't understand. Why would your father say that?"

"I suspect there were two reasons. First, he wanted be sure Toby was really in love, and he thought that time would either prove or disprove that. Secondly, he wanted me to find a wife. He and Ma were concerned that I hadn't expressed an interest in any of the ladies I met in Houston. I told them none had caught my fancy."

"But you agreed to court someone here. That's dishonest if your only reason was to help Toby." And that was one of the things

185

that bothered Greta the most about Beulah's revelation. She had believed Matt to be an honorable man.

"That's exactly what I told Toby. I said I wouldn't deceive anyone, but I would consider courtship if I met someone I felt attracted to."

That sounded more like the Matt Greta thought she knew, but how could she tell if he was being honest or simply saying what he thought she wanted to hear? After all, she'd deluded herself before.

"Toby and I were still having this conversation when you arrived." Matt continued the story. "I always scoffed when my brother talked about love at first sight, but for the first time in my life, I understood how he felt."

More pretty words designed to convince her. If she hadn't had a similar experience with Nigel, Greta might have believed them. "I don't believe in love at first sight," she said firmly. "Attraction at first sight is possible"—she'd certainly been attracted to Nigel's good looks—"but love is like a seed. It takes time to germinate and grow, and it has to be based on more than physical appearance."

"I agree. What I felt scared me. I was afraid I was more like Toby than I realized and that the attraction would soon fade." Matt leaned forward, his expression seemingly sincere. "It didn't fade. The more time I spent with you, the more I was attracted to you."

As she had been to him, but that was something Greta wouldn't say. Not tonight, probably not ever.

"But you never said anything. You never hinted that you wanted us to have a future together." The future that had started to appear so appealing to her had been nothing more than a mirage.

Matt nodded. "You're right. I didn't tell you about my dreams, because until tonight I had no future to offer you. I knew I wouldn't be happy spending the rest of my life on the ranch, and I wouldn't ask you to share that life. Otto might enjoy the goats and the cattle, but you and I wouldn't have been happy there. That was no way to start a marriage."

Under other circumstances, Greta would have been thrilled that Matt was discussing marriage, but what she'd learned tonight made her question what he said. "So being elected sheriff changed everything." Though she hadn't intended it, her words rang with skepticism.

"It did. It meant I had a job I would like for at least three years and that I have a home to offer you and Otto. The apartment over the sheriff's office is large enough for the three of us. The morning I saw it, even though I'd met you only a couple days earlier, I could picture us living there. I was hoping I could convince you and Otto to stay in Sweetwater Crossing and make your home with me."

He sounded sincere, but Greta could not forget that Matt always sounded sincere, even when she now knew he was hiding important things.

"I'd like to believe you," she said slowly, "but what happened with Nigel has shown me that pretty words are often empty words."

Matt was silent for a moment, the furrows between his eyes testifying to his displeasure with the way the conversation had gone.

"How can I convince you?"

"I don't know. All I know is that you weren't completely honest with me. When you asked me to help you chaperone Toby and Rose, you didn't tell me the whole story. That makes me wonder what else you haven't told me."

He shook his head, as if to say there were no other omissions.

"I'm not sure I can trust you, Matt." And trust had to be the foundation for any lasting relationship. "Even if I could trust you, I can't trust my own judgment. I thought I'd learned lessons from Nigel, but apparently I didn't. I feel like a fool to have let myself be tricked twice. I thought you were honest and sincere, but I believed that about Nigel too until I saw the truth behind the façade he showed me." Though she hadn't intended to tell Matt how she felt, the words gushed out seemingly of their own volition.

"There was no trickery involved. What you saw was the real me, the man who cares about you and who still hopes we can have a future together. Won't you give me a chance to prove that? Tell me what you need."

She needed so many things, but first and foremost, she needed to rebuild her trust in herself. "I need time by myself."

Matt's lips thinned, signaling his unhappiness with her response. "How much time?"

"I don't know." Though it was the coward's way, right now the only thing Greta wanted was to climb into bed, pull the blankets over her head, and try to forget that today had happened.

"I think it's best if you leave and don't come back."

Matt started at her for a long moment before nodding. When he rose and walked toward the door, Greta knew that whoever had said hearts can't break was wrong. Hers had.

Chapter Twenty

He ought to be happy. He'd been elected sheriff by what could only be called a landslide. He'd accepted the keys to his office and new home, and in a few minutes he would unload the few things he'd brought from the ranch and move them into the apartment. This was what he'd wanted for months, the dream he'd harbored well before Greta Engel had arrived in Sweetwater Crossing. He ought to be, if not happy, at least satisfied by what he'd accomplished. Instead all he could think about was what he'd lost.

Perhaps that was why he found himself striding north on Center. When he reached Creek Road, though he wanted nothing more than to turn right, march up the front steps of Finley House, and demand that Greta give him another chance, he forced his feet in the opposite direction. It was still too early for Greta to have gone to the tearoom, too early for anyone to be stirring, but when he glanced to the right, he spotted a small figure moving through the cemetery, stopping to crouch next to one of the monuments.

Why was a child out so early and why was she—for there was no mistaking the skirts she wore—in the graveyard? Not wanting to frighten the girl, Matt walked as quietly as he could. It was only when he was a few feet away that he realized what she was doing. The child placed a flower that Matt was certain had been growing in Mrs. Sanders's yard only an hour ago next to the gravestone, then pressed a kiss on the marker.

The grass had yet to cover the grave, and the engraving confirmed that the death had been recent.

Melinda Palmer
Beloved Wife and Mother
January 2, 1861 – October 15, 1884

"You loved your mother, didn't you?" he asked softly.

The girl turned, tears streaming down her cheeks as she nodded. "Mama loved flowers."

She couldn't be more than seven years old, with hair so poorly braided that Matt suspected she'd snuck out of the house without her father's knowledge. Though his heart ached for the child's loss, Matt couldn't ignore what she'd done. "What's your name?"

"Sally."

"That isn't your flower, is it, Sally?"

"No, sir." She blanched when she spotted the star he'd pinned to his coat. "Are you gonna arrest me?"

"That depends on what Mrs. Sanders says. It's her flowers you've been stealing." He reached for Sally's hand and drew her to her feet. "We're going to pay Mrs. Sanders a visit."

The child's hand trembled, telling Matt she was afraid of what was in store for her. Though he was grateful that he'd been able to resolve the minor mystery of the missing flowers, he didn't know Mrs. Sanders well enough to predict her reaction and could only hope that whatever punishment she demanded would not be severe.

"Matt, or I should say Sheriff Nelson, what are you doing here so early?" the town's most accomplished gardener asked when she opened her door.

Matt looked down at the girl whose hand he still held. "Sally has something to say to you."

"I'm sorry, ma'am." The tears that had stopped as they walked from the cemetery began to flow again. "My mama always said your flowers was the prettiest in town. I know what I done was wrong, but I didn't think you'd miss one or two."

Mrs. Sanders's expression was stern, and for a moment Matt thought she was going to strike the child, but then she said, "You're right, Sally. What you did was wrong. Stealing is a crime, and crimes need to be punished."

The way the widow bit her lip made Matt wonder what emotions she was trying to suppress. Was she remembering how harsh Sheriff Granger had been to her son? Slowly, she nodded at Sally. "You've taken something that was valuable to me. That means you need to give me something valuable in return."

The girl made no effort to hide her fear. "What is that?"

"Your time. I expect you to spend every Saturday afternoon working in my garden with me. Maybe once you see how much effort is involved in growing flowers, you'll be less inclined to steal them."

"Yes, ma'am." Sally's relief that her punishment did not involve the jail was obvious.

While Sally kept her eyes on the ground, Mrs. Sanders winked at Matt. "And, Sally," she continued, "if you do well, I'll give you one of my wild rose bushes. It should grow nicely next to your mother's grave."

Sally looked up, her eyes filled with hope for the first time since Matt had found her in the cemetery. "Thank you, ma'am. I promise I'll work extra hard and I won't steal again."

"See to it that you keep your promise. And, Matt, thank you for keeping your promise. You told me you would discover who was taking my flowers, and you did. Good job, Sheriff."

Matt only wished he could solve all his problems this easily.

⇥ ⋯•⋯ ⇤

"Aren't you and Matt going walking tonight?" Emily asked at the end of supper Wednesday night. Mrs. Carmichael had taken Otto, Beulah, and Noah for story time in the parlor, and Prudence was happily waving in the direction they'd gone, ignoring her parents and Greta.

Waving, Greta had noticed, was Prudence's favorite thing to do these days. Most of the time, it was a cute gesture, but when the waving included a spoonful of mashed peas, the results were less amusing. Even normally placid Beulah had complained when the peas landed in her hair.

Thinking about the baby's antics was more pleasant than answering Emily's question. Unfortunately, Greta couldn't avoid it. "No, not tonight." Not ever again. "I told Craig I'd work on the script for the pageant. We need to start rehearsals this weekend." All that was true, even though it wasn't the reason Greta was staying indoors.

"I see." The furrows between Emily's eyebrows told Greta she wasn't happy with the answer. "In that case, I could use your help with the dishes. Craig mentioned he wanted to give Mrs. Carmichael a break and that he'd read the story tonight."

Though Emily's words formed complete English sentences, they made no sense. Not only did Craig appear surprised by the notion that he was tonight's storyteller, but Mrs. Carmichael hadn't seemed in need of a rest. Furthermore, if Emily had believed Greta's excuse, she would not have asked her to help, since that would limit the time she had to plan the pageant. This was reminiscent of the day Matt's mother used mashing potatoes as an excuse for a private conversation.

"Certainly." Greta rose and began to stack the dishes.

Once they were in the kitchen, Emily turned to Greta. "Craig tells me I need to be more tactful, but I believe in plain speaking." She reached for the bar of soap, then laid it back down rather than shaving pieces into the dishwater. "I can see that you're trying to hide it, but you look miserable. What happened between you and Matt? Surely you're not upset about the so-called bargain."

"It wasn't a so-called bargain. It was a real one." The words came out more forcefully than Greta had intended, betraying how deeply the knowledge that the reason Matt had spent so much time with her was that he'd been trying to help his brother, not that he'd been attracted to her had hurt her. Though he'd claimed that that had changed almost immediately and that he did indeed care for her, she was afraid to believe him. Memories of Nigel and how he'd deluded her were too fresh. Greta couldn't—she wouldn't—let herself be hurt that way a second time.

"Yes, I'm upset, not so much about the bargain itself but mostly that Matt didn't tell me about it." It had been humiliating to learn the truth from Beulah.

Emily gestured toward the table, waiting until Greta settled in one of the chairs before she took a seat, apparently willing to delay the dishwashing until she'd said whatever it was she wanted Greta to hear.

"Have you considered that Matt might not have wanted to look foolish in front of you? The agreement he and Toby made was one I would have expected from boys half their ages."

Emily was trying to appease her, but it wasn't working. "I'm the one who looks foolish. I trusted him." She swallowed, wishing this conversation were over. "More than trusting him, I trusted myself not to make the same mistake I did with Nigel, imagining myself in love with a man who doesn't love me."

Greta understood wanting to do everything possible to help a brother. Hadn't she done that for Otto? But her efforts to keep her brother alive and to make his dream come true hadn't hurt anyone else.

Reaching forward, Emily laid her hand on Greta's. "You didn't make a mistake. Matt loves you. Craig's known him almost his whole life, and he says he's never seen him like this." When Greta did not respond, Emily continued. "I've seen the same thing. His expression changes when he looks at you. It becomes softer, more tender."

But that wasn't proof of anything. "Nigel was good at fooling people too. The smiles he gave me would have melted any girl's heart, but they were as false as the sweet letters he wrote."

"Matt isn't Nigel," Emily insisted.

"How do you know? You've never met Nigel."

"That's true, but I met someone who sounds a lot like him." Her lips curved downward into a frown. "I did more than meet him. I married him."

For a second shock left Greta speechless. "You're not talking about Craig." He was *nothing* like Nigel.

"Craig is my second husband. I was married to George for longer than I want to remember. Marrying him was the biggest mistake of my life."

Greta leaned back in the chair, trying to reconcile the happily married woman who'd welcomed her into her home with the woman who claimed to have married someone like Nigel.

"How did that happen?"

Emily sighed. "When George came to Sweetwater Crossing, it seemed he only had eyes for me. He told me I was the most beautiful woman he'd ever met, the one he'd been searching for for years."

That sounded like something Nigel would have said.

"I was so flattered by his words that I didn't question anything George said. It was only after we were married that I learned what he'd been searching for was a woman with blonde hair and blue eyes who'd give him blond, blue-eyed children."

Greta stared at her friend, horrified by the revelation. She knew men married because they wanted children to carry on the family name, but she'd never heard of a man choosing a bride simply because of the color of her hair and eyes. "I have trouble believing that. What kind of man would marry for a reason like that?" Surely even Nigel wasn't that shallow.

"A man like George."

"But you don't have any children from that marriage."

"No I don't. George was convinced it was my fault." Emily bit her lower lip as if trying to hold back tears. "Let's simply say that he made his displeasure evident."

The way Emily clutched her arm told Greta that her husband had been violent. Poor, poor Emily. No one deserved to be treated that way.

"It's probably awful of me," Emily continued, "but when George was killed, my first thought was that I was finally free."

Greta had had similar thoughts the day she and Otto left Houston and again when she'd burned Nigel's letter. Though she'd feared what Nigel might do to Otto, Greta's situation had been less serious than Emily's. "Your marriage sounds horrible."

Emily nodded. "It was, but I didn't tell you my story so you'd feel sorry for me. I wanted you to know that I understand what you're feeling. After what happened with George, I was afraid of men. I was also afraid of my own judgment, wondering how I could have made such a mistake. I was afraid I would do it again."

"But you didn't. Anyone can see that you and Craig are deeply in love." All three Vaughn sisters had found wonderful men to marry.

"We are in love." Emily's frown turned into a smile as she thought of her husband. "Now that Craig's part of my life, I can't imagine how I lived without him. We're two pieces of a puzzle, incomplete unless we're together."

It was a lovely image, the kind of relationship Greta had always dreamt of. "How did you know you could trust Craig?"

"I watched him. I saw how he treated other people, and gradually I realized that he would never hurt me. More than that, I saw that the love he offered me was true and lasting." Emily was silent for a moment, perhaps wanting Greta to think about all she'd said. "I don't claim to be an expert, but I believe that what Matt feels for you is the same kind of love that Craig has for me. Trust him, Greta. Trust yourself."

"I wish I could."

∗ ∗ ∗

"Are you planning to hide out here?" Toby demanded as he flung open the door to the apartment that Matt now called home.

"I live here," he said as mildly as he could. He'd moved in yesterday an hour after he'd taken Sally Palmer home and suggested that her father might want to accompany her on future visits to the cemetery. Arranging his belongings had taken little time, and though Matt had spent a restless night, today his new quarters felt more like home.

The apartment was pleasant enough. While it could not compare to Finley House, when he'd first seen it, he'd thought it would be large enough for him, Greta, and Otto. They could live here until they wanted or needed more space. But now it seemed likely that he would be the only occupant.

When Toby did not respond, Matt said, "You know that the town expects the sheriff to live here, not out on a ranch."

This time his brother wrinkled his nose. "That may be true, but it seems to me you're avoiding chances to see Greta."

There was more than a little truth in Toby's accusation. Although Matt made what he intended to become daily rounds, walking along each of the streets, talking to residents, ensuring that everyone knew their sheriff was on duty, he avoided going near the tearoom when he knew Greta might be outside. There was no point in deepening the wound she'd inflicted.

"Greta made it clear that she didn't want anything to do with me."

"And you blame me for having suggested the bargain."

This time Matt shook his head. "I blame myself for not telling her the whole story. She deserved the truth, but because I didn't do what I should have, I lost her and you may have lost your chance to marry Rose. I'm sorry, Toby. I know you love Rose."

"And you love Greta."

There was no reason to deny it. "I do. It's bad enough that I ruined my chances with Greta, but I hate the idea that I'm responsible for your unhappiness. I plan to do whatever I can to change that."

The spark of hope that lit Toby's eyes was quickly extinguished. "Have you ever known Pa to change his mind once he's given us an edict?"

"No, but there's always a first time. Let's talk to him."

Half an hour later they were seated in the parlor with both Ma and Pa. Though Matt had planned to begin the conversation, his brother gave him no opportunity to speak.

"I did something selfish and it's hurt Matt."

"Toby's wrong," Matt told their parents. "I was the one who made a stupid mistake, and now it's hurt him."

Ma remained silent, but Pa's expression appeared almost amused. How could he find anything amusing when the situation was so serious?

"Suppose one of you tells me exactly what happened." Pa looked at Ma, who nodded her approval of his approach.

"I wanted to marry Rose." Once again, Toby spoke first.

"And I wanted to become sheriff."

"But I knew you wouldn't agree unless Matt was married or at least courting."

This was turning into one of the duets Matt had heard where two people alternated singing lines from the song.

"So we struck a bargain," he said. "Toby would help me campaign."

"But only if Matt pretended to woo a woman."

Though Ma's hiss left no doubt of her opinion of the bargain, she said nothing.

"I thought it would be pretense, but it wasn't." Matt had to ensure that his parents knew how deeply his emotions were involved. While he wasn't proud of what he'd done, there was no question that the bargain had benefited him greatly. "I love Greta and want to marry her."

"But she learned about our bargain." Toby's frown was almost a scowl.

"And was justifiably angry, possibly even hurt." Ma spoke for the first time, her words sounding like nails in a coffin. "No woman would be happy about something like that. It makes her feel as if she's an object, not a living, breathing person."

Ma's chastisement hurt Matt almost as much as Greta's rejection. "She doesn't want anything to do with me."

"And now Rose isn't sure I'm the right man for her."

Matt blinked in surprise. This was the first he'd heard that. He'd believed that the obstacle to Toby's happiness was his own failed courtship.

Pa looked at Ma for a second, their expressions inscrutable to him, although Matt was certain they could read each other's thoughts.

"I had hoped that your shenanigans would have ended when you grew up, but I was wrong." Pa's voice was calm yet firm. "You two have gotten yourselves into a pickle."

When both Matt and Toby nodded, acknowledging the mess they'd created, Pa continued. "If you can convince your lady to trust you, Toby, I'll give you my blessing."

"Even without Matt marrying first?" The hope in Toby's voice said this was more than he'd expected.

Pa nodded. "I should never have imposed that restriction. It was obviously a mistake, but I thought I was protecting you. You fancied yourself in love so many times that I wanted to keep you from rushing into marriage and then discovering that you'd mistaken attraction for love."

That was the explanation Pa had given Matt the evening they'd discussed what Pa had believed was Toby's infatuation with Rose.

"Your bargain may not have turned out the way you expected," Pa continued, "but it showed me that your feelings for Rose are deep. If you were willing to go to those lengths to win her, your love is true." He exchanged another quick glance with Ma. "Your mother and I will dance at your wedding."

A smile wreathing his face, Toby nodded. "Thank you, Pa, but what about Matt?"

Pa turned toward him. "You'll have a harder time winning Greta's trust again than your brother will with Rose. I don't know what happened to her in Houston, but I can tell that she doesn't give her trust easily. Still, nothing worthwhile is easy. My advice is to do everything you can to win her. She's the one for you."

Matt nodded. "I know."

Chapter Twenty-One

Greta was smiling when she walked out the front door of Finley House Friday morning, but the smile faded when she saw Matt standing at the end of the driveway.

"May I escort you to Porter's?" he asked, bending his arm so that she could place her hand on it.

She stood silently for a moment as emotions warred within her. She wasn't ready to be near him again, but the manners Mama had instilled in her told her it would be rude to refuse him. Just as importantly, Greta knew it was time to start trusting herself, and her instincts said she and Matt had unfinished business.

"Yes, of course." She laid her hand on his arm, trying not to recall the times she'd done that when they'd strolled with Toby and Rose. Those had been pleasurable occasions. Today ... she wasn't certain what this morning would bring, but she doubted it would be pleasant.

Matt's gaze met hers, his brown eyes filled with pain as they took their first steps down the street. "I know you said you didn't want to see me, but I can't go on any longer without apologizing to you. I never meant to hurt you."

"But you did." Perhaps she shouldn't have been so blunt, but they owed each other honesty. Complete honesty.

A brief nod was his first acknowledgement of her words. "I'm sorry. If I could do it over, I would not have agreed to Toby's bargain. It was a foolish one." He paused for a second, as if debating whether to continue. "The truth is, Greta, I can't regret it completely, because it gave me a chance to spend time with you."

He sounded sincere. He looked sincere. She wanted to believe he was sincere, but could she?

"Because of that bargain, you're now the sheriff. I'm glad about that." Whatever else she might think about him, Greta knew Matt would be an honest, honorable lawman.

"So am I, but I'd be happier if I hadn't destroyed our chance at a future together. That's what I want more than anything."

He laid his hand on top of hers and squeezed it ever so briefly. Though the touch was fleeting, the warmth it sent through her arm surprised Greta with its intensity. She shouldn't feel this way, and yet she did. Though she hadn't admitted it to him, she had once shared Matt's hope that they'd build a future together. That had been her dream, but now she was wary, just as Emily had been wary after her experiences with George.

"I'm no longer certain what I want my future to be," she said softly. As much as she enjoyed living at Finley House and being treated like a sister by Emily, Louisa, and Joanna, that was only a temporary home. She didn't need a house as large as the Vaughn sisters' childhood home, but she wanted one that would be hers, a place where Otto could grow to adulthood, a place she could share with her husband ... if she found a man who made her heart sing the way Mama's had whenever Papa was close, a man she could trust. But that seemed as ephemeral as frost on a sunny morning.

Matt nodded, as if he'd expected her response. "Can we start over? Can we forget the past and begin anew?"

"I don't think that's possible." Though Greta didn't shake her head to totally dismiss the idea, she didn't want to raise any false hopes. "I know I can't forget the past. It's what made me the person I am. What I need to do is forgive myself for the mistake I made."

When Matt started to speak, Greta held up her hand to stop him. "I'm as much to blame as you are. Maybe more. The problem is, it takes time for me to forgive, and time is one thing I don't have. Almost every minute of my day is taken by the Christmas teas, the pageant, and preparing for the caroling." If those sounded like excuses, perhaps they were. What Greta knew was that she wasn't ready to move forward.

They'd reached Porter's. As Greta approached the steps, Matt laid his hand on hers again. "When all those events are over, will you at least consider what I've said? Will you think about me? Think about us?"

The problem would be *not* thinking of him and the future she'd once dreamt of. Greta already thought about Matt more than she was willing to admit.

"Maybe after Christmas." She had a decision to make before the year ended. A week ago she had thought it would be an easy one. She would take Otto to Pikes Peak so that he could see the mountain and experience snow. They'd spend a week or two there, then return to Sweetwater Crossing so that Greta could continue to run the tearoom. Now she was no longer certain that that was the right decision.

Greta turned to meet Matt's gaze. "Until then, please leave me alone."

His eyes darkened again, but he inclined his head. "If that's what you really want."

"It is."

⇥ ⋯ ✦ ⋯ ⇤

"I want to be Joseph, and Beulah wants to be Mary."

Matt bit the inside of his cheek to keep from smiling at the way Otto fisted his hands on his hips and glared at his sister. When he and Craig had discussed the pageant, Craig had predicted there would be some disgruntled children. That was one of the reasons they were having the first rehearsals in the schoolroom instead of

201

the church. "I'd rather have the shouting here," Craig had said, and so even though the schoolhouse was not normally open on a Sunday, once the church service ended, all the children who sought roles in the pageant had rushed across the street.

Matt had followed at a normal pace, wishing Greta were as enthusiastic about his participation as Craig was. She'd pursed her lips when Craig had announced that Matt would be helping, then nodded, deferring to Craig as the head of the pageant committee.

Matt hadn't cared what tasks Craig assigned him. Even if they included sweeping up hay after the performance, it would be a small price to pay for spending more time with Greta. Perhaps it was foolish, but he hoped that being together would help wear down Greta's resistance to him. He wouldn't force proximity, though. That was why he waited quietly in the back of the schoolroom while she and Craig stood in front, surrounded by eager pupils.

Greta kept a smile fixed on her face as she looked at her brother and Beulah. "I know you do, but those roles are reserved for the oldest children." Her voice, though low, carried clearly.

Otto shook his head. "Mitch is the same age as me, and Susan's the same age as Beulah."

"That's not true." Greta's smile did not falter. "They're both a few months older."

While Beulah remained silent, Otto pouted. "That's not fair."

"We need wisemen. That's an important role, because you have to carry precious gifts."

Apparently mollified, Otto turned to Beulah. "We won't drop them, will we?"

She shook her head, then whispered so loudly that even Matt could hear her, "My mother said not to tell anyone, but the wisemen's costumes are the best."

This time Matt made no effort to hide his smile at how easily these children were pleased. From what Emily had said, the costumes Beulah's mother and grandmother were sewing would surpass the ones he remembered from his childhood. Now if only the designated Joseph would meet Craig and Greta's expectations.

Craig had explained that Mitch Sanders had been a troublemaker during Craig's first months in Sweetwater Crossing but that he seemed to have reformed. It was Craig's hope that having Mitch in such a prominent role would show the town that the boy could be trusted. His mother had already regained the town's trust through her position as the manager of the teashop, but Mitch was still regarded with suspicion.

Though he claimed that he did not anticipate any problems, Craig had chosen Susan Johnson to play the role of Mary not only because of her age but also because she could be depended on to help keep Mitch in line if needed.

Craig moved to the front of the classroom and clapped his hands to get everyone's attention. "Now that you know your roles, let's start practicing. Sheriff Nelson will help the shepherds and the wisemen in the back of the room. Everyone else, stay here with Miss Greta."

Spinning around, Otto stared for a second, then scampered toward Matt. "Mr. Matt. You're here! Where have you been?"

"I've been busy." Though there had been no serious crime since he'd become sheriff, a number of residents had come to his office to ask his opinion about everything from how to handle a neighbor whose dogs trampled a flowerbed to the possibility that someone was stealing from the church offering plates. When he took his daily walks around town, others came out to greet him and wish him well.

Matt's days were full, with each interaction confirming that he'd made the right decision in running for office. The work might not be exciting, but it was rewarding in its own way, satisfying him as life on the ranch had not. The one thing that would make his life much more satisfying would be an end to his and Greta's estrangement.

Otto wrinkled his nose. "Busy. That's what Greta said when I asked her about you. I wish you'd come, cuz I miss you."

"I miss you too." Matt turned to the group of children standing in front of him and reached for the pages Greta had given him. "Let's see what the script says."

The hour-long rehearsal went faster than Matt had expected. When it ended, Craig and Greta thanked everyone, reminding them that they would practice again next Sunday and that the actual performance was scheduled for Saturday the 20th at the church.

They'd been inside the schoolhouse for more than an hour and not once had Greta spoken to Matt. It was as if he was invisible, for if she'd looked his way, he wasn't aware of it. He bit back a sigh. Winning her was going to be even more difficult than he'd feared.

◦──·◦·──◦

Greta could not recall the last time an hour had passed so slowly. The rehearsal had gone as well as could be expected for the first time. She should have been—and she was—happy about that, but having Matt there had made it almost impossible for her to concentrate on coaching Mary, Joseph, the innkeeper, and the angels. It had taken every ounce of discipline she possessed not to keep glancing at him, but she hadn't been able to block the sound of his laughter as one of the shepherds pleaded for live sheep rather than the wooden cutouts Craig had said they'd use.

Greta was grateful for the inanimate animals, since being close to sheep might have given Otto another asthma attack. Burke had declared him completely healed from the last one, and she wanted that to continue.

Why had Craig asked her to help with the pageant when he knew she was working long hours to accommodate the extra holiday teas? Greta stifled a wry laugh. Emily must have been responsible. She was convinced that Greta and Matt belonged together, and nothing would dissuade her. If she and Otto stayed in Sweetwater Crossing, Greta had no doubt that Emily would continue her matchmaking efforts.

She turned toward her brother, who was staring out the window now that their work was done. Though Craig and Matt had offered to help her straighten the desks, Greta had insisted that she and Otto could do it, and so the men had gone outside with the other children.

"Come along, Otto. We need to go home."

"Can't Mr. Matt come with us?" Otto's persistence was one of his most endearing traits, but today it was annoying.

"You know that Finley House belongs to Mrs. Emily and Mr. Craig. We can't invite guests."

"But they wouldn't mind."

That was true. Emily had said that the night rain had kept her and Matt and Toby and Rose indoors, but Greta wouldn't tell Otto that. She put a hand on his shoulder and motioned him toward the door. "No more arguments."

Otto was still sulking when they entered Finley House through the kitchen. With barely a word of greeting for Joanna and Emily, both of whom wore beaming smiles, he stormed up the stairs to his room, leaving Greta with the two sisters.

"She's beautiful!" Joanna's brown eyes sparkled with happiness.

"You'd say that even if she was the ugliest baby you've ever seen. She's our niece, so of course she's beautiful."

The reason for the sisters' happiness was now clear. "Louisa had her baby."

Joanna nodded. "Two hours ago. My stubborn sister wouldn't send for Burke until she was almost ready to deliver. She said she didn't want to bother him before breakfast."

Greta wasn't surprised by that. As a midwife, Louisa would have known what to expect and when she would need help, but she was a bit surprised that she hadn't wanted at least one of her sisters with her during her labor. Perhaps she hadn't wanted Joanna to miss playing the piano at church or Emily to disrupt her Sunday morning routine. That would be characteristic of Louisa.

"Now that you're here," Emily said, inclining her head toward Greta, "the three of us are invited to admire the next generation of

Porters. Joanna had a sneak peek, because she stopped there after church, but we're supposed to go now."

"Are you sure I should? You're family, and I'm ..."

"Family," Joanna said quickly. "We adopted you, remember?"

Ten minutes later the three women were in Louisa's bedchamber where she wore a radiant smile as she nestled her daughter close to her.

"I want you to meet Josephine," the proud mother announced.

Emily's eyes widened in surprise. "So you and Josh finally decided on a name. I thought you preferred Theodora and he wanted Priscilla."

"That's what we wanted you to think." Louisa pressed a kiss on her baby's forehead. "After you honored our mother by naming your daughter Prudence, we decided our child would be either Joseph or Josephine. I wanted both of our parents' names to live on in this generation." When Joanna and Emily nodded, Louisa turned toward Greta. "Would you like to be the first to hold her?"

Overwhelmed by the gesture, Greta struggled to speak. "Yes, but ..."

"Don't worry." Louisa was quick to reassure her. "They'll get their turn."

Greta bent down to reach for Josephine, then held her close, her heart filled with joy. Was there anything more beautiful than a newborn child? All three Vaughn girls had been blessed with these precious gifts from God, a legacy of their love and of God's goodness.

As she stared at the tiny infant in her arms, Greta said a silent prayer that one day she would experience the joy of holding her own child.

→→ ··•··◄◄

"Sheriff Nelson."

Matt looked up as the woman entered his office. Though she was taller than many women, today her shoulders were bowed as if she carried an enormous weight, and she breathed heavily, as if she'd been running.

"I've got a crime to report."

He rose and offered her a chair. "What happened, Mrs. Oberle?" Matt had met the Oberles when he first arrived in Sweetwater Crossing. When she'd introduced Herb as the man who brewed the finest beer in the county, her husband had chuckled and said that was an easy title to win, since he was the only brewer in the county. The Mrs. Oberle who'd laughed along with him had seemed almost girlish in her mirth. Today no one would call her girlish.

"It's my silver candlesticks." She wrung her hands in obvious distress. "They were my mother's and her mother's. Someone stole them."

Though theft wasn't common in town, it did happen. Matt nodded to acknowledge Mrs. Oberle's distress. "I'll do my best to get them back for you."

"I hope you can find the thief. It won't feel like Christmas without those candlesticks on the table."

As tears filled the woman's eyes, Matt rose and walked to her side. "I know how important traditions are. Suppose you show me where you usually keep the candlesticks."

To his surprise, Mrs. Oberle remained in her chair. "Aren't you going to write a report?"

"Later. I don't want to waste time that could be better spent searching for your candlesticks."

"That makes sense." She rose, then led him to her house, saying nothing other than "I hope you can find them" as they covered the distance in half the time it would normally take.

When they reached the modest home, rather than going to the front door, Mrs. Oberle stopped and gestured toward the backyard. "I'll let Herb know I'm home. He worries about me, you know."

Matt wasn't surprised. The few times he'd met her, Mrs. Oberle had struck him as slightly scatterbrained. "Certainly." He followed her behind the house to the building whose yeasty smell left no doubt that this was where Herb brewed his beer.

"I'm back," she called as she opened the door.

The heavyset man wiped his forehead as he emerged from the brewery, his confusion apparent when he saw Matt. "Where did you go, and why is the sheriff with you?"

"I had to report what happened. We have a thief here. Someone took my candlesticks."

Herb Oberle's expression changed from confusion to chagrin. "No, they didn't." He shook his head and walked back inside, returning a few seconds later with two tall candlesticks in his hands. "You left them here. You said you were going to get a cloth to polish them. Someone told you that beer was good for polishing silver, and you wanted to try that."

Mrs. Oberle's face flushed with embarrassment. "That's right. I said that." She turned to Matt, her eyes beseeching him. "I'm sorry, Sheriff."

"There's no need to apologize. I'm glad you found them."

This problem had been easy to solve. Unfortunately, he saw no easy resolution to the one that kept him awake at night.

❧ ⸱⸱•⸱⸱ ☙

"Sleep in heavenly peace."

Greta smiled as the carolers sang *Silent Night*. Though some of them couldn't carry a tune, and the youngest children were obviously anxious for the promised cookies and cocoa, the smiles on the parents' faces as they led their children told Greta the caroling had been a success.

As the last notes faded, one child cried, "Cookies! I want cookies!" Her cry was echoed by a dozen others.

"And you shall have them." Greta gestured toward the porch that connected the tearoom to the teashop. She'd placed two tables on it, one with pots of cocoa, the other with trays of cookies. When Louisa had learned that Greta proposed serving a hot beverage, she'd suggested Greta ask each family to bring their own cups, reasoning that that would make the preparation and cleanup easier, not to mention that the tearoom's delicate china cups weren't suitable for young children.

Louisa's idea proved to be an excellent one. No one complained about having to bring their cups. To the contrary, Greta overheard two women say they were relieved that they didn't have to worry about their children breaking something. Everyone seemed to enjoy the food, and although several children spilled their cocoa, since they were outdoors, there was no reason to worry about cleaning table linens or carpets. While it was different from caroling at her parents' restaurant, the result was the same: townspeople enjoying the holiday spirit.

An hour later after the last of the carolers had left, though she'd insisted she didn't need assistance and had sent the waitresses home to spend the rest of the evening with their families, Josh joined Greta on the porch and grabbed one of the cocoa pots. When they were both inside, he laid the pot on the counter in the back room, then turned to face her. "I can't thank you enough for all that you've done here. I thought the tearoom was doing well last summer, but you've shown me how much better it can be."

The words warmed Greta as much as the parents' and children's smiles had. "I'm glad I could help. I've enjoyed every minute I've spent here."

Josh's smile faded. "I don't like the sound of that. It sounds as if you're not planning to stay."

She hesitated. Though she didn't want to spoil what had been a successful evening, Josh deserved a response. "I haven't made the final decision. I promised to take Otto to Colorado, and I need to keep that promise. You know he's dreamt of seeing Pikes Peak. I want to make that dream to come true."

That would be good for Otto. As for Greta, even though she knew she would never forget what had happened here or the hopes that had taken root in her heart, there would be fewer reminders of how those hopes had withered if she were living in Colorado Springs. That would be good for her.

Josh's expression said it wouldn't be good for him. "You could come back after Otto sees the mountains."

They could. That had been Greta's plan, but that was before everything changed. Now she knew that if she left Sweetwater Crossing, there would be no returning. "I don't think so."

She heard what sounded like a gasp, but it hadn't come from Josh.

"You may not want to hear this, Greta, but one thing I've learned is that dreams can change. I thought I knew exactly what I wanted from life until breaking my leg made me reconsider everything I once believed was important."

Greta had heard how Josh's horse had thrown him, leaving him on the road with a badly broken leg and suffering from heat stroke. If Louisa hadn't been traveling the same road that day, he wouldn't be here now.

"I believe that was God's way of getting my attention. He showed me what was truly important, and that was building a life here with Louisa." Josh paused again, then touched Greta's hand. "You've made a difference—a positive difference—in Sweetwater Crossing. You've brought the town together and you're making this a special Christmas for everyone. I hope you'll reconsider."

"I don't know, Josh. I honestly don't know what's the best path forward."

He tightened his grip on her hand. "Keep praying. You'll find your answer."

»—•◆•—«

"I hate you!" Otto raced into Greta's room, stomping his feet with each step. She'd thought he was asleep, but she'd been wrong. "You said you love me, but if you do, you wouldn't make us leave."

Had he overheard her conversation with Josh? As she recalled the gasp she'd heard, she wondered if Otto had been outside the back of the tearoom. There was no reason for him to have been behind the building, but boys Otto's age sometimes did unpredictable things.

"I want to stay here forever." The stubborn set to his chin told Greta he was both angry and determined to convince her of the error of her ways.

"What about seeing the mountains and playing in the snow? You told me that was your dream."

Otto let out a sigh that said she ought to understand but that, since she didn't, he'd explain. "I don't care about that anymore. I like it here. Mr. Craig is a good teacher, and Mrs. Joanna is teaching me to play the piano. That's better than looking at mountains."

Greta repressed her own sigh. When Otto made up his mind about something, he often took days to change it. There was no point in trying to argue with him.

"I haven't decided."

Otto stomped his foot again and glared at her. "Yes, you have. I know you have. But you're wrong. You can't make me go if I don't want to." Another stomp punctuated his words. "I don't care about those stupid mountains. I want to stay here with Beulah and Noah and everyone else."

It had been a long time since Otto had been this angry, but Greta was angry too. She was the adult; she was the one who had to make the difficult decisions.

"Sometimes we can't have everything we want."

"We could. You're being selfish. You aren't thinking about me."

"I am, Otto. I am."

He clenched his fists. "It doesn't seem like it. I hate you."

When he stormed out of the room, slamming the door behind him, Greta burst into tears.

Chapter Twenty-Two

Greta sighed as she unlocked the front door to the tearoom Monday morning. She had to stop crying. Hadn't she learned that tears solved nothing when first Papa and then Mama died? There was no reason to cry now. No one had died. It was only her dreams that were gone, but still the tears came. Fortunately, she'd managed to control them during the day. It was only at night that she succumbed to weeping.

She hung her cloak in the back room and was preparing the batter for the scones when she heard the front door open. Realizing it was too early for her helpers to be here, Greta's heartrate increased and she hurried into the main room, startled when she recognized her visitor. This was the first time Caroline had come to Porter's since Junior was born, yet here she was, holding her baby in her arms and frowning at Greta.

"I was going to say 'good morning,' but one look at you tells me it's not a good morning. What's wrong?" the former manager of the tearoom asked.

"Nothing."

Caroline studied Greta's face for a few seconds. "You look tired," she said. "I am too, but you don't have a little one waking up every two hours and demanding to be fed."

"That's true." The likelihood that Greta would ever have a child was slim, because that required a husband and after what had happened with first Nigel and now Matt, Greta couldn't imagine herself agreeing to marry anyone. It was difficult to picture herself caring about anyone the way she did about Matt, and look how wrong she'd been in thinking he cared for her.

It was true that he'd said he did. His words had been eloquent and might have convinced her if she hadn't been all too aware of the difference between words and actions. Words came easily. Look at the words—both written and spoken—that Nigel had given her. They'd been designed to win her heart, and they'd almost succeeded. But then his actions, banishing Otto to the stable and planning to send him to the poor farm if Greta did not capitulate to his demands, had shown her how empty those words had been.

Matt had said the right things, but there had been no actions to prove that his words were any truer than Nigel's had been. Was it any wonder she cried? But that was not something Greta would tell Caroline.

"I may not have a baby." Hoping to allay the other woman's suspicions, Greta continued, "But between the extra hours here, arranging last week's caroling, and helping with the children's pageant, I haven't had much time to sleep." And when she did, her dreams were filled with unhappy scenes that led to her waking with tears on her cheeks. It was more than Otto's anger with her, which had not abated. That was bad enough, but even worse was the feeling of having a hole inside her, one that nothing could fill. She hadn't realized that the loss of Matt's friendship would leave her so bereft.

Trying not to let Caroline see how unhappy she was, Greta forced a smile onto her face. "It's only temporary."

"You're right Everything will be back to normal soon." Caroline returned Greta's smile. "I can hardly believe it's only ten days until Christmas." Her smile broadened as she gazed at her son. "Thanks to him, it'll be extra special this year."

Caroline's son was a safer subject than Greta's mood, and so she seized on the topic. "Will you bring Junior to the pageant?" As she asked the question, Greta's mind began to whirl. She'd finished crocheting the angels for Otto and her new family. Perhaps making one for Caroline's baby would give her something to do other than weep.

Caroline shook her head. "I can't predict when he'll start crying, and no one needs a screaming baby. It would destroy the mood."

"That's why we're using a doll instead of a live child in our manger." When they'd heard about the pageant, several of Louisa's patients who'd recently delivered baby boys had volunteered their sons and had been slightly miffed when Louisa had told them Greta and Craig planned to have a doll in the manager.

Unlike those mothers, Caroline nodded her agreement. "That's a wise decision." She looked around the room, studying the holiday décor. "So are the changes you've made here. Everyone I've talked to says they hope the Christmas teas will be an annual event. A new tradition."

"I expect they will be." Even though she wouldn't be here to organize them. "It's been a lot of work, but Josh is pleased with the reaction to them." And so was Greta. There was no denying that it was reassuring to see how well her suggestions had turned out. She might not be a good judge of men, but the evidence indicated that she understood what other women would enjoy.

"Josh should be pleased." As Junior began to wail, Caroline slid her forefinger into his mouth to quiet him. "That's his hungry cry. I'd better get him home." She wrapped her free arm around Greta's shoulders in a quick hug. "I'm glad you came to Sweetwater Crossing."

⇒⇒ ·•·•· ⇐⇐

Matt was leaning back in his chair, trying to decide whether he should have lunch at Ma's Kitchen or try to cook something for himself. It was hardly a momentous decision, but thinking about meals kept him from dwelling on his failure to make headway with Greta. Go out or eat here. Those were his choices. As he reminded himself that while Mrs. Tabor's pot roast was delicious, if he ate there, he might have to fend off questions about why he no longer strolled through the town with the woman who occupied so many of his thoughts, someone knocked on the door.

That was odd. No one knocked on the sheriff's door. If they needed him, they simply walked inside. Curious about the visitor's identity, Matt rose and opened the door.

"Otto." Shouldn't he be in school? When Matt looked across the street and saw the children playing outside, he realized that it was recess time. While Otto shouldn't have left the others, at least he hadn't skipped out during classes.

"What's wrong?" The frown that etched the boy's face left no doubt that he was upset about something.

"Everything!"

Stepping back, Matt gestured toward his desk. "Come in and tell me about it." This was not a conversation to be held on the boardwalk.

After he'd plopped into one of the chairs in front of the desk, Otto glared at Matt. "It's Greta. She's being mean."

That was not a word Matt would have used to describe her, but a ten-year-old's perceptions were different from an adult's. "What's she done?"

"She says we gotta leave." Otto clenched his fist, stopping short of pounding it on the desk. "She won't listen when I tell her I don't care about Pikes Peak anymore. I want to stay here with all my friends and you."

Though his heart warmed at the thought that the boy included him on that list, Matt knew better than to smile, lest Otto misunderstand him and think he was laughing at him. "I'd like you to stay too, but Greta must have good reasons."

Matt could only hope that his foolish bargain wasn't the cause for her decision, but he suspected it was. She'd told him she didn't want to see him again, and leaving Sweetwater Crossing would ensure that she didn't. He wished—oh, how he wished—he could convince her of how much he regretted agreeing to Toby's plan, but she wouldn't listen to him any more than she would listen to Otto. Instead, she put Matt in the same category as Nigel, and if that wasn't infuriating, Matt didn't know what was.

"What did Greta tell you?"

"She says I'm too young to understand why we have to go." His face flushing with anger, Otto glared at Matt. "She's wrong, Mr. Matt ... er ... Sheriff. I think Greta knows she's wrong and that's why she cries every night."

"Your sister cries?" The shame Matt felt over his role in Greta's decision turned into alarm. He'd known she was angry, but tears? That put a different spin on everything.

Otto nodded. "She doesn't think I hear her, but I do. Can't you fix it?"

"I wish I could." There was no point in telling Otto that he'd tried, but that so far he'd failed.

"You're a grown-up. You should know what to do."

If only it were that simple. "Grown-ups don't have all the answers."

"They should."

"I agree."

»···•·—·••«

The conversation with Otto had taken place Monday morning. It was now Saturday evening. The pageant was about to begin, and Matt still had no idea how to persuade Greta to remain in Sweetwater Crossing, much less how to convince her that he loved her and wanted to marry her.

"I wish I could help you," Craig had said when Matt had gone to the schoolhouse Monday afternoon to seek his friend's advice, "but I can't. Emily says Greta's determined to leave. All three sisters have tried to convince her otherwise, but it's like she doesn't hear them." Craig shook his head slowly. "Emily said words aren't enough."

"I'm not surprised. The man in Houston wooed her with words that proved to be false. It makes sense that she no longer trusts words."

As he'd reflected on Craig's explanation, the adage that actions speak louder than words echoed through Matt's brain. He needed to do something, but here he was days later with no idea what that something should be.

"Beulah and me are ready."

Otto strutted toward Matt, his pride in being part of the pageant obvious. Rather than correct the boy's grammar as Greta or Craig might have, Matt simply nodded. "You certainly are. I've never seen such fine wisemen." Beulah's mother and grandmother must have spent almost every waking hour sewing the costumes, but if they'd grown weary, there was no evidence of it. Not only had they created garments that would last for years, but they'd ensured that each was unique.

When the third wiseman arrived, trailed by the four shepherds, Matt spoke again. "You wisemen know what to do." He pointed to the first pew on the right. "Sit here until it's your turn." Turning to the shepherds, he asked, "Are you ready?" The quartet nodded, then walked to the right of the altar.

Greta and her players were on the opposite side, preparing for their roles. Mary and Joseph would seek room at the inn, then take their places in the carefully constructed stable where a doll wrapped in swaddling clothes was already lying in the manger. Only when they were in position would the angel appear to the shepherds.

As Craig had predicted, every pew in the church was full, leaving some of the late-coming adults to stand in the back. Matt heard a low buzz of conversation but could distinguish no words, perhaps because Joanna was playing Christmas hymns while the parishioners assembled. When Craig moved to the center, both the music and the conversation ceased.

"On behalf of my pupils, I would like to welcome you to our first annual Christmas pageant. Everyone has worked very hard to learn their parts in the story of the greatest gift the world has been given." Craig paused for a second before saying, "I ask you all to remain silent until the end, but first let's have a round of applause for the effort the children of Sweetwater Crossing have put forth."

Not only did the adults clap, but some parents shouted encouragement to their children. Though it was an unusual beginning, Matt couldn't fault Craig, because the audible approval had a visible effect on the players. Some stood taller; others grinned. Everyone seemed eager to show the adults what they'd learned.

Matt stood at the end of the pew where the wisemen waited and watched the pageant. Everything was going smoothly. Mary and Joseph were inside the stable. It was time for the angel to appear.

She stood silently for a moment as if she'd forgotten her lines, then cried out, her voice carrying clearly to the back of the church, "'Fear not: for behold I bring you good tidings of great joy, which shall be to all people.'"

The words from the gospel of Luke touched Matt's heart as they always did. This was the heart of the Christmas message. Good tidings. Great joy. All people. Even without the heavenly host joining in, it was a powerful message. And as the shepherds stared at the angel in awe, Matt began to smile. He'd found his answer.

◦◦────◦◦

"I was a good wiseman, wasn't I, Mr. Craig?" Though Greta had assured her brother last night that he'd done well, he seemed to need confirmation and posed the question while the rest of the family began to eat their scrambled eggs.

Craig smiled. "You certainly were. So was Beulah. You were both fine wisemen."

"We had fun." Otto slathered jam on a piece of toast, then stuffed half of it into his mouth.

Though Greta thought the conversation would turn to other subjects, Craig wasn't finished. "I'm glad you did, since you were responsible for us having a pageant."

Otto was responsible? How had that happened and why didn't she know about it?

"Me?" Her brother was as surprised as she.

"Yes, you." This time it was Emily who spoke. "You told Matt that the town should have something for the children, so he suggested that there should be a pageant."

Greta stared at Emily, shock rendering her temporarily unable to speak. Though both Emily and Craig had known that the concept had been Matt's, neither had mentioned it to her.

"Why didn't you tell me?" she asked at last.

"He didn't want to take credit for something that was a community project," Craig explained. "According to Matt, the work everyone else did was more important than making the suggestion."

But without his idea, there would have been no pageant and Greta's brother would not be sitting here, grinning at the thought that Matt had listened to him and cared enough to try to make this a special Christmas for him.

Greta took a deep breath. She might not see him before church, but once the service ended, she would tell Matt how grateful she was.

⋙ ·•·•· ⋘

It had been only a little more than twelve hours, but the church no longer bore any signs of the pageant that had taken place here. The props were gone, the hay swept away. The only reminders were the grins on the children's faces as they entered the sanctuary with their parents. Those had not faded. The children were justifiably proud of their performance. Oh, there had been a couple minor mistakes. The third wiseman had mispronounced frankincense, calling it Franklin's sense, but no one had minded. The congre-

219

gation had been caught up in the dramatization of the story that would never grow old, no matter how often it was told.

Good tidings of great joy. Yes, indeed. And soon Greta would be able to tell Matt that the tidings she'd heard at breakfast had brought her great joy. She settled back in the pew and let Joanna's music soothe her spirit, then listened intently when Pastor Lindstrom began to preach.

This morning he based his sermon on the events leading up to Mary and Joseph's journey to Bethlehem, asking his parishioners whether they would have had the faith both Mary and Joseph had shown when angels appeared to them. "Would you have thought it nothing more than a dream?" he asked. "Would you have praised God the way Mary did? Would you have been as obedient as Joseph?" There were quiet murmurs, but no one answered.

At the conclusion of the final hymn, the minister reminded the congregation of the times for the Christmas Eve and Christmas Day services, then said, "I have one further announcement. Byron Winslow has asked me to tell you that he will be serving as sheriff until Sheriff Nelson returns."

Greta felt the blood drain from her face. Matt was gone? She turned to look behind her, seeking confirmation that the minister was wrong. But though his parents and Toby sat in their normal pew, Matt was not there. Where could he have gone, and—more importantly—why had he left Sweetwater Crossing?

"When will he be back?" a man in the rear of the sanctuary demanded.

Byron rose to respond. "He wasn't certain."

"Where did he go?" another asked.

This time Byron shrugged. "He didn't say."

"Sheriff Granger never left town. Sheriffs are supposed to be here, protecting us." The first man was obviously unhappy with Matt's behavior.

Toby stood to face the man. "My brother wouldn't have left unless it was important."

"So, where did he go?"

"I don't know any more than Mr. Winslow—pardon me, Acting Sheriff Winslow—does. All anyone knows is that Matt took his horse. We don't even know which direction he went."

The low murmur grew louder as Sweetwater Crossing's residents considered their elected lawman's uncharacteristic actions, and the conversation continued during the Finley House dinner.

"He didn't say anything to me," Craig told Greta.

She turned to her brother. "Mr. Matt talked to you after the pageant. Did he tell you he was leaving?"

Instead of meeting her gaze, Otto kept his eyes fixed on his plate. "No."

He sounded truthful, but Greta wasn't satisfied. "Then what did he want?" Though he'd congratulated all of the children, he hadn't singled out any of the others.

"He told me I was a good wiseman."

Greta suspected there was more to the discussion, but though she pressed him, Otto would say nothing more. Perhaps it didn't matter. What mattered was that Matt was gone.

‹‹·›·—·+·—·‹‹·

Matt frowned as he pulled out his watch. The train was an hour behind schedule, thanks, the conductor told him, to a problem at the last water stop. *Take a deep breath*, he urged himself. There should still be enough time, assuming there were no problems in Houston. Otto had said that the Carmons were nice neighbors, not mean like Nigel Channing and his mother. "They never made Greta cry," the boy had said, his expression indicating that the Channings had caused his sister to shed tears more than once. Unfortunately, so had Matt. He couldn't undo the past. What was important was ensuring that the future held no more tears for Greta.

Matt hoped that the Carmons would agree to what he had in mind. If they did, if there were no delays on the train trip, and if his horse didn't go lame between Austin and Sweetwater Crossing, Matt should be back by Christmas Eve.

The problem was, those were a lot of ifs.

Chapter Twenty-Three

The parlor wasn't crowded. Even though Emily had invited her sisters and their husbands to join them, both Joanna and Louisa had declined, saying they had their own trees to decorate. And so Emily, Craig, Noah, and Prudence, who was decidedly unhappy that her mother had stopped her from putting one of the tree branches in her mouth, sat in front of the tree, with Mrs. Carmichael, Greta, Otto, and Beulah beside them. These were the usual residents of Finley House, and yet the noise level in the room was higher than usual, because Beulah, Otto, and Noah had raised their voices in excitement, and Prudence, not to be outdone, had started wailing.

This was far different from the tree decorating Greta and Otto had done with their mother. Though Mama had overseen the placement of ornaments on the large and impressive tree the Channings had in their parlor, Mrs. Channing had made it clear that that tree was for the family. If servants wanted one, they'd have to buy it themselves.

Mama had done exactly that each year, choosing a small and often spindly tree and inviting the rest of the staff to participate in decorating it. There'd been no costly ornaments like those that adorned the Channings' tree, but in Greta's estimation the humble tree that stood in the corner of the servants' dining room was far more beautiful, particularly when Otto placed their grandfather's angel on top.

While the fact that the angel would grace another family's tree this year brought tears to Greta's eyes, she took comfort from Otto's renewed health and the warm atmosphere that filled the Finley House parlor.

"Thank you for waiting." As normally quiet Beulah practically shouted the words at Emily, both Otto and Noah fell silent.

When they'd discussed the plans for the tree last week, Emily had explained that the family usually decorated it the Sunday before Christmas, but Beulah had been so disappointed that she couldn't participate last year that Emily and Craig had delayed the activity until Monday night when Beulah would be staying with them.

In an attempt to distract Prudence, Emily handed her daughter a rag doll while she smiled at Beulah. "We should have thought of this last year. After all, you're like one of the family. You should be here."

Beulah's smile was so bright it might have outshone the sun. Trust Emily to say exactly the right thing to make the girl others had once treated as an outcast feel welcomed.

"What about Greta and me? Are we part of the family?" Otto's voice was only slightly quieter than Beulah's had been.

"Yes, of course you are." Once again it was Emily who offered reassurance.

"Good." Visibly pleased, Otto gave Greta a look that seemed to say, 'See. I told you. We should stay here.'

"Boxes! Open boxes." Noah had no patience for the pleasantries the others were exchanging.

"Yes, son, we're going to open the boxes. You can help me." Craig turned toward Emily, nodding when she gestured toward one. "Let's start with this one, Noah." When Craig opened the box, Greta understood why Emily had indicated that one. Rather than containing fragile ornaments, it held strings of red and green beads. There was little danger of Noah breaking them.

"Beulah and me want to help."

Emily rose to carry her now-sleeping daughter upstairs. "You two have an important job," she told Otto. "After Greta and Mrs. Carmichael unwrap the ornaments, you have to decide where to place them on the tree."

Greta gave Emily a cautionary look. "They might drop them."

"That's possible, but I doubt it. Look at how carefully they're carrying them."

When Mrs. Carmichael handed each of the children a single ornament, Beulah and Otto walked slowly, holding the baubles in both hands as if they were priceless treasures.

"Besides, what's important is that they're having fun." Emily shrugged. "One or two broken ornaments won't matter. We have more than enough decorations for the tree."

And they would have even more when they received the angels Greta had crocheted. Those were wrapped and ready to be distributed. The only question was when. She was still debating whether to give them on Christmas Eve or Christmas Day.

It took the better part of an hour, but when the last box had been emptied, the tree looked beautiful. If one side had more ornaments than the other and if several strings of beads drooped in places rather than being evenly draped over the branches, none of the adults cared. As Emily had said, what was important was that the children had fun.

"Where's the star, Emily?" Craig asked. "Noah and I are going to put it on top."

As Emily reached for a box that she'd placed underneath her chair, Otto abandoned his post next to the tree and raced to stand in front of Craig, his hands fisted on his hips. "You can't do that, Mr. Craig. Not yet. That's for Christmas Eve."

Craig's confusion was evident. "I don't understand."

"That was our family's custom," Greta explained, a familiar pang clenching her heart. "We had an angel rather than a star, but though we decorated the rest of the tree earlier, the angel didn't go on top until Christmas Eve. My parents said that made it special. The angel didn't appear until the Christ child was born, and neither did the star."

As Otto nodded solemnly, confirming Greta's story, Craig exchanged a brief look with Emily, then nodded. "All right. We'll wait."

"Thank you, Mr. Craig." Otto unfisted his hands.

Beulah, who'd been watching and listening intently, moved to Otto's side. "You're smart, Otto. You're the best friend I ever had." She punctuated her words with a hug.

The hug from normally undemonstrative Beulah brought a smile to Otto's face. "You're my friend too," he said softly.

And as he did, the words from one of Mama's favorite hymns echoed through Greta's brain. "Was blind but now I see." The author of *Amazing Grace* had it right. Greta had been blind, so blind.

⋙ ⋅•⋅ ⋘

The house was dark. Frustration mingled with worry, and for what seemed like the hundredth time Matt feared that he would fail. The hours were ticking by. Ticking? They were racing, and so far he had nothing to show for them.

He'd finally made it to Houston, but he hadn't accomplished what he'd sought to do. Either he hadn't been clear when he'd spoken to Otto or the boy had been confused. The reason wasn't important. What was was that Matt had made his way to the address Otto had given him only to discover that was the location of the Engels' former restaurant.

The new owner wasn't certain where the family had gone once Mrs. Engel sold the restaurant to him, but when he summoned his wife from the kitchen, she recalled the Channings' name and the street where they lived. That was where Matt was now. Though he was tempted to knock on the door of the brightly lit mansion and tell Nigel and his mother what he thought of the way they'd treated

Greta and Otto, nothing would be gained other than venting his anger, and he didn't have time to waste.

What he sought was next door, but that house was dark. Though it was too early for the occupants to be asleep, Matt knocked anyway. As he'd expected from the lack of lights, there was no answer. The couple he'd come all this way to meet were not home. But somehow, someway he had to find them.

As much as Matt hated the idea of asking any favors from the Channings, he knew he had no other good alternative. If he was fortunate, he wouldn't encounter either Nigel or his mother. When Matt rapped on the door to the servants' entrance, there was a lengthy delay before a harried looking woman with flour on her face opened it.

"What do you want?" Her voice held no welcome, and her expression radiated suspicion.

Matt gestured toward the neighboring house. "I was looking for Mr. Carmon, but no one seems to be home."

"They ain't."

"Do you know where they went?"

"Why should I tell you?"

When she started to close the door in Matt's face, he gave her his warmest smile. "Because I'm trying to make sure the woman I love has a happy Christmas."

"Oh." She stared at him for a long moment, appearing to assess his sincerity. "All right," she said at last. "Their cook told me their daughter just had a baby and they went to be with her. I reckon they plan to spend Christmas there."

"Do you know where the daughter lives?"

The woman shook her head. "No. I ain't been here long enough to know much about the neighbors. Miz Channing keeps me busy."

"Would anyone here know?" Matt had no intention of leaving Houston until he'd followed every possible lead. If he failed, it wouldn't be for lack of trying.

The woman pursed her lips, then pointed to the left. "Maybe Hank. He's in charge of the stables."

The stables where Otto was supposed to spend his final days. "Thank you, ma'am. I'll ask him."

According to Hank, a kindly older man who asked about Otto's health and seemed genuinely relieved that the boy was still alive, the Carmons' daughter lived on the opposite side of town. It would take another half hour to get there, meaning that Matt would miss the last train to Austin today, but if everything went well, he could still be back in Sweetwater Crossing by Christmas Eve. If everything went well.

When he reached the daughter's house, his spirits rose at the sight of the modest but well-lit dwelling. Maybe things would work out after all. If the elder Carmons intended to celebrate Christmas here, it was likely they'd brought what Matt sought with them.

"It's here," Mr. Carmon said when Matt explained why he'd come. "I'd like to help you, but I can't agree to what you're asking. The missus and I figured the angel would be our Christmas gift for Susanna. We waited a long time for our first grandbaby and we want her first Christmas to be special. The missus calls her our little angel. That's why we reckoned that would be the right present for her."

Just as it would be the right one for Greta, proof of how much Matt loved her. He'd known this might not be easy, but he hadn't thought he would be dealing with doting grandparents. That was different from someone who viewed the Engels' angel as nothing more than a beautiful piece of porcelain.

"I'm not a grandfather or even a father, so I can't pretend that I understand everything you're feeling. I wouldn't ask you to part with the angel unless it was important. That angel is the only thing Greta and Otto have left from their family. Their grandfather made it and even when times were hard, he wouldn't consider selling it. It was going to be his legacy to his son and his son's children. Greta wouldn't have sold it if she hadn't been desperate."

Though Mr. Carmon listened politely, Matt saw no sign that he would agree to part with the angel. He paused, mustering the words to convince the older man. "Otto would have died if Greta hadn't taken him away."

Furrows formed between Mr. Carmon's eyes. "She didn't tell me that. I knew something was wrong when they were in such a hurry to leave Houston, but I figured it was because the Channing boy was making a nuisance of himself. His ma let him do whatever he pleased and didn't care if he hurt others along the way."

Mr. Carmon chuckled. "It's wrong of me to gloat, but the boy got his comeuppance. The way I heard it, that pretty gal from Galveston broke off their engagement."

Thank you. Matt offered a silent prayer of thanksgiving that his letter to Mr. Berger had had the desired effect. Adelaide might be disappointed now, but she'd been spared an unhappy marriage.

Unwilling to confirm Mr. Carmon's assumption that Nigel was the reason Greta had fled Houston, even though it was correct, Matt said, "The doctor told Greta Otto would die within a couple months. For years he'd been talking about Pikes Peak, so she decided to take him there, because she didn't want him to die without seeing it."

The older man's grin faded and his eyes glistened with unshed tears. "You've convinced me. Greta and the boy deserve every bit of happiness they can find." He took a deep breath and straightened his shoulders. "Give me a couple minutes to tell the missus what I've decided. I know she'll agree that this should be our Christmas gift to Greta and her brother."

A gift? That was far more than Matt had expected. Almost speechless at Mr. Carmon's generosity, he shook his head. "Let me at least give you whatever you paid Greta for it."

"It wouldn't be a gift then, would it?"

The man's logic was faultless. "You're right about that." Matt pulled out the roll of bills he'd brought with him. "I know Greta and Otto will be grateful. I'd be grateful if you'd let me give your granddaughter a little something for her first Christmas."

For the second time Mr. Carmon chuckled. "You're trying to get the better of me, aren't you? You know I can't refuse something for Susanna. All right, sir. You've got yourself a deal."

At least he hadn't said bargain. After all the trouble his bargain with Toby had caused, Matt wasn't certain he'd ever agree to another one.

A few minutes later, Mr. Carmon returned and handed Matt a cloth-wrapped object that was perhaps a foot tall. "Here you go. I know I don't have to remind you to be careful with it."

"I brought a blanket to cushion it on the trip back."

Now that he'd missed the train, there was no reason to rush. Before he bade Mr. Carmon farewell, there was one more thing to do. He needed to see the angel that had been such an important part of Greta's life. Ever so carefully, Matt pulled it from the cloth sack and unwrapped it, his breath catching in wonder when it was revealed.

The angel was the size he'd expected with hair the same shade as Greta's, flowing white robes, and golden wings. All of that made it memorable, but what made it unforgettable was the angel's expression. Never before had Matt seen such joy and adoration depicted on a figurine. Greta's grandfather was indeed a master of his craft, a man whose love for the Lord was clearly displayed in his art.

"It's even more beautiful than I expected."

"A masterpiece," Mr. Carmon agreed, "but you're right. It belongs with Greta and Otto." He narrowed his eyes, then smiled. "Judging by the way you look, so do you."

⚜

Greta stared out her bedroom window, wishing her thoughts were as clear as the night sky. The moon was no longer full, but it still illuminated the sky. The stars twinkled. The trees swayed in the light breeze. An owl hooted. It was a peaceful night in Sweetwater Crossing, a night to rejoice in the beauty of God's creation. On another day, her heart would have been filled with joy, but not tonight.

How could she have been so blind? She'd done the same thing her mother had after Papa died. She'd made plans, so certain she knew what was best for herself and Otto. Not once had she asked God what plans he had for her. How disappointed her father would have been.

It had been a week or so before he died. Greta didn't recall where Mama and Otto were, but she and Papa had been washing dishes after the restaurant closed.

"I love you, Greta," Papa said as he handed her a plate. "So does your heavenly Father. His Word tells us that he wants only good things for us."

Greta paused, the dishtowel motionless as she considered what her father had said. "You mean John 3:16, 'For God so loved the world, that he gave his only begotten Son, that whosoever believeth in him should not perish, but have everlasting life.'" That was one of many verses she'd memorized.

"That's many people's favorite and for good reason, but there's another that comforts me, Jeremiah 29:11." Papa's blue eyes were serious as he recited. "'For I know the thoughts that I think towards you, saith the Lord, thoughts of peace, and not of evil, to give you an expected end.'"

Though Greta knew that verse, she had never found comfort in it. "Those are only thoughts," she protested. "The verse from St. John is about an action."

"That's true, but some people believe 'thoughts' should be translated as 'plans.' God has plans for us, but it's up to us whether we listen to him and follow those plans."

Greta nodded slowly as her father continued. "If you remember only one thing I've told you, let it be this: ask God what his plans are and then listen."

She hadn't asked. She hadn't listened. Instead, she'd forged ahead, confident in her own judgment, and all the while she'd been blind to the opportunities God had placed before her, clear evidence of his plans for her.

It hadn't been a coincidence that Otto had been taken ill so close to here. It hadn't been a coincidence that she'd turned right at the crossroads and had come to Sweetwater Crossing. It hadn't been a coincidence that Matt had been across the street when she and Otto arrived and that he'd been the first to help them. All of those had been part of God's plan.

She had tried to ignore it, but seeing Otto and Beulah together today had shown her that this was what God had planned for her and her brother. He'd led them to a new home. He'd restored Otto's health. He'd brought Matt into Greta's life. And how had Greta reacted? She'd planned to take Otto from his newfound friends. She'd been willing to abandon the three sisters who'd welcomed her into their family. She'd rejected Matt.

She'd told him she put little faith in words, that only actions would convince her that his feelings for her were genuine. But she'd been blind, horribly, inexcusably blind. She'd been so angered by the bargain Matt had made with Toby that she'd ignored all the things he'd done, the actions that had demonstrated the kind of man he was. Actions did speak more loudly than words, but Greta had ignored Matt's actions.

From the very beginning, he'd shown himself to be a man who cared about others. Why else would he have rushed to help her get Otto into the doctor's office? Other men might have done that, but how many would have taken Blackie and the wagon to the livery and arranged for Blackie's stabling without any thought of being repaid?

How many men would have taken a young boy to their ranch simply because they realized the boy might enjoy it? How many would have proposed that the town have a Christmas pageant so that the same boy would have a role in it and feel as if he was part of the town?

The answer was simple: not many, perhaps not even one other than Matt. He might not have been courting her in the usual way, but everything he'd done had shown that he cared for her. She'd simply been too blind to see that Matt was part of God's plan for her. It was time for her to admit her mistake and take the next steps on the path God had set before her.

Greta took a deep breath, exhaling slowly as she said a silent prayer of thanks that she hadn't given Josh her final decision about continuing as the tearoom's manager and that Emily's offer of a home at Finley House was open-ended. She would stay here where God had led her; she wouldn't uproot Otto; she wouldn't leave the three women who'd become the sisters she'd always longed for.

Those were easy. Now she could only pray that it wasn't too late to make amends with Matt.

Falling to her knees, Greta began to pray. "Thank you, Lord, for showing me your plans. And please, if it's part of your plan, bring Matt back so that I can tell him how much I love him." Once she'd done that, she would tell Otto, Josh, and Emily that she planned to remain in Sweetwater Crossing.

Tuesday passed more quickly than Greta had expected. It was the last day the tearoom would be open until after Christmas, and the women who came were filled with excitement over the upcoming holiday. Greta took pleasure in seeing them so happy. She'd be happy too, if only she could talk to Matt.

Where was he? Surely he wouldn't miss Christmas with his family, but there'd been no sign of him, no word of why he'd left. Toby had stopped by Finley House this morning to ask whether Greta had heard anything from his brother.

"I'm as mystified as you," she told him, unsure why Toby thought she might have news before he did.

"This isn't like my brother." Toby made no effort to hide his concern. "He's never done anything like this." He paused, as if trying to decide whether to continue speaking, then gave a quick nod. "I wanted his opinion on something, but maybe you can help me."

Almost sheepishly Toby pulled a small box from his pocket. "I plan to ask Rose to marry me tonight. Matt may not have told you, but our parents became engaged on Christmas Eve. I want to continue the tradition." He opened the box and held it out to Greta, revealing a cluster of diamonds in the newly popular floral style. "Do you think Rose will like it?"

Greta's smile was genuine. "It's gorgeous. I'm sure Rose will love it." She handed the ring back to Toby. "What a wonderful Christmas you'll have."

"If Matt returns."

Chapter Twenty-Four

"Look what the wind brought in."

Matt was too exhausted to respond to his brother. It was taking every ounce of energy he could muster to get Neptune unsaddled. Everything was off-schedule. When the train had been hours late arriving in Austin, he'd considered waiting until morning to leave, but all he could think about was seeing Greta, and so he'd saddled his horse and headed west.

"Let me help with that. You look worse for the wear." Toby entered the stall and lifted the saddle off Matt's horse.

"You would too if you'd ridden through the rain for as long as I did." It had been one of the most challenging rides he could recall between his fatigue and the weather. Fortunately, Neptune was sure-footed and acted as if he knew the route as well as Matt.

When Toby reached for one of the saddlebags, Matt shook his head and unbuckled it. No one else was handling the package that he'd wrapped in oilskin for extra protection from the elements.

"I'm glad you're home. Christmas wouldn't feel right without you." As he started to groom Neptune, Toby wrinkled his nose. "You look like you're in a hurry, but let me give you a word of advice. You need a bath before you go courting."

"Who said I was going courting?"

"Aren't you?" Taking a step back from the horse, Toby patted his pocket. "That's where I'm headed. It's the morning of Christmas Eve, and I can't wait another hour to ask Rose to be my wife." He pulled out a box that could only hold a ring and opened it so that Matt could see the diamonds. "I'd ask where you went, but I have a feeling you won't answer, so instead all I'm going to ask is whether you brought a ring for Greta."

"I have something better."

→→ ·•◦•· ◄◄

Greta smiled when she saw that the rain had finally stopped. Even though the weather didn't change the message of hope that Christmas brought, clear skies boosted people's spirits—especially hers. Now that she'd made her decision, she was filled with peace. She hadn't told anyone, not even Otto, because she wanted Matt to be the first to hear it. Where was he?

Breakfast was finished, and since there was no school, Beulah was home with her parents and Otto was with Mrs. Carmichael and Noah, reading a book in the library. Emily had insisted she didn't need help in the kitchen, and Craig had gone on a mysterious errand that Greta suspected was related to Emily's gift. That left Greta alone and restless.

She grabbed her cloak, then stopped in the kitchen. "If you're sure you don't need me, I'm going out for a walk."

Emily nodded. "Fresh air will do you good."

When she reached the end of Finley House's long driveway, Greta started to turn right as she did every morning when she headed to the tearoom, then stopped. She had no destination in mind, but somehow turning right felt wrong, and so she headed left, then turned south on East Street. She was in front of Joanna and Burke's home when she noticed a man turning the corner of Main onto East. Not just any man. Matt. There was no mistaking his gait. Matt was back!

"Matt!" Greta wouldn't run. That would be unseemly, and Mama had insisted that a lady never do anything unseemly, but though Greta did not run, she increased her pace to a fast walk. Oh, how she wanted to see Matt, to tell him everything she'd learned about herself and to ask his forgiveness for her rejection of him.

Apparently feeling no compunction to adhere to society's rules of proper decorum, Matt sprinted toward her, his long strides closing the distance between them in seconds. "Greta, I'm so glad to see you," he said when they were only a foot apart.

Lines of exhaustion marred his face, but those brown eyes that had figured in so many of Greta's dreams sparkled with warmth as he smiled at her. If he remembered the way they'd parted, he gave no sign. This was the Matt who'd walked with her most evenings, the Matt who'd told her he wanted them to have a future together.

As happiness blossomed inside her, Greta returned Matt's smile. "You can't be as glad as I am to see you. I was worried about you. So was everyone in town. No one knew where you went or why you left." Greta hoped she didn't sound as if she was scolding him.

Matt shifted the bag he held in his left hand. Though it didn't appear to be heavy, he seemed unusually protective of it. "I had something to do in Houston."

Whatever Greta thought he might say, it wasn't that. "Houston? You went all the way to Houston? How did you get there and back so quickly?" It had taken her and Otto close to a week to travel the distance one-way.

Tightening his grip on the bag, Matt began to explain. "I rode Neptune to Austin and took the train from there. That made the trip a lot shorter than riding all the way or going by stagecoach. Trains can go thirty miles an hour."

That was something Greta didn't know. On another day, she would have asked Matt for details of the journey, but this wasn't another day. "I want to hear about your trip, but first there's something I need to say."

Should they go to Finley House? Greta looked around. Though this was a public street, there was no one else in sight, which meant they'd probably have more privacy here. As she glanced at Joanna and Burke's house, she nodded, then led the way to the small bench Joanna had placed in the front yard, knowing neither she nor Burke would mind that Greta was using it. It was no coincidence that she and Matt had met here. Once again, Greta had been led.

When she and Matt were seated, Greta continued. "I'm sorry for the way I treated you and the way I refused to talk to you, especially after you described the future you wanted us to share. I should have realized that when you agreed to Toby's bargain you were simply trying to help him just like I always try to help Otto. It's what we do for our brothers."

Greta suspected that even when Otto was an adult, she would still be protective of him and that she would do whatever she could to make his dreams come true, the way Matt had tried to ensure that Toby's dream of marrying Rose came true.

"There's no excuse for it," she continued. "I should have trusted you. I should have believed everything you said, but I let my pride get in the way. I was so sure that I was right, but I was wrong." Greta paused for a second, then asked the question that was foremost in her mind. "Can you forgive me for being so unkind?"

Though his expression had remained inscrutable while she was speaking, Matt's response was immediate. "There's nothing to forgive. I knew Nigel hurt you and that you were afraid I would do the same. I hope by now that you know that I'm not like Nigel and that you can forgive me for causing you to worry while I was gone." Chagrin colored his face as he continued. "I should have realized that leaving without an explanation would be a problem, but I didn't want anyone to know what I intended to do because I wasn't certain I'd succeed. It would have been cruel to raise your hopes and then have to dash them. Fortunately, I was successful."

Matt's voice resonated with satisfaction, telling Greta whatever he'd done was important, but she still did not know what had taken him to Houston.

As if he'd heard her thoughts, he said, "I went to Houston to get something for you." He smiled as he held out the bag that he'd been carrying. "Merry Christmas, Greta."

She stared at it, wondering if it was possible that it held what she thought it did. There was only one thing she wanted from Houston, but how did Matt know that? She couldn't recall having told him about it. Her fingers trembling with anticipation, Greta pulled the oilskin-wrapped object from the sack and began to unfold the wrapping. Even before she'd removed the final layer, she knew what Matt had brought.

"The angel! It's our angel!" Her voice cracked with emotion. Matt, wonderful, caring Matt had somehow found the one thing that would make this Christmas perfect.

She studied the angel, running her fingers over the gilded wings, caressing the face that Mama had said bore a strong resemblance to Greta's grandmother. The angel that had been her family's most prized possession was even more valuable now, because as one line of *Amazing Grace* said, it had been lost and now was found.

Greta turned her gaze to Matt, hoping he would see how much the gift pleased her. "How did you know how much I missed this and where to find it?"

"Otto mentioned the angel the day I took him to the ranch. When I decided to try to get it, I asked him what happened to it and where you used to live."

The pieces of the puzzle were starting to fit together. "So that's why you singled him out after the pageant. I asked him, but he wouldn't tell me anything. He claimed all you'd done was congratulate him."

Matt shrugged. "I told him it was a secret and only big boys knew how to keep secrets."

Greta nodded, realizing how well Matt understood her brother. "That would have ensured silence, but what made you think of the angel?"

"I knew words wouldn't convince you that I loved you. Only actions would. I needed to do something. The problem was, I didn't know what that something was. Then when I watched the angel in the pageant, it was almost as if I heard a voice saying, 'The angel is the key.' That's when I remembered Otto saying you'd sold your family's angel so you could take him away from Houston. Otto didn't say a lot, but it sounded as if the angel was an important part of your Christmases, so I wanted to see if I could get it back for you."

Tears of happiness prickled Greta's eyes. No one had ever done something so loving for her. Matt had left Sweetwater Crossing, possibly irritating the people who'd elected him, and had traveled a substantial distance, all in the hope of returning her grandfather's legacy. Was there ever such a wonderful man?

Retrieving the angel couldn't have been easy, because in addition to the long and undoubtedly arduous journey, he would have had to convince Greta's former neighbors to give up something that was almost as valuable to them as it had been to Greta.

"I'm surprised the Carmons agreed. When I offered to sell it to them, Mrs. Carmon said she'd admired the angel from the first time she saw it."

"I didn't meet Mrs. Carmon," Matt admitted. "All my dealings were with her husband. He told me they have a new granddaughter and were going to give her the angel, but when he heard the whole story and realized how much it meant to you, Mr. Carmon agreed the angel belonged with you and Otto."

Matt reached over to touch the figurine's blonde hair. "I was prepared to offer him more than he paid you for the angel, but he said it was a gift from him and his wife. Though I argued, he wouldn't let me pay for it."

Tears filled Greta's eyes as she looked at the porcelain figurine in her lap. "When we left Houston, I told myself I'd done the right thing. Otto's life was more precious than my grandfather's masterpiece. I knew that, and yet there were times when I wished I hadn't had to sell it. I never dreamt that I would see it again, much less own it, but now I do, and it's all because of you. Matt, I don't know how to thank you."

His eyes darkened, and his expression grew more intense. "There is a way," he said slowly. "It's something I've dreamt of. What I want more than anything is to court you. Will you give me a chance to show you how much I love you and that I want to spend the rest of my life with you? I know I'm rushing you, but—"

This was twice now that he'd said he loved her, twice that Greta's heart had skipped a beat at the realization that this wonderful man who'd stolen her heart felt about her the way she did about him.

"You're not rushing me," she told him, willing her voice to remain even. "While you were gone, I did a lot of thinking and spent a lot of time on my knees. I realized I'd been wrong about so many things. I realized it was only pride—my foolish, selfish pride—that kept me from admitting I cared for you." She paused for a second, wanting him to see the love shining from her eyes before she pronounced the words. "I love you, Matt. I love you more than I thought it was possible to love anyone. So, yes, I would be honored to be courted by you."

The smile that had started when she'd said she loved him widened. "It seems like we both know what we want from life and what we want our future to be. The way I understand it, the point of courtship is to determine whether a couple is ready for marriage."

When Greta nodded, Matt continued. "We've already spent time proving that to each other. Why waste any more time courting?" He rose, then bent one knee and took her hands in his. "Will you marry me?"

When the stories Greta had read had described proposals of marriage, they'd involved moonlight evenings or candlelight with soft music in the background. Not once had the heroine received her proposal during daylight on a public street. It was unconventional and broke every rule of etiquette, but Greta didn't care. This was the man she loved, making a declaration of love, asking if she would agree to the thing she wanted most.

"Yes. Oh, yes."

"Then there's only one thing to do." Matt rose and tugged her to her feet. "We need to seal it with a kiss."

"Here, where anyone can see?"

"Why not?"

Greta couldn't think of a single reason.

Slowly, ever so slowly, Matt drew her into his arms. For several long seconds, he looked at her. Then he smiled and lowered his lips to hers. And there, where passersby could see them, Greta and Matt pledged their love, a love that would stand the test of time.

Chapter Twenty-Five

"Star." Noah tugged on Emily's arm, then pointed to the tree. "Wanna hang star."

His mother gave him a fond smile as she shook her head. "We're going to wait a few more minutes."

When Greta had told Emily how Matt had brought her family's angel, she'd agreed that Matt should be here when Otto saw it.

"You look especially happy today," Emily had said.

"It's wonderful having my grandfather's angel again," Greta had told her. But though that was only a small part of the reason she was happy, Greta had made no mention of their engagement. Both she and Matt had agreed that Otto should be the first to learn of it.

"I don't wanna wait."

"Me neither." Otto echoed Noah's complaint.

Fortunately, before anyone could admonish them to be patient, there was a knock on the door. It had to be Matt.

Greta rose. "I'll go." She'd been counting the hours—no, she'd been counting the minutes—until she would see him again. As she opened the door, her heart began to pound and she wondered whether her smile would cause her face to crack. In all her life, she could not remember having such a wide smile.

His smile matched hers. "I'm sorry I'm a little late. The things I had to do at the ranch took longer than I'd expected."

She wouldn't ask what they were. Instead she continued smiling as he hung his coat on the rack. "You're here now. That's what's important."

Wordlessly, Matt extended his hand and she placed hers in his, savoring the warmth as he entwined his fingers with hers. Linked together, they walked into the parlor. If the adults noticed, no one said anything, perhaps because Otto's shout distracted them.

"Mr. Matt!" He leapt to his feet and raced across the floor to stand so close to him that Greta wondered if he intended to knock Matt over with his enthusiasm. "You're back! Did you bring ...?" When he saw that Matt's hands were empty, Otto's smile faded. "I guess you're gonna help us hang the star."

Though she hated to see her brother so disappointed, even though it would only be temporary, there were things Greta wanted to do before she showed Otto the angel. She led the way to the settee she'd appropriated for her own and waited until she and Matt were seated before she spoke. "We'll hang the star, but first there are some gifts to open."

She reached into the bag she'd stowed under the settee and pulled out four sacks of varying sizes, then handed the largest to Mrs. Carmichael, a medium-sized one to Noah, and a large as well as a tiny one to Emily. "The little one is for Prudence," she explained. She had given Caroline, Joanna, and Louisa theirs and had sent Beulah's home with her mother.

Predictably, Noah was the first to pull his crocheted angel from the sack, but it was Mrs. Carmichael who spoke. "This is beautiful." She placed the angel on her palm and studied it from all directions. "Your workmanship is excellent."

"Thank you." Greta waited until the others had unwrapped theirs before she began her explanation. "Emily told me there've never been angels on the Finley House tree. I wanted to change that this year."

When he noticed that there was a hanging loop, Noah suspended his angel from his forefinger. "Wanna put it on the tree."

"We'll do that," Craig agreed.

Before he and Noah could approach the tree, Otto glared at Greta. "Where's mine? Didn't you make one for me?"

"I did, but you might prefer this." Greta pulled the final item from the bag and unwrapped the angel that had held the place of honor on her family's tree for longer than she'd been alive.

Otto stared, his frown turning into a smile that rivaled hers. "Our angel!" He reached out to touch the porcelain figurine, as if to assure himself that it was real.

"That's why Mr. Matt was gone," Greta told him. "He went to Houston to get it for us."

"I know." Otto's smile turned into a smirk. "I told him where to go, but I didn't think he'd gotten it."

"He gave it to me earlier," Greta explained. "I wanted him to be here when you saw it."

"Oh, okay." Apparently mollified, Otto watched as the adults exclaimed over the beauty of his grandfather's masterpiece.

When they finished, Greta turned to Emily and Craig. "I hope you'll let Otto put it on your tree. I know you always have a star, so ..."

Emily shook her head as she interrupted Greta. "It's time for a new tradition. For as long as you're living with us, this will go on top."

"And Otto should place it there." Craig turned to Matt. "Will you lift him up?"

That was what Greta had hoped would happen, but her brother had other ideas. When he saw the obvious disappointment on Noah's face, he shook his head. "I want Noah to do it. You'll be careful, won't you, Noah? It's important."

The little boy nodded, his expression revealing his pleasure as well as his awe that he was being entrusted with such a valuable item. Though Mrs. Carmichael was obviously dubious, there was no danger of Noah's dropping the angel, because Craig kept one hand on it while he lifted his son and helped him position the angel at the top of the tree.

"Pretty." Noah said.

"Yes, it is." His father lowered him to the floor.

"And now we should get ready for church."

Though everyone else rose, Matt remained seated. "If you don't mind, I need a little time with Greta and Otto."

After exchanging a quick look with his wife, Craig said, "Of course," and ushered the others out of the parlor.

When Otto was seated across from him and Greta, Matt spoke. "That was a fine thing you did, letting Noah hang the angel. It shows me that you're becoming a man."

Otto flushed at the praise but said nothing, because it was evident that Matt wasn't finished.

"Tradition says that when a man wants to marry a woman, he asks the man of the family for permission."

As the words registered, Otto's eyes widened, but he remained silent. So did Greta, though her heart was overflowing with love. She hadn't believed anything could increase her love for Matt, but the way he was treating her brother did. Only a truly loving man would have thought to include Otto in one of the most important days in their lives.

"I love your sister and I want to marry her," Matt continued. "You're the man of the family, so I'm asking whether I have your permission."

Though Greta had expected Otto to answer Matt, he turned to her. "Does this mean we're not gonna leave Sweetwater Crossing?"

"It does. Mr. Matt wants us to live with him."

"Me too?" Otto's voice quavered, telling Greta how deeply the prospect touched him.

"Of course." It was Matt who spoke. "You're part of our family."

Otto nodded solemnly. "Then I agree. You can marry Greta."

Leaning forward, Matt extended his hand to shake Otto's. "Thank you." He tipped his head toward the door. "You'd better get ready for church."

Confusion crossed Otto's face. "What about you and Greta?"

"We're almost ready."

As comprehension dawned, Otto wrinkled his nose. "So you want to be alone with her."

"I do."

"Okay, but you better not make her cry."

Keeping his face solemn, Matt said, "I'll do my best not to."

Otto rose. When he reached the door, he turned, his smile turning into another smirk. "It's okay if you smooch."

Once the door was closed, both Greta and Matt began to laugh.

"I did ask for permission," Matt admitted. "As much as I want to smooch you, there's something I want to do first." He rose, then faced her and bent one knee as he had earlier today. "Ma told me it's all right to ask a woman twice, so that's what I'm going to do. I wanted you to have an official proposal in a private setting."

Since her answer would be the same, Greta wasn't certain why Matt wanted to propose a second time, but she wouldn't argue with him. Sweet words of love were always welcome.

He fixed his gaze on her, his eyes radiating the love that made her heart beat faster. "Greta, I love you, and I'll be the happiest man alive if you say you'll be my wife. Will you marry me?"

She nodded. "All I've thought about since the first time you asked me is how much I love you and how much I'm looking forward to being your wife. Yes, my darling, I'll marry you."

She'd thought he would seal their agreement with a kiss, but instead Matt reached into his pocket and pulled out a small pouch. "I hope you'll wear my ring. It's not as fancy as the one Toby gave Rose, but this one has a special meaning for me. It's the only thing I have from my first mother."

Matt extended the ring for her inspection. A small diamond was centered in a setting some would call old-fashioned. Greta called it perfect.

"It's beautiful," she said, touched beyond words by the gift. "I'm honored that you would give me something your mother wore. Like my grandfather's angel, this is priceless."

She extended her hand so that Matt could slip the ring onto her finger. "It's a perfect fit."

"And you're the perfect wife for me."

Matt drew her to her feet, and as he pressed his lips to hers, Greta realized that Mama was right. Christmas was the season of miracles. Otto's health had been restored; they had a new home; and Greta had discovered the miracle of true love. This was indeed a special Christmas.

Author's Letter

Dear Reader,

I'm often asked what inspired a particular story, and more often than not, I have to say, "many things." That wasn't the case with *One Special Christmas*. When I finished writing *Into the Starlight*, although I'd resolved all the major questions that plagued the residents of Sweetwater Crossing, I realized that I'd created a new one: what happened to the Albright ranch?

My first thought was to add a paragraph to the epilogue in *Starlight*, but that didn't work well. It felt tacked on and detracted from the epilogue, so I abandoned that idea.

I still wanted to answer the question, so it was time for Plan B. Since the answer needed more than a paragraph, I decided to write a Christmas novella featuring the new residents of the ranch. No doubt about it. That was a better idea than trying to shoehorn the explanation into an epilogue, but once again I ran into a problem. I'm notorious for being challenged by a maximum word count on my novels, so I shouldn't have been surprised when the story grew and grew and grew. Before I knew it, I had a full-length book.

That, of course, took longer than I'd expected and delayed my next project, but when I typed the final words of *One Special Christmas*, I smiled as I realized that Greta wasn't the only one who'd been led. I'd been led to write this particular story at this particular time.

If you're one of my newsletter subscribers, you know that my husband died earlier this year. Even though I was grateful that his suffering had ended, it was a difficult time for me. Everyone's grief journey is different, but mine was made easier by writing this book. As I crafted Greta and Matt's love story, I was buoyed by memories of my own love story, of the many years that my husband and I shared, and of the countless ways he supported my dream of becoming a writer. I was blessed!

I am also blessed by having you as a reader. I know you have many other books and activities competing for your time, and so I feel honored that you chose one of my stories.

If this is your first visit to Sweetwater Crossing, you might want to read the entire **Secrets of Sweetwater Crossing** trilogy. *After the Shadows* tells the story of Emily's return home, while *Against the Wind* brings a reluctant Louisa back to town. The trilogy concludes with Joanna's story, *Into the Starlight*, which reveals the final secret, namely what really happened to Clive Finley, the man who built Finley House.

I also encourage you to visit my website, www.amandacabot.com, to learn more about my books and to sign up for my newsletter.

Thank you again for spending some of your time in Sweetwater Crossing. I've said it before, and I'll say it again: you're the reason I write.

Blessings,
Amanda

In Case You Were Wondering

Were you surprised when Burke ordered coffee to treat Otto's asthma? Did you think I invented this remedy? I didn't.

If you've read my earlier books, you know that I've been fascinated—and often horrified—by nineteenth century medical knowledge and treatment. Fortunately, by the time *One Special Christmas* takes place, few doctors still practiced what had been called heroic medicine. That was the use of purging, bleeding, blistering, and other treatments that made me shudder each time I read about them. Since that period had ended, the question became, how were doctors treating patients in 1884?

It took a fair amount of searching, but I found my answers in a book entitled *Domestic Medical Lectures* by John Kean, M.D. It has the subtitle, *A Thorough Treatise on the Cause, Prevention, Treatment and Cure of the Most Prevalent Diseases.* Sounds comprehensive, doesn't it? At more than 500 pages long, the book covers symptoms as well as recommended treatments. And, since it was published in 1879, it was likely Burke would have been familiar with many of the techniques in it.

To say that I was excited when I discovered this book would be an understatement. It's become my primary source of medical information for all of my books set in the late nineteenth century. I've spent hours reading about various ailments and the recommended treatments so that my fictional doctors' actions would be as realistic as possible.

Getting back to the coffee and asthma question, Dr. Kean lists a number of other ways to treat asthma, including inhaling the fumes of burning nitre paper, but I liked the idea of coffee, which is why I had Burke prescribe it.

And, yes, if you were wondering, Dr. Kean also recommends inhaling steam for capillary bronchitis.

About the Author

Amanda Cabot's dream of selling a book before her thirtieth birthday came true, and she's now the author of more than forty novels as well as eight novellas, four nonfiction books, and what she describes as enough technical articles to cure insomnia in a medium-sized city. Her stories have appeared on the CBA and ECPA bestseller lists, have garnered starred reviews from *Publishers Weekly* and *Library Journal*, were a *Woman's World* Book Club selection, and have been finalists for the ACFW Carol, the HOLT Medallion, and the Booksellers Best awards.

One of Amanda's greatest pleasures is hearing from readers, and so she invites you to find her online at www.amandacabot.com.

Printed in Great Britain
by Amazon

54700429R00148